Tales from the Black Chamber

A Supernatural Thriller

Bill Walsh

A LIBERTY ISLAND BOOK
ISBN: 978-1-947942-04-2

Tales from the Black Chamber:
A Supernatural Thriller
© 2017 by Bill Walsh
All Rights Reserved

LIBERTY ISLAND
LET YOUR RIGHT BRAIN RUN FREE

Liberty Island
libertyislandmag.com

Published in the United States of America

TABLE OF CONTENTS

For Julie,
who hates untranslated Latin
and *sine quā non*.

1

Anne Wilkinson pressed the ⬚ button with a right middle digit whose confrères were mostly occupied with clutching a paper bag containing a hummus-and-sprouts bagel sandwich. She tucked her tall frame into the elevator's back corner without lifting her eyes from the paperback in her left hand. Unnoticed, the elevator filled in front of her. New Yorkers one and all, no one so much glanced at the attractive young woman, or they'd have noticed her eyes narrow, then widen in surprise, followed by her right eyebrow rising to Spockian heights as she shook with restrained laughter.

When the doors opened on the lobby of Hathaway & Edgecombe, Anne was alone again. She wiped some tears from her eyes, tucked the book under her arm, and stepped onto the broad oriental carpet.

"Hi, Lindsay," said Anne to the reed-thin girl with trendy eyeglasses behind the mahogany Louis Quinze desk.

"Hi, Anne!" Lindsay replied with eager enthusiasm. "That was a fast lunch."

"Takeout," said Anne, lifting the bag for inspection.

"No messages for you. How's the book?"

"Oh my God. You know the premise? *Roman à clef* about Kate Warne, the first woman Pinkerton, and the Transcontinental Railroad?"

"Yep. I've been thinking about picking it up."

"It's really well-written, good plot, etc., but I'm in the elevator and all of a sudden, I hit this." She handed Lindsay the open book. Lindsay opened her mouth to read, and Anne whispered, "Not too loud."

> *"Her corset, bustle, and crinolines crumpled in the corner, useless as a knight's armor after a joust, quintessence and symbol of the old, guarded maiden she'd be no more, the rough-hewn boards of the caboose floor vibrating beneath her back, she felt his thick piston head reciprocating in her cylinder, pulling its long connecting rod in and pushing it out again, acceleration and power growing imperceptibly with each mighty stroke."*

"Are you kidding me?" Lindsay laughed.

"Keep going," said Anne.

> *"Their breaths came in syncopated heaves, chuffs from the engine of flesh they'd become. She felt the pressure in her smokebox growing and growing. It had to find a release."*

"Oh my God, this is—"

"Keep going."

"No ..."

"Yes!"

> *"Then, as the shuddering wood and their frenzied bodies merged in an incandescent, pulsating explosion, she thought, no, felt, no, knew what it meant to have that golden spike pounded into Promontory Point: All became one. Union Pacific,*

*Central Pacific. East, West. Atlantic, Pacific.
Rancher, farmer. Cowboy, Indian. Crow, Sioux.
Man, woman. Christian, Jew, heathen. America!"*

Lindsay was laughing so hard she was crying, her sides aching from trying to be quiet.

"One more line," said Anne.

*"And by the trackside, a prairie dog cocked its
ear at the unaccustomed scream of the train's new,
throaty whistle."*

Lindsay had to grip the desktop to keep from falling off her chair.

Anne laughed. "Seriously, what the? I'm guessing her publisher made her stick in a sex scene."

"That is priceless," said Lindsay.

"You can have the book when I'm done."

"Thank you!"

"Not at all, this place was built on books' changing hands."

"Yeah," grinned Lindsay, "though Dad was always smart enough to charge people for the privilege."

When Anne arrived, still smiling, at her office—not a corner office, yet, but not too many doors down and with a big window overlooking Union Square—her heart gave a little leap at the brown-paper-wrapped box on her desk, covered with lurid foreign postage, lots of insurance paperwork, and an unintelligible customs declaration on which she could only make out the words *antik könyvek*, which was the sum total of her Hungarian, her consuming vocation, and the raison d'être of Hathaway & Edgecombe—antique books.

Without sitting down, Anne set her bagel bag and novel on a side table, opened her desk drawer for the very sharp scissors she kept for just such occasions, and went at the package like a demolitions expert defusing a time bomb—quickly, deftly, and expertly, with just enough caution to ensure that everything emerged unscathed.

Once the packing was dispensed with, she slipped on a pair of cotton gloves and removed the contents. She smiled unconsciously as she opened the first volume, a 1558 incunabulum of Giambattista della Porta's *Magiæ Naturalis*, valuable in itself. As she turned the pages, a frisson ran up her spine as she noted the copious marginalia in a crisp, bold italic hand. These notes, in a mixture of German, Latin, and Greek, made the book priceless, as they showed it to be the personal copy of Rudolf II, Holy Roman Emperor, King of Hungary, King of Bohemia, Archduke of Austria, &c. &c. &c., famous patron of art, science, and alchemy, annotated by the man himself. Anne had tracked it down at no small expense and prized it loose from a collector in Székesfehérvár whose family had acquired it in the mid-nineteenth century. *Hello, beautiful,* she thought. *You're going to help make me a partner here.* Priceless it might be to her, but the market could value it very exactly. She planned to make it the centerpiece of H&E's next auction of occult and esoteric books, which was her bailiwick. The other volumes in the box were interesting but minor bits of Rudolfiana that would help fill out the catalog.

After a couple of hours of reading della Porta's book and trying to decipher Rudolf's comments, Anne decided that real work awaited, slipped the books into acid-free bags, and placed them in a wall safe hidden behind a hinged bookshelf. For the rest of the day, she plunged herself with the energy of the ambitious into drafting catalog descriptions and estimating values for the new arrivals and some of the other items for the Rudolf auction.

The phone rang at a little after four o'clock. Lindsay announced with her crisp, perfect, prep-school enunciation, "Mildred Garrett is here."

"Great, send her back, Linds."

"I'll make some tea."

"Thanks."

Mildred Garrett was a tiny woman somewhere in her eighties who wore her hair in an old-fashioned coif and peered out at the world through cat-eye glasses with tiny, tasteful rhinestones in the corners that must have been the height of matronly fashion in the '60s. Anne had come to learn, however, that the eyes behind the glasses missed nothing. Mrs. Garrett was the head of some sort of private library foundation in Washington, D.C., and she regularly made trips to New York to check out auction lots she might be interested in bidding on. An odd mix of vinegar and charm, Mrs. Garrett had become such an enjoyable visitor that Anne found herself inviting her to stop by H&E's offices to check out books before they went up for sale—sometimes even before they were announced for sale. Mrs. Garrett always looked them over with an enthusiasm that seemed to belie a methodical examination. However, when she was done, she'd invariably make a comment or two that were profoundly informed and shrewdly figured. Anne had never come away unenlightened, and Mrs. Garrett's comments frequently ended up making her substantial amounts of money for what they added to the eventual sale prices.

Over the course of their acquaintance, Anne had slowly figured out that the sharp-tongued little old lady knew more about rare books on the occult than she did—more, in fact, than anyone she'd ever met. Mrs. Garrett rarely bought books, though when she did they were a collection of excellent classics and some very off-the-wall bits that were either valuable on some level that no one else had perceived, or that specifically fit whatever her foundation was interested in. Mrs. Garrett was a bit cagey on what exactly that was, saying that she was merely doing the bidding of its trustees, and Anne never pressed.

Anne went to her safe, brought out all the books it held, and arranged them on the long mahogany table in the conference room across the hall. Mrs. Garrett was seated in her office when she returned, clutching a white beaded purse with lines of tiny artificial pearls snaking around its snap-clasp and handle. She did not rise but removed her gloves and offered her hand to Anne.

"How are you, dear girl?"

"Very well, Mrs. Garrett, and you?" Anne had never been tempted to call her "Mildred," and "Millie" was unthinkable.

"Fine, thank you. I could regale you with the horrors of Amtrak these days, but I shan't."

"Have you tried the Acela? I hear it's much nicer."

"I have, thank you. It is better, but it's one of the tragedies of being old that oftentimes, nostalgia aside, you remember when certain things were unquestionably better. And rail travel, my dear, was once much, much better. So was air travel, for that matter. People dressed for it, however shocking that may sound to your tender young ears."

"Well, I can't say I remember that myself, but my parents have mentioned it."

"Well, enough small talk, dear. You're a busy woman, and you shouldn't waste your time exchanging pleasantries with elderly people without enough to do."

"I never think it's a waste of time to talk to you, Mrs. Garrett. You're too kind to drop by when you're in town. Let me show you some of our new books."

Ordinarily, leaving a person off the street unaccompanied with tens of thousands of dollars worth of antique books was, to put it mildly, *streng verboten* by H&E. However, Anne had over the years become persuaded of Mrs. Garrett's absolute honesty and had received permission from the partners to allow her to spend time examining books. And, in fact, far from cutting out pages and stuffing them in her socks, Mrs. Garrett had on occasion brought to Anne's attention a document or other valuable item that had been slipped between the pages of a book, sometimes hundreds of years before, that might have gone unnoticed before auction.

Anne returned to work at the computer, looking up in surprise twenty minutes later when Mrs. Garrett's voice said, "Anne, dear?"

"Yes, Mrs. Garrett?"

The petite woman made her way to a chair and sat down. Anne noticed that, contrary to custom, she'd carried a book in with her.

"First of all, congratulations on finding Rudolf's *Magiæ Naturalis*. That's a coup of the first order. It was an honor to be able to look at it."

"I thought you might like that, Mrs. Garrett." *Oh, thank God*, Anne thought. *If she recognizes it's the real deal, it's the real deal.* The terror of forgeries haunted dealers unremittingly. "If I'm remembering right," she continued, "you've bought some things from his court before."

"I have." While she paused, Anne's mind went back. Some documents belonging to the great British magus John Dee she remembered, and even an oddball "Enochian" text in the hand of Dee's con-man assistant, Edward Kelley. *Those were some cool pieces. And man, did they help me establish myself. There's nothing better than a smart customer to make a dealer look good.* "However," Mrs. Garrett spoke up, "I had a question about this book."

She handed Anne a small book, a half-*octavo*-format Latin breviary from Aldus Manutius's press, primarily of interest to collectors of Aldine works and of Catholiciana, as it contained a number of rites, like exorcisms, not ordinarily included in a breviary, and which had endowed it with its name, the *Breviarium dæmonologicum*, the sex appeal of which added a few dollars to the price of a fairly dull, common book.

Anne's brow furrowed; it was not a particularly interesting or valuable book, as far as she knew. It was a filler lot for some neophyte collector and a vaguely spooky name for the catalog. "What can I tell you?"

"Well, it's not the book itself, as I'm sure you're aware. I was wondering where this copy came from. There's something oddly familiar about it, but I just can't place it."

"If I'm remembering right, it's supposed to have been brought to England back from the continent by an English Jesuit who was eventually executed. On his death it was confiscated by the Crown and ended up at the Bodleian. It was deaccessioned in the 1830s sometime as they had—and have—several better copies, and it's been in a series of private collections. I got it from the Archdiocese of New York, of all places. They'd received a bequest of a lot of books, couldn't handle them all, and called us. There were a couple vaguely interesting ones, but nothing special, I didn't think."

"Oh, well, then, I must be mistaken. Well, keep it safe, dearie, I may want to bid on it, if I can figure out why I've got such a sentimental attraction for it."

"No problem, Mrs. Garrett." *Is she being cagey?* Anne wondered, then dismissed the thought. *She's never played any games with me. And I've been all over that book. It's nothing special.*

Lindsay brought in the pot of tea and box of sugar cookies that tradition required Mrs. Garrett and Anne share while talking books. To Anne's surprise, Mrs. Garrett got up to leave.

"I'm sorry, Anne dear, but I've got to go. I have a hot date with the Library of Congress, if I get back before it closes tonight. Lindsay, dear, since it's after five already, would you be so kind as to share those cookies with Anne?"

"Sure, Mrs. Garrett."

Almost out the door, Mrs. Garrett turned around. "Oh, Anne, check the title page of that 1525 copy of *De libero arbitrio diatribe sive collatio*. The inscription that says 'Sod. Staup.' means it belonged to the Nuremberg philo-Protestant club called the *Sodalitas Staupiziana*, and if you check I think you'll find the handwriting is Albrecht Dürer's. You might advertise that to fine-art collectors as well." Anne's jaw dropped. "Goodbye, dear! See you soon."

"Do you want any of this tea?" Lindsay asked a minute later.

"My God, she's amazing," said Anne, still staring after Mrs. Garrett. Then Lindsay's question registered. "Sure, why not. Pour us some while I go get the books."

As Anne replaced the books in the safe, she double-checked their condition and contents, as Mrs. Garrett's behavior struck her as odd. However, everything looked perfect, so she decided that old ladies were allowed a little eccentricity now and then. She locked up the books, sat down with Lindsay, and enjoyed some tea, cookies, and gossip about whom various people at the firm were dating, the latest doings of various celebrities, and the books they were reading or thinking of reading. They rarely talked shop, but Anne had received some of her best advice from Lindsay over the last couple years, as Lindsay's father was Richard Edgecombe, founder and eponym of H&E, and Lindsay had absorbed more information about the rare-book business by osmosis during her childhood than most professionals gleaned in a decade of experience.

At the beginning of their acquaintance, Anne worried that Lindsay would decide that she'd want a partnership in H&E and bump her and her peers back a year or more. However, as she'd gotten to know Lindsay and like her very much, she realized her fear was unfounded. She learned that Lindsay loved rare books, but had no particular attraction towards the business of buying and selling them, and was taking a couple years after Yale to decide what to do with her life. Her father understood and had made her one of the six most overqualified receptionists in Manhattan with the firm agreement that she had three years in the job, not a day more, after which professional employment, continued schooling, or an entry-level position at H&E was mandatory.

Anne had availed upon Lindsay for advice any number of times and never found her less than forthcoming and helpful. On the basis of this collegiality, a genuine friendship had grown up, even though Anne was almost a decade older than Lindsay, and Lindsay's privileged East Coast upbringing was a world away from Anne's youth in the high mountains of northern New Mexico.

"So, did you see *Grey's Anatomy* last week?" asked Anne.

"Oh. My. God," Lindsay elaborated.

ᴂᴂ

Anne sat in the back of the firm's auction room watching the Rudolfiana auction poker-faced. Inwardly, she was giddy at the excellent prices the major pieces had fetched. Her partnership offer was now a mere formality. She'd established herself as acquirer, evaluator, and seller. She expected to have job offers from Sotheby's and Christie's on her voicemail by the close of business. Though she had no intention of leaving H&E, it would be nice to feel courted.

When the final gavel fell, Anne slipped out the door, adding up the sale prices in her head. Arriving back at her office, she found Mrs. Garrett sitting at her table with a pot of tea and plate of cookies at the ready, and the Aldine *Breviarium dæmonologicum* she'd paid a healthy but not unreasonable price for.

"Hi, Mrs. Garrett! Congratulations on getting that breviary. Nothing else interested you?"

"Oh, everything else interested me, dear. I'm just a little old lady who saves her pennies. Or rather, the Foundation's pennies. But congratulations to you, Anne. I haven't seen a better-run or more entertainingly contested auction in, well, twenty years."

"Thanks, Mrs. Garrett. I was pretty happy with how it went."

"You're too modest, my darling. It was a *coup* of the first order. Please, have some tea and cookies to celebrate. I'm sorry I didn't think to bring a port to celebrate, but you didn't let me know what a day it'd be for you."

"Thank you, Mrs. Garrett. It is a little more than my average day at the office."

Mrs. Garrett chatted with her about the books and the prices. Anne was, as always, amazed; this time, at the elderly lady's knowledge of not only the book market but of the oddball milieu of Rudolf's Prague, as well as an enormous amount of history and art to which she alluded offhandedly and unselfconsciously.

After a relatively brief chat, Mrs. Garrett excused herself. "I should leave you to the company of your peers, now, Anne. I suspect they'll have lots to say to you."

Their probable congratulations (laced with well-concealed envy) flashed through Anne's mind, but she said with absolute sincerity, "Nothing as interesting as a talk with you, Mrs. Garrett."

"I see you have mastered the art of flattering your customers," Mrs. Garrett deadpanned. Then drawing herself up to her full four-foot, eleven-and-three-quarters inches, she placed a hand on Anne's arm, an unexpected intimacy, and said, with a smile, "Celebrate your success with the élan of youth, dear."

Anne saw her out, then settled in for a delicious afternoon bath of praise and celebration. Her peers were genuinely happy for her (if indeed a little envious and worried that she'd set the bar very high), the partners were ecstatic (if clearly doing the math on enlarging the partnership and feeling a little old and mortal), and her voicemail and e-mail boxes were full of "I'd be interested in talking to you about ..." e-mails from firms around the world. News travels fast when your auction is simulcast on the Internet.

At just after five, however, her almost-perfect feeling of happiness and self-satisfaction was abruptly punctured by the appearance of a gaunt man with a grim visage and empty eyes, wearing a gray suit and a flat black tie, the texture of which contrasted with the shiny black hair slicked down against his skull.

In a raspy, affectless baritone, he said, "The Jesuit breviary. I understand it was sold today for three thousand dollars. I will pay ten thousand for it right now. You may return the buyer's money, give three to your firm in payment, and keep four yourself."

"I'm sorry, sir, but all sales are final at Hathaway & Edgecombe."

"I understand that, which is why I am offering you that inducement."

"I appreciate your candor." *Though why you're willing to flatly admit you're bribing me to put my career at risk and break the law*

11

is something I don't think I want to know. "Nevertheless, I must decline."

He took a step forward, his face tightening so that something like cruelty could be seen skulking behind the blank features. "No, you must not. More money? Or, must we discuss this further?"

A flashing, freezing, atavistic dread shot through Anne. She felt the hair on her arms rise. "No, I'm sorry. I mean, it's impossible. The book has been sold, it's in the buyer's possession. There's nothing more we can do."

"The buyer's name," he stated flatly. "I would like to make him an offer."

"I'm sorry," she lied quickly and fluently. "The buyer paid cash, and we did not take his name. It's not a particularly valuable book, and it's not worth our time to keep records on the vast majority of unremarkable pieces that pass through our hands. I'm sure any reputable book dealer will be able to find a copy of the *Brevarium dæmonologicum* for you, and Aldine copies come on the market fairly frequently. I'm sorry not to be able to help you, sir. I appreciate your enthusiasm for antiquarian books, and I hope Hathaway & Edgecombe will be able to serve you in the future. Good evening." She moved behind her desk, tapped a few computer keys and looked up with what she hoped was an are-you-still-here? look.

The skeletal man stood stock-still for a long, unnerving moment before speaking. "Yes. I understand. Thank you." He turned and left without another word.

Anne picked up the phone and dialed zero.

"Lindsay, it's Anne. A really creepy guy just left my office. Is he hanging around?"

"Nope. He's gone. Walked right to the elevator, totally ignoring me when I said goodbye, and went straight down. What was his deal?"

"Wanted to buy a book we'd already sold."

"Dork. Hey, you didn't hear it from me, but the partners had me make a dinner reservation at Le Cirque tonight, and they're currently headed for your office with some champagne that costs more than my suit."

Anne was embarrassed to hear herself squeal slightly. "Awesome. Your secret is safe with me. Thanks, Linds."

"Congrats!" said Lindsay in a stage whisper, before hanging up the phone.

Anne hung up and put on a poker face. When they came in, she didn't bother faking surprise, she just let out a little of the elation she'd been holding in all day and beamed like a movie star.

2

Anne spent the next day in bed, nursing an epic hangover and an oceanic feeling of well-being and success, having been offered and accepted a partnership at H&E over a seven-course meal that was by miles the best and by leagues the most expensive she'd ever eaten. Over the course of the night, with the food and drink arriving like magic, she'd probably had a couple bottles of vintage cabernet herself—she was a little unclear on the details—and she'd slept in until well after two in the afternoon.

Once sufficiently hydrated and caffeinated to open the window shades, she called her parents in Albuquerque and shared the good news. They were elated, though she could hear a tiny unarticulated undertone of grief that she was more firmly anchored to New York than ever. Around five, she called Lindsay at work and invited her out for a non-alcoholic celebration ("Non-alcoholic only on your part, Anne"), then called a few other friends, intentionally skipping peers from the office just to give them a little breather for any awkwardness to pass. She'd take them out for lunches or dinner sometime later. Tonight she just wanted to relax and not worry or think about work in the least.

She had everyone rally in Midtown for boatloads of Chinese at Ollie's, the new Johnny Depp flick on an enormous screen at the big AMC theater off Times Square, and a cab ride down to

Bowlmor near the Village for some midnight bowling and beers (or decaf cappuccino, in her case).

As she climbed into bed, she thought, "With apologies to Kundera, that was the perfect evening of laughter and forgetting." Sleep never felt so deep or restful.

ཕ༷ ༷

The next day was Saturday, and after some time on Citibank's website and doing a little math, Anne decided that she could afford to do a little shopping, so she spent the day picking out a couple "partner suits" and some "partner shoes" and having some seriously frivolous fun.

Sunday, she hit the gym to sweat out some of the weekend's excesses, then called her ex-boyfriend Dave to share the good news. Dave and she had remained friendly, against the odds, largely because of their shared love for 1930s horror movies, which kept them running into each other at revival houses. After a while, they decided they might as well sit together. Then, they revived their old habit of watching them on TV late at night together—by phone or Internet chat instead of in bed.

She and Dave had steaks at Carne on the Upper West Side, and he grabbed the check.

"Hey, wait, I'm the new titan of, um, antiquarian book auctions."

"I know," he said, smiling, "but it's on me."

"Dave, I don't want to be callous here, but I'm going to be making a *lot* of money fairly soon."

"Yes, but for the moment, you have to buy into the partnership, which I imagine will involve some massive loan on your part. So it's on me. Because I'm really happy for you."

She looked at him asquint for a moment, then exhaled. "Okay. Thank you. That's really very kind of you." *Damn*, she wondered, not for the first time, *did I screw up badly in dumping him?*

Dave gave her a brief peck as she got into the cab, which let her wallow a bit more in romantic nostalgia and no small amount of fantasy about the future. Maybe she could finally stop being so obsessive about the job. Maybe there was someone out there— maybe even Dave again?—with whom she could actually settle down, move to the suburbs, have a kid or two. Possibility beckoned seductively.

ཕ᷅ᩓᩛᩃ

Monday morning, Anne strolled into the office and humbly accepted the further congratulations and plaudits of all her coworkers. After pouring herself a coffee, she was relieved and pleased to shut her office door and just sit down to work. She opened up her e-mail. As she was typing an enthusiastic response to a man in Chillicothe, Ohio, who claimed to have a 1601 copy of Trithemius's *Steganographia*, the first printed edition by Johann Berner, an itch between the third and fourth fingers of her right hand began to bother her. She rubbed at the web between her fingers and kept typing. A touch-typist, she could do ninety-five or a hundred words a minute if she needed to. Perhaps two hundred words later, the itch returned. And then worsened.

Annoyed, she looked down at the keyboard, and noticed there was a hair protruding from between the K and L keys. She pulled it out and immediately noticed it was not one of her medium-length, light brown, slightly wavy hairs. It was coarse, black, dead straight, and slightly greasy. She was briefly baffled, then she remembered the unpleasant man who'd shown up wanting to buy Mrs. Garrett's breviary. Could he have used her computer before she'd found him in her office? Or come back over the weekend? It wouldn't have been any problem whatsoever for him to call up the firm's database and check the auction-lot number. The record would contain not only the sale price, but the buyer's name, address, phone number, and e-mail. In Mrs. Garrett's case, she wasn't listed personally in favor of her employer, the Coolidge Foundation for Rare and Intriguing Books.

Anne picked up the phone and called Mrs. Garrett's cell phone, getting voicemail. "Mrs. Garrett, this is Anne Wilkinson from Hathaway & Edgecombe. I just wanted to let you know that there was a strange and rude man here last week who wanted to contact you about buying the breviary you purchased. He was very unpleasant, and I told him it was impossible for us to give any information. However, now I'm worried that he may have obtained the Coolidge Foundation's name from our records unethically, and I wanted to warn you and the Foundation that he might be contacting you. I can't apologize enough that this happened on our watch. Please call me back, and I'll let you know who to look out for. Or … out for whom to look?" She giggled. "Hope you're well, Mrs. Garrett. Oh, and I have some good news I'd love to share with you. Talk to you soon."

When five o'clock came and she hadn't heard back, Anne called again, got voicemail again, and hung up. She called Mrs. Garrett's home number: answering machine. Anne left messages there and on Mrs. Garrett's cell phone, leaving her own home and cell numbers.

Tuesday came and went without any word from Mrs. Garrett, and Anne began to worry. Wednesday passed as well, by which time Anne was genuinely concerned the elderly woman might have fallen ill or passed away and had no one to find her. With that grim thought and the realization that as a partner, she no longer required approval for such things, she booked herself onto a Thursday-morning shuttle flight to Reagan National to go look for her favorite client. She rented a car at the airport, plugged Mrs. Garrett's address into her iPhone, and drove up Rock Creek Park to Connecticut Avenue and then into Mrs. Garrett's quiet neighborhood in Northwest. She pulled up in front of a white-painted brick house on Linnean Avenue, maybe just shy of being called a mansion, walked up the front walk past two enormous oak trees growing together, and rang the doorbell. She heard it chime and waited. She called all Mrs. Garrett's numbers from the doorstep, then walked around the front of the house, but both side yards were closed off with locked wooden gates the height of doors, and the backyard was surrounded by a brick wall. Returning to the front door, she rang the bell again, and in frustration, opened the glass storm door and tried the front door handle. It stuck, but with a pull and then a push, it swung open.

With rising alarm, Anne looked at the door jamb and noticed paint missing around the height of the locks. Were they tool marks? She wished she'd been fonder of mystery novels and the recent proliferation of forensic-cop shows on TV.

She swung the heavy wooden door open, jumped when the ornamental knocker clicked next to her ear, and started to say, "Mrs. Garrett?" when she froze. A tiny pair of feet in cream-colored leather pumps stuck out of the doorway up a single step and to the right.

Anne leapt up the stair but stopped when she saw all the blood. Some very old part of her brain immediately recognized death. And then she smelled decomposition. She choked back tears and vomit, stepped outside, shuddering uncontrollably, and called 911.

3

The police kept her standing out on the lawn for two hours. Eventually, they asked her into the house and sat her down in a little breakfast room off the front hall that looked like a large butler's pantry set off by swinging doors from the kitchen and a formal dining room.

The detectives, a tall white woman and a shorter black man, asked her questions for a half hour, with a stenographer taking a statement. Then for another half hour, they asked the same questions again. And then once more. Yes, she'd come down here out of concern for her client; no, she didn't know who the strange man was or have any concrete reason to believe he was involved other than a suspicion he'd used her computer; no, the book was of no great value; and no, she had just walked in.

Finally, they asked her to look around the house for any valuable books that might be connected with the crime. She was shown upstairs, downstairs into a finished basement, and upstairs again to a finished third floor. Books were omnipresent but not overwhelmingly so. The library in whose doorway Mrs. Garrett's body had lain had two walls of built-in bookshelves. Anne confessed to the police that, in fact, she hadn't noticed a single really rare, old, or valuable volume in the entire place. There were books about books—enough to write several doctorates on early printing, calligraphy and illumination, and manuscript authentication.

Even more numerous were vast numbers of secondary sources on Renaissance printers, authors, sages, clerics, magicians, alchemists, and the whole rogues' gallery of the world of knowledge from the sixteenth century or so. Anne's admiration of Mrs. Garrett grew. Not only did she have a charmingly formal, old-fashioned sense of décor, she'd assembled Anne's dream library, or at least the secondary-source stacks of it. But there wasn't a single piece she'd bought from H&E nor a solitary antique book.

The police thanked her for her expert opinion, asked her to stay in Washington for a couple days in case they had any more questions, and told her they'd like her to check and sign the statement she'd given once it was typed up.

Anne got back in her rental car and poked around on her iPhone for the number of a hotel—there was an Embassy Suites that seemed like it'd be fine a mile and a half away in an upscale shopping center in Friendship Heights right on the Maryland line.

She checked in, got in the shower, and wept.

ༀ༷ༀ

Cried out, Anne was sitting in bed wearing the hotel's complimentary robe, which she loved—hard as it was for a New Yorker to admit, it was fully as nice as the one she'd worn the one time she and Dave had checked into the St. Regis for a romantic weekend—when her cell phone rang.

"Ms. Wilkinson, I'm Stephen Hunter from the Federal Bureau of Investigation," announced a slightly gravelly baritone. "If you wouldn't mind, I'd like to ask you a few questions about the death of Mildred Garrett."

"I'd be happy to cooperate, but I've already spoken to the D.C. police."

"Yes, they gave me your name. Where are you now?"

"I'm at the Embassy Suites in the mall in Friendship Heights."

"Mazza Gallerie?"

"No, a different one. Chevy Chase something?"

"Pavilion. Sorry for the confusion. That's right across the street from the other mall. I'll meet you in the hotel lobby in half an hour."

"All right."

She'd just gotten dressed and was wondering where she'd buy some changes of clothes for the next couple days when her cell phone rang again. Another 202 area code.

"Hi, is this Anne Wilkinson of Hathaway & Edgecombe?" Anne was relieved that it sounded like business. She needed a distraction.

"Yes, who's this?"

"Sorry to bother you, Ms. Wilkinson, but my name is John Ashton and I work for the Coolidge Foundation for Rare and Intriguing Books."

Oh, damn, thought Anne. "Hello, Mr. Ashton, I'm so sorry about your colleague, Mrs. Garrett."

"Thank you. And my condolences to you. I know Mildred considered you a friend. And I'm told you … found her. That must have been awful."

You have no idea. "Thank you. What can I do for you?"

"Well, I just had a few questions about Mildred's purchases from Hathaway & Edgecombe, and I was hoping I might sit down with you before you return to New York. Are you leaving tonight?"

"No, the police have asked me to stay around for a little while. I'm staying in Friendship Heights."

"Well, then, can I take you to dinner tonight? On the Foundation. You've been such a great help to us and a good friend to Mildred, it's the least we can do."

Anne's first inclination was to stay holed up in her hotel room, but she thought for a moment. *Going out would be less morbid and might even be interesting.* She had always wondered about the Coolidge Foundation. *And my appetite's starting to come back. Food sounds good.*

"Yes, thank you, Mr. Ashton. That would be nice."

"Oh, good. You said Friendship Heights, right?"

"Yes, the Embassy Suites."

"Okay, I'll pick you up out front at the corner of Wisconsin and Military at seven thirty. I'll be driving a red Honda Accord. Not exactly limo service, but it'll get us there."

"Sounds just fine, Mr. Ashton. I look forward to it."

"Me too, Ms. Wilkinson. Talk to you then!"

Anne hung up, feeling a bit better. She did, after all, have to consider retaining the Coolidge Foundation; and, she had to admit, this John Ashton sounded fairly young, bright, and nice. *Two birds with one bourguignon?* she thought and giggled.

ཨ༵་༃

The thought of a pleasant dinner with a guy got Anne dressed and downstairs to the mall for some makeup and toiletries. By the time she met the FBI man, in the lobby of the hotel, she was looking and feeling great.

Hunter was a tall blond with a neat haircut and the athletic stride of a wide receiver; Anne was put in mind of a leopard she'd seen in the Bronx Zoo. He wasn't unattractive, either, with intelligent blue eyes and solid features. However, Anne's incipient attraction evaporated as soon as he opened his mouth; his persona was pure Joe Friday, to the point that she wondered if he was putting her on.

Without any apparent regard for her ordeal, he ran her through the facts of her discovery of the body, her relationship with Mrs. Garrett, and why she'd come looking for her. He then returned to the mysterious man, prodding her on details of his appearance, clothing, and asking a variety of other questions, some of which seemed to Anne to be a bit out of left field, and to all of which she had to confess she had no answers. Ordinarily, she'd have chatted with him a little and tried to glean what he was getting at, but he was such a drip to talk to and her dinner with Ashton so on her mind, she really had no desire to spend any more time in his presence than necessary. They exchanged business cards, and she watched him slink across the lobby. *Too bad the prose is so awful,* she thought, scowling, *because that's one hell of a cover.*

ཟ˅ི

Anne hadn't been standing on the corner for more than three minutes when, as promised, a red Honda Accord pulled up to the curb. The driver's door opened, and Anne quickly appraised the man who got out: six feet or so, dark hair, large greenish-brown eyes, and decent dress sense. He wore a smart green blazer with brown twill pants, and a beautiful parchment-colored silk tie that, upon closer inspection, had a pattern that was actually manuscript calligraphy. She thought it might be a Carolingian minuscule hand, but didn't think it'd be a great first impression were she to grab and scrutinize his tie.

"Hi, are you Ms. Wilkinson?"

"Call me Anne." They shook hands.

"John." He opened the passenger door for her. "Hop in."

The car was quite new and had all sorts of sleek instrumentation. "You underplayed how nice your car is, John," said Anne as he pulled away.

"Hey, thank you. I like it a lot. I've got a bunch of dinner options for you. You have any preferences?"

"Whatever you like. At the risk of appearing indelicate, I'm starved."

"Do you like steak?"

"Very much."

Ashton drove them downtown to the Capital Grille, an old-fashioned steak house that catered to Washington's well-heeled population of lobbyists, real-estate developers, and attorneys.

Anne ordered a rare Delmonico, much to Ashton's evident satisfaction.

"Wow, you really do like steak."

"I do. Rare, like my books."

"Ow." He laughed.

"Too cheesy? Actually, I'm a New Mexican. Well-done meat is a Class B felony in the state. Speaking of books, that's a great tie."

"Thank you. It's *The Death of Simon Magus* from a colored version of the *Nuremberg Chronicle*."

"Wow, that's really cool. Where did you have that made?"

"I actually found it in a hotel gift shop."

"Crazy! I actually saw a 1491 Latin first-edition in person once. During my year abroad, by coincidence, I went to the Ny Carlsberg Glyptothek in Copenhagen while they were having this exhibit of medieval esoterica. It was just amazing. Did you know that it's possible that a young Dürer worked on the illustrations as an apprentice?"

"I did not."

"It's true. My girlfriends went off to Tivoli, but I stayed the whole afternoon, even though they only had nineteen books on display. I'd get to the end, then start over. That was probably the moment at which it became inevitable that I'd end up as a rare-book nerd."

"Oh, so your interest extends beyond their monetary value?"

"Truth be told, as much as I like my job, it's mostly a pretext to get my hands on lost, old, and rare books. It's just for a short time, usually, but there's nothing like actually reading them while you can touch them and smell them and hear the pages turn. It's electric; it's like a little time machine. But I'm babbling. I'm sure working for the Coolidge Foundation, you're no stranger to the charms of old books."

"Love them. But hey, if you don't mind my saying so, aren't you a bit of a real expert on some of this stuff? I Googled you to find out your contact information, and found you've actually got a bibliography."

"Well, yeah." Anne took a drink of her Zinfandel. "I don't really consider myself a scholar, but I got interested in the content first, then the books as art and craft, and finally as a way to make a living."

"A pretty nice one, I take it. Congratulations on making partner."

"How did you know about that?"

"I spoke to Richard Edgecombe when I was trying to track you down."

"Oh. Well, thanks."

"Back to your articles—they're all about esoteric, occult, and unique books. Is that your thing?"

"Yes. When I was a girl, I was really interested in magic and ghosts and vampires and all of that, and it stuck with me."

"Really? I find it hard to picture you as a Goth."

"Oh, hardly, no, I was math team, debate, all that sort of stuff. I got into it all when I was really young, like sixth grade or so. I had enough sense to conceal my continued interest while in high school. And this was before the web took off, so it was a mostly solitary pursuit. Easy to conceal. Not that I was Miss Popularity, but I got through high school pretty unscathed. Except for never asking out the guy I had a crush on. Wow, I'm talking a lot about myself. I'd better slow down on the wine. So tell me about the Coolidge Foundation. Mrs. Garrett never really talked about it much."

"Well, there's not much to tell. We are a private foundation that acquires the occasional 'rare' or 'intriguing' book for a library that we run for the benefit of a small membership."

"Who's the membership?"

"Can't say. Sorry. Rules."

"What's in the library? I know Mrs. Garrett was mostly interested in esoterica, though she did buy a couple other books from us that were pretty far afield."

"I wish I could tell you. The Foundation was set up with very specific and, let me say, strange rules. Still, it's a nice place to work."

"So, going forward, will the Foundation still be in the market for books?"

"Of the kind you deal in? Absolutely. And I'm sure we'll be happy to work with Hathaway & Edgecombe."

Business portion of dinner, check! "That's very nice to hear. We'll be happy to help you or whoever replaces Mrs. Garrett however we can."

"Thanks. Speaking of Mildred, here's a question I have for you. I know she was excited about a book she was going to buy from you last week, but I hadn't talked to her in a few days. Did she end up buying something?"

"Yes, but to be frank, it's the first one of her purchases I don't quite understand. It was an Aldine breviary once owned by a martyred English Jesuit."

"Hmm. Doesn't sound too exciting. Any interesting marginalia or inclusions?"

"No, there was some marginalia, but it was pretty much all just religious stuff, the odd practical shopping-list-type note—you know, 'buy bread,' 'launder shirt,' that sort of thing—and doodling."

"So why do you think Mildred wanted it?"

"I couldn't tell you. I mean, it has the very sexy title of *Brevarium dæmonologicum*, but that's not because it relates to witchcraft or demonology, just that it includes a few unusual prayers for exorcism, protection from demons, and the like. There are any number of copies floating around. It was sort of popular in the late sixteenth and early-to-middle seventeenth centuries. I think her purchase price was three thousand, which wasn't out of line, as it was a very well-preserved copy with an interesting history, but it's hardly the stuff of legend."

"So, did they find the book at her house when she died?"

"No, I don't think so. Why, is it not at the library? Or can't you tell me that?" She smiled, lifting her wineglass to her lips.

He laughed. "No, it never arrived at the library."

"It wasn't at the house unless there's a hidden safe or something."

"I doubt it. Mildred almost never kept books at her house for more than a day or two before bringing them into the library. Sometimes she'd bring them straight in. So, do the police think she was killed for the book?"

"No idea. They didn't tell me anything. I had an FBI guy interview me for some reason, though."

"Really? What did he want to know?"

"Well, there was this creepy guy who showed up at my office after the auction, asking about the breviary, wanting to buy it directly from us, and asking about who won it. I stonewalled him, but it turns out he may have gotten the information off my computer when no one was looking."

"Oh my God, that's awful."

"I know." Anne stabbed at her food distractedly. "And I forgot all about it over the weekend—I *just* made partner, so I was kind of, you know, wrapped up in myself—and by the time I called Mildred on Monday, she might already have been dead. I'm really, really worried that this guy did it, and that I inadvertently helped him." She sniffled and wiped at an eye. "I'm sorry. Too much wine."

"Not in the least. Look, don't feel the least bit guilty. If this guy was involved, there was no way you could know he was a murderer, for God's sake. You did everything a reasonable person would to hinder him, anyway. Mildred always thought of you as a good friend, a real up-and-coming expert, and, I don't know, but I always got the sense that she thought of you a little like the granddaughter she never had."

"Now you're really going to make me cry."

"I'm sorry. Can I buy you dessert to make up for it?"

"As long as it's chocolate."

4

A week later, Anne was back into the swing of work. She had a pile of furniture catalogs sitting on the corner of her desk, the sole sign that she'd made partner, but the sight was enough to make her smile. When John Ashton called, she was excited to hear from him. Not only did it mean he was serious when he'd said the Coolidge Foundation would continue to use H&E for esoterica purchases (and potentially sales), but maybe, she thought, he enjoyed dinner as much as she had. They'd gotten along very, very well, talking about books (professional), books (for entertainment), movies (he liked monster movies too!), and even waded a little into politics. He was a Republican, apparently, which gave her pause, but he clearly seemed to be a sane one, so, she'd decided, she was willing to overlook that blemish on his résumé if he ever decided to ask her out.

"How are you holding up, Anne?" *Sincere concern!*

"I'm well, thanks, John. It catches up with me a little when I think about Mrs. Garrett, but honestly, it's so crazy at the moment with having made partner and working on the firm's annual general auction, personal thoughts just haven't really been getting much time. Except at home—and I'm not there much. You?"

"About the same. There's the grief, and I'm still shocked and appalled. The police really don't seem to have any leads on the 'who,' yet, other than there were two sets of men's footprints in the carpet. Near as they can tell, the bad guys were in the library, Mildred surprised them, and they shot her. They were cagey on the details, but I think something about how she was shot—the gun, the bullets, or something—makes them think the killers were professionals. Anyway, because the 'who' is giving them fits, they've moved on to the 'why,' and so they keep asking me about the breviary you sold us. I keep telling them that it was an interesting but not uncommon book that Mildred took a fancy to. But, you know, the more I think about it, the more I wonder if maybe it was the reason she was killed."

"Really, why?"

"Well, nothing else was taken. Mildred had an inventory of all her personal books on that computer on the library desk. All present and accounted for. There's no sign they touched her jewelry—of which she had a lot—or any of the silver or other valuables she had out in plain sight."

"Maybe they got scared and ran?"

"Maybe, I don't know. But as I said, for some reason the police seemed to think these were very cool characters. And the neighbors didn't hear a thing. So maybe they used a silencer.... Then again, the walls in those old houses are incredibly thick. It'd be hard to hear much from next door."

"So you think they found what they were looking for, killed Mrs. Garrett almost by accident, and left."

"Could be. But I wonder if they didn't kill Mildred on purpose. If the book is the key, then she clearly saw something significant. Maybe they didn't want anyone knowing what it was. I mean, Mildred is—was—four-foot-ten or-eleven? And she couldn't have weighed more than about a hundred pounds at most. If you are two big, bad armed criminals, how hard is it going to be to manage a little old lady? I know Mildred knew how to shoot—and well— but her gun was still in her purse on the little couch in the hall."

Mildred carried a gun? Something to ask about later.

"Well, if it's something *in* the book, I mean, on the page, rather than in the binding or covers, we could look for it."

"What do you mean?" he asked, confused.

"I've got a copy."

"Of the breviary?" John asked, excited, then continued, his voice dropping in disappointment, "No, I mean, if it's as common as you say, there's no reason that they had to kill Mildred for that particular one."

"No, no, I'm sorry," Anne explained, "I mean, I've got a digital copy of the book she bought. I make it a practice to take high-resolution photos of every page of every book that passes through my hands in order to have a record for authentication in the future. Occasionally you get someone who'll buy a valuable book from you, then modify a less-valuable copy until it resembles the expensive one, then try and sell it back to you as the original. So early on, I made it a practice to build a private archive of all the books I've sold. I put it in the contract any seller has to sign, but it's a tiny little clause and no one even notices, I don't think. Plus, since it's only for my legitimate business use—I'm not publishing facsimile editions of their books—I don't *think* there are any copyright issues. I mean, I haven't run it past a lawyer. I probably should now that I'm a partner; I don't want to get the firm in trouble ..."

"You have *pictures* of *every page* of that book?"

"Yep. And the covers, end papers, spine, too. Do you think I should tell the police?"

"Ah, no.... I don't know that they'd be able to evaluate them." John paused, thinking. "In fact, don't tell *anyone*. Here's the thing—if she was killed for knowing something about what was in the book, if the killers know you have a copy of the book and were friendly with her, they might think you could know the same thing. And then ..."

"Come after me. Oh, God. Do you think that's possible?"

John paused a moment, then said, "I have no idea. But that's why you shouldn't tell anyone. Do a lot of people know about your archive?"

Anne thought for a moment. "No. A couple people at work. The computer guy who got me all the storage space and off-site backup. But it's really just a personal thing of mine, like a Rolodex or whatever."

"Okay, well, tell you what, I'll go home, throw some stuff in a suitcase, and get in my car. I'll be up there late tonight. I'll check into the Marriott at Times Square, and tomorrow we can see if we can figure out what Mildred saw. That ok with you?"

Anne noticed she was smiling and had to laugh. "Actually, it sounds like a heck of a lot of fun. I mean, not to make light, but seriously, this sounds like a Nancy Drew book—*The Clue in the Jesuit Breviary!*"

"You're not worried?"

"Well, that there's a non-zero chance someone could try and kill me is inherently worrisome, sure. But my chance of getting hit by a crosstown bus on my way home is probably much higher."

"Probably."

"Okay, then! Nerdy Rare-Book Girl gets pulled into exciting intrigue revolving around a mysterious tome! Seriously, who wouldn't want to be her?"

John cracked up. "Okay, Nancy, I'll see you tomorrow."

"'Night, Ned!" Anne said chirpily and then hung up quickly, even though she heard him saying, "Huh?" Ned Nickerson was, after all, Nancy's famously smitten boyfriend.

ᗡᡭᡎᡭ

Anne's cell phone rang at eight the next morning.

"Hi, Anne, I hope I didn't wake you."

"Nope. I'm so worked up over all this, I didn't sleep well. I've been up for a couple hours."

"Sorry about the insomnia. You want to meet for breakfast?"

"Only if we can get to work on this over the food."

"Okay, your place or mine?"

Anne laughed. "I thought about that. If it was the guy who was in my office, they definitely know where I work, and they might even know my apartment, right?"

"That's not out of the question," John said cautiously.

"So, why don't I come down to Times Square, mingle with the crowds, and meet you in the lobby of your hotel. We can pick a place to eat then."

"Sounds good. See you in a bit."

Less than an hour later, John and Anne shook hands in the lobby of the Marriott. After exchanging pleasantries, he pointed to the manuscript box under her arm.

"So, is that it?"

She nodded. "So where do you want to eat?"

"How about here?"

"I don't know, if this is cloak-and-dagger, a restaurant might not be the best. And, nothing personal, but I'm not really comfortable with going up to your room."

"Oh, no problem. I checked with the business center, and they've got a free conference room. I figured if we needed to spread things out, a big table would be great. And the room-service breakfast menu looked good. Murderously overpriced, but good. They'll bring it right to us in the conference room."

"Sounds perfect."

Comfortably ensconced in a black leather chair at a polished oval cherry wood conference table with a futuristic-looking speakerphone in the middle, Anne opened the box.

"Wow, those are beautiful pictures," John said, as she took the top few pages out. "Was the book really *this* big?"

"No, the breviary was a fat little book that would fit in a pocket. I just printed these scaled up for eight-and-a-half-by-eleven paper on the theory that if we were looking for something small, it'd be easier to spot."

"Good idea. Nice printing and paper, too."

"We have a high-resolution printer in the office for printing off last-minute signs and labels for things for auctions. Okay, now look here where the file name is printed in the corner. The three numbers after the P tell you the page number, starting with the inside front cover as 001."

"And the V and R after the numbers?"

"Verso and recto. Left- and right-hand pages. It's redundant in most cases, since odd-numbered pages are always left-hand, or verso, and the even ones are recto. But sometimes you have some odd fold-out pages, or printer's errors that leave blank pages, and the like. It's just another way to triple-check you've got the right book."

"So, maybe we should start with the cover—" John had begun when a knock at the door startled them. Room service brought in their breakfasts and two pots of coffee. John insisted on the Coolidge Foundation's picking up the tab. Over Belgian waffles and eggs Benedict, Anne explained she'd been up since six or so, drinking less-good coffee and going through a number of the pages at her breakfast table. She hadn't come up with a thing. The type and the content were exactly what you'd expect, and the marginalia were pretty conventional stuff. Devotional remarks, underlinings. Occasional explication of a word in Latin or Greek. As she remembered and the photos showed, the cover and binding were also unremarkable.

John asked a few questions but mostly just needed to be brought up to speed on sixteenth-century books. He was obviously not the expert Mrs. Garrett had been, but Anne found his rapt attention to her explanations a more than slightly pleasurable compensation.

His suggestion of dividing up the book into sections by content seemed to make a lot of sense in terms of how to work through it. Anne chose to start at the beginning, and John in the "demonological" section. His Latin was evidently excellent, Anne noted, occasionally looking up to find him engrossed in the text, sometimes chuckling, sometimes nodding his head gravely.

"How's it going?" she asked him an hour or so into reading.

"Well. This is really neat stuff. I love how they've got exorcisms for individual, named demons. I'd think the trick would be finding out their names. Who knows, maybe they'd get cocky and answer to them. Or maybe you just run through them all and hope one works?"

"Got me," Anne said. "I do know that they believed that when you called a demon by its name, it had to answer."

"Is that right?"

"Yes," said Anne, warming to one of her favorite topics. "And, in fact, a demon's name was one of the keys to controlling it. Necromancers and the like spent a great deal of time trying to figure out the names of demons from the Bible and other sources in order to be able to summon them and bend them to their will."

"Hmm." John frowned. "If they were real, I think I'd want to keep my distance from them as much as possible."

"Really?" Anne smiled. "Not even to gain power over your enemies? Or obtain forbidden knowledge? Raise the dead? Contact Mrs. Garrett and ask her who killed her?" Anne stopped as she heard her own words, her joke suddenly leaden and dreadful.

John spoke up quickly, rushing past the discomfiture. "No, no, I mean, I just wouldn't want those things knowing where I lived."

"Well, there's two things there," Anne said, her feet back on academic ground. "First, if you're a necromancer, in the context of the day, you're doing science. You're doing experiments on the nature of life, death, and so forth. Secondly, you might—and it's a big might—even consider yourself a Godly person, since the essence of controlling a demon is harnessing some of the Divine to compel the demonic. Some necromancers were priests."

"Still." Did John shiver? "Still. I don't like the idea."

"Why?" asked Anne. "Are you superstitious?"

John paused, then carefully said, "No."

He must be religious, thought Anne. *Not sure how I feel about that.* "Do you want me to look at those instead?" she offered.

"No, no, as I said," John smiled, "it's great stuff."

They sat together in silence until they ordered some sandwiches for lunch, then compared notes over food. Neither of them could come up with anything, though they had covered only a fraction of the book's pages. They spent the afternoon in companionable silence, occasionally discussing a point of Latin syntax or typesetting. They shared a bottle of wine and some very good sole for dinner, bouncing ideas off of each other, then ordered lots more coffee and dessert for the caffeine and sugar.

Anne heard the knock on the door and John saying, "Come in" to someone who she assumed was Milton, their Ugandan room-service waiter. What happened next was a blur. Thinking back later, she thought she'd seen, out of the corner of her eye, John's head come up in shock. She heard some soft whistling sounds. John lunged across to the far side of the conference table and pulled it over towards them, just missing Anne's ankle. Papers flew everywhere. Anne's first thought was to scream, "What are you doing?!" at John, but when she looked over again, he'd produced a black semiautomatic pistol from somewhere and began firing it over the table. The sheer incongruity of the sight of him standing there in a shooter's stance, pulling the trigger incredibly rapidly, with everything she thought she knew about him stunned her into silence.

John dropped down below the tabletop to load a fresh magazine and noticed her, frozen. "The pages!" he said in a stage whisper she made out through the ringing in her ears. "Get all the pages!" then popped back up and began firing the gun again, this time more slowly and precisely. As Anne tried to gather all the hundreds of pages and stuff them haphazardly back in the manuscript box, she noticed for the first time the pocking sound coming from the table. She realized there must be bullets hitting the underside. *They must have silencers*, she thought. She'd been around enough guns in New Mexico to know that she was only hearing John's pistol.

John changed magazines twice more, firing more slowly and carefully each time. Anne surmised he was trying to hit someone through the doorway and buy her time. He went to change the gun's magazine again and whispered, "Last one. You ready?"

Anne nodded, though she wasn't sure there weren't a few pages on the far side of the table. John pointed at a door on their side of the conference room. "Go left to the 'employees only' door." He stood and fired a shot. "Then turn right and run to the end of the hall. There's a freight elevator." He fired again. "If I'm not there in two minutes, take it all the way to the garage and head for the subway." He fired again. "Ride to the end of a line and call the Foundation's number and tell them what happened." He fired again. "Go!" he ordered.

Anne crouched and ran for the door, following his directions exactly. A small part of her brain posed the interesting question, *How did he know an escape route?* but Anne was in no mood to ponder. She got to the elevator and had started punching the down button repeatedly when she heard footsteps. John was sprinting down the hall behind her, gun in hand. The doors opened. She slipped inside into a front corner next to the control panel, and held the ◀ | ▶ button until she saw John, a blur, leap through the door, and land flat on the floor.

Anne jabbed at the ▶ | ◀ button for what seemed like an eternity as John rolled to the far side of the elevator. She heard the faint whistling sounds again, the dull cracks of bullets ripping through the wall padding and striking the back of the elevator, and sharper reports as others struck the wall out front. Finally the doors closed in what seemed like slow motion and the elevator began to descend.

Anne was still breathing hard, but she was pleased at how calm and rational her voice sounded when she said, "What was *that*?"

"I don't know," said John, his eyes slightly wild and darting hyperactively with adrenaline.

Cold fear flooded her. She hugged herself. "Those men are trying to *kill us*."

"Yep."

"Who *are* they?!"

"I swear to you, I have no idea." His eyes looked right into hers, wide, honest, and a little frightened.

"But how did you know to ..." she waved her finger around to indicate their flight.

"Contingency planning. We knew there was a chance someone was looking for you."

"But not a *big* chance!" Anne felt tears stinging the corners of her eyes, and it made her mad. "And what's with the *gun*?!" She pointed at his weapon. "And you said *Mrs. Garrett* had a gun and could shoot. What the hell kind of foundation are you people running?!"

"Long story. A very strange one, as I think I mentioned."

The elevator chimed and the display read G.

"Our stop," said John. "Ready?"

Anne bit her lip, drew a deep breath, and nodded, feeling a bit of steel in her spine. She gripped the manuscript box to her chest. Her eyes narrowed and as the doors began to move, she said, "You'd better have a hell of an explanation ready when we stop running, Mr. Ashton."

They ran.

ཕ་ར་ར

After an incredibly nerve-racking trip around the subway system, doubling back, switching cars, crossing platforms to slip between closing doors, they ended up on the Long Island Rail

Road out of Grand Central en route to MacArthur Airport. Anne wanted desperately to interrogate John on what in God's name was going on, but he'd indicated early on that they couldn't talk in public, and she just didn't have the heart to chat. John made a few cryptic cell-phone calls, but otherwise just scanned everyone in sight watchfully. They passed almost the entire time in silence. Occasionally Anne caught John staring off into space for a second with a haggard look on his face. *God, I'm dead on my feet after just running*, she thought. *He was in a* gunfight.

They walked up to the US Airways counter at MacArthur Airport, and John said to the agent, "We're John Ashton and Anne Wilkinson. I'm told you're expecting us." After he showed a piece of identification, Anne was surprised when the gate agent led them through an unmarked doorway next to the security turnstile. Down a long hall was a small, but comfortable lounge. "Someone will come get you when your plane is ready," the agent said and left, after they thanked her.

"Where are we?"

"VIP lounge," he said, collapsing, exhausted into a chair. She stood, arms crossed over the manuscript box.

"We didn't have to go through security?"

"A lot of law enforcement use this lounge."

"Are you a cop?"

"No. I work for the Coolidge Foundation. And I can't really say more than that. I'm sorry. I really am. I *really* am after today."

"I appreciate that. But, you know, it's time for me to go. Obviously, I don't know you anywhere near as well as I thought I did—and that wasn't very well to begin with—but there's no way on God's green earth that I'm hopping off on some airplane with you to who knows where—"

"Washington."

"It doesn't matter. But, look, John, from my perspective, you've gone from being an interesting colleague to Some Crazy Guy With a Gun. Look, here, keep the manuscript." She dropped it on the seat next to his with a little vehemence. "Do whatever you want with it. Just leave me out of it."

"You're not safe, Anne."

"No shit, Sherlock. I'm going to take a couple flights and maybe visit my parents in Albuquerque or some friends in Jackson Hole. Someplace far, far away. If you need me, call my cell phone. Or better yet, don't."

"Anne, I don't mean to alarm you, and I realize you're being asked to take an awful lot on faith here, but I swear to God I'm just trying to keep you safe at this point. This—" he waved at the box, "this is secondary. I mean, honestly, I don't know if we're going to be able to figure it out without you, so I have a selfish reason for keeping you around. I mean, other than that I like you a lot."

"I *liked* you too. But, look, you're not telling me crap, you're acting like some library foundation is the freaking CIA, and you've got a gun. I know you were never a teenage girl, but when we get our first training bra, they give us a booklet that says *never cross state lines with a stranger with a gun*. So I'm done. Goodbye."

"Anne, wait. Do you have your cell phone?"

She stopped, halfway to the door. "Yes."

"Do you have that FBI agent's number?"

"Yes."

"Call him."

Moments later, Anne's head spun even more when, having explained the situation to Agent Hunter, he said, "Go with Mr. Ashton, Ms. Wilkinson. We know him. He's trustworthy. Let me make a few calls to the New York field office to find out what the state of the investigation of the shooting is, and I'll be in touch with you later tonight or tomorrow. But for now, come down here to Washington. You'll be much safer. And Mr. Ashton is no threat to you. I promise."

After hanging up, Anne grabbed a beer out of the refrigerator and plopped angrily into a chair. She tried to formulate a fierce accusation. "You're not a librarian."

"No, I'm not. Mildred was our Librarian. I'm the Historian."

"For the Coolidge Foundation, about which you can tell me nothing—but that arms its librarians and historians."

He shrugged helplessly.

"Okay, fine. We won't talk about you. But we're awfully alone here. You *owe* me the benefit of your knowledge about what happened at the hotel," she said angrily, hoping she wouldn't burst into tears and ruin the effect.

"Absolutely. But I swear to you, I really don't know. I'm guessing those are the guys who killed Mildred and, like we thought, they're trying to kill you because they think you know something about the book. And, if we left any pages behind, they'll know we have it. Which can't be good. But, look, all I know is that I thought Milton had brought the coffee and chocolate mousse, so I raise my eyes and there are two guys in the doorway holding H&K MP5SDs."

"Those are guns, I assume?" she asked, a little abashed at the sarcasm leaking into her words.

"Yes. German-made nine-millimeter submachine guns with integral silencers. Extremely accurate and the weapon of choice of hostage-rescue and commando teams—"

"Not interested. So, they had guns. What did they look like?"

"White guys in suits. That's all I got."

"I wonder if one of them was Creepy Guy from my office."

"Could be," said John, taking a deep breath. "Okay, so, thank God they didn't have their guns aimed or we'd both be dead. So I'm guessing that they're not ex-commandos or the like. Anyway, I turned over the table, trying to dump all the pages towards us, pulled my gun and fired as much as I could to try and keep them out. That seemed to work. They looked surprised as hell. Then they hid behind the doorframes, shooting at me every so often. I think I winged one guy in his arm, but it must have just been a graze, because it didn't faze him. And this," he drew his gun, "is a Glock 37 chambered in .45 GAP." John popped out the magazine and unloaded a bullet onto the side table, then pulled the slide back and placed the bullet's ejected twin next to it. "If you get hit solidly with one of these, you drop your gun and go down."

"You're not going to take that on the plane," Anne said, incredulous, as he reloaded the two bullets, chambered one, and holstered the weapon.

"I am. We're not going through security. And if those guys can ambush us with automatic weapons in midtown Manhattan, they could jump us on a plane with a plastic shiv or garrote just as easily."

"But they don't know we're here; and, how...?" Her voice trailed off.

"I hope they don't know we're here. But hey, what if they put a transmitter in your wallet or shoe? It's awfully hard to know. And as to how I can get on a plane with a gun, again, I'm going to have to tell you I can't tell you how." He raised his hands in helpless apology.

Anne was amazed as they were led onto the plane, the door closed behind them, and they were seated in the first row of first class. John spent most of the flight standing with his back to the cockpit door, ostensibly reading a magazine, having pled a bad back to the flight crew (who treated them with solicitous gingerliness, as if they were celebrities or spies).

When the plane set down at National Airport, the passengers were told there would be a brief delay before deplaning, and that they were requested to stay in their seats. Anne and John, however, were led right off, through another series of restricted-access corridors until they were met by a tall blond man in a dark suit. Anne did a double take.

"Oh, Agent Hunter! Thank you so much for helping us out."

"Glad to see you're well, Ms. Wilkinson." He turned to Ashton. "John."

"Agent *Hunter*. Yes, thank you."

"You're welcome, sir. Now, please come with me," the FBI man said flatly.

They walked out an inconspicuous side entrance where a black SUV with tinted windows sat at the curb. Agent Hunter opened the back door and they both climbed in. Anne didn't know whether to be comforted or alarmed to see an M16 and a shotgun on the front passenger seat.

Hunter turned on the headlights, as dusk was turning to night, started the engine, then reached into a glove compartment and handed Anne a small, very heavy box. "Could you hand that to Mr. Ashton please, Ms. Wilkinson?"

"Sure." She did so, noticing in the process that it had the Winchester company's logo on it and .45 GAP just below that.

"Thank you, ma'am."

"You're welcome."

They drove in silence as John began laboriously loading each of the four empty magazines from his pockets with ten rounds of ammunition and topping off the one in his pistol with nine more.

Eventually, watching them cross the American Legion Bridge into Maryland, Anne said, "Okay, am I allowed to ask where we're going?"

"We have a nice safe house in Maryland where you'll be able to look more at the book," said Agent Hunter.

"Oh my God, that's the last thing I want to do right now. I can't even think straight, and you want me to do paleography?! In freaking *Latin*?!" Her voice began to crack, so she shut up quickly.

"Ma'am, that may be the one way we're going to get onto these guys at this point."

John put his hand on hers, and she instinctively yanked hers away. "Anne, look, this is the best way to keep you safe, and maybe we can get back to our mystery."

"Mystery?! Nancy Drew never got shot at with fucking *machine guns*. One minute, we're looking at a rare book, the next minute it's the fucking *Bourne Identity*. Only you're no Matt fucking

Damon." She saw Hunter crack a sardonic half smile. "No offense, John. I mean, well, sure, take offense. I don't know anymore." She shrank into a corner, arms crossed, glowering fiercely at the Beltway traffic out the front window.

Neither of the men seemed inclined to essay conversation after that, so Anne sat in furious stillness as they got off the Beltway at Connecticut Avenue and drove into a suburb just off Rock Creek Park. They drove through a neighborhood until they got to the last street before a ravine, on the other side of which rose the Mormon Temple, an Emerald City in luminous white, surmounted by orange spires on the top of one of which stood the Angel Moroni, his trumpet at the ready for the end of the world.

At the L-shaped intersection of two streets sat a house behind a wall and a long, gated driveway. Agent Hunter took a garage-door opener out of the glove compartment, flipped it open like an old cell phone and entered a code on a keypad. The gate slid open quickly and silently, and the SUV rolled past.

Anne saw the outline of a two-story house in the headlights. Hunter opened the garage door and parked the SUV next to a Camry. After he'd closed the door behind them, he unlocked the doors. Anne made no move to get out.

"Anne, look," pleaded John. "Give Agent Hunter the manuscript box. He'll sit on it here, and we'll take the other car out to a mall and buy you some clothes and toiletries. On me. Heck, I'll buy you dinner. Or give me your sizes, and I'll go. You can shower and take a nap and I'll bring something back. Or you can take the car. It's got a GPS navigation thingy. You're not a prisoner."

Anne exhaled and leveled her gaze at him. "Look, you. None of those sound appealing *at all*. I want to be back in my apartment in New York watching TV with no one trying to kill me. Or on my parents' couch in Albuquerque. The last place I want to be is this dump with you two. But. I am hungry, and I'm not taking a shower until I have clean clothes to change into. So, let's go, you and I. We'll shop. We'll eat. What we won't do is chat. In fact, I don't think I'd like you to speak unless spoken to. Are we clear?"

"Pellucid," he said solemnly. She had to fight hard not to show a little amusement at the baroque vocabulary. From Nancy Drew to *The Bourne Identity*—what fresh hell was this, Wodehouse?

She turned to Agent Hunter, who was again smiling his ironic little smile, enjoying Ashton's dressing-down. She picked up the heavy manuscript box and lifted it over the seat, setting it down on the long guns. "Agent Hunter, here's the book." Her lips curled into a vicious little smile of her own. "So that you aren't bored in our absence, by the time we get back, you will have all these pages in numerical order according to the file name printed on each page's bottom corner, and you will carefully document all the missing pages on a notepad in legible script."

Hunter scowled and opened his mouth when John patted him on the shoulder and said, "Hey, thanks, Agent Hunter," and slid out of the SUV.

5

They'd spent a good hour or more walking around White Flint, an expensive mall on Rockville Pike a few miles from the safe house. John did a good impression of a deaf-mute servant. He stayed a pace behind her, and dutifully tendered the Foundation's Amex card at each cash register. Anne still felt a bit vindictive, so she made sure all her purchases were expensive, including a pair of earrings with a tangle of sterling stems ending in little diamond buds, an original design from the Khoury Bros. store near the foot of the escalator to Borders, her last stop. She picked up what few reference volumes they had on Latin, Renaissance magic, and cryptography. Actually, the last were plentiful, which confused Anne a little until she remembered that the National Security Agency was somewhere around Washington.

Done at last, she turned to John and said, "Okay, I'm ready to be wined and dined. Take me somewhere nice."

"You like French?"

"I do."

"After you."

La Miche, a country-French restaurant in Bethesda, was not far. When they arrived Anne said, "*La Miche? Comme ça?*" and put her hand on her rear end.

"Um, I thought it meant 'loaf of bread,'" John said, a tad abashed.

"It does. A round loaf. Which is why it's slang for 'buttock.' Where'd you learn French?"

"My German's better," John truckled.

Not willing to let him off the hook, she said, "Well, let's hope it doesn't taste like ass."

Quite the contrary, she found out. She happily ordered for both of them. Baked brie and white sturgeon caviar to start, goat cheese *salade maison*, and *filet mignon au poivre et bourbon* for her and *cuisse de canard Grand-mère* for him. As she placed the order she said, "We'd also like the soufflé. But no hurry."

Seeing John wince a little, thinking about what must already be the mother of all expense reports, she waited until the waiter was gone, took a sip of wine, and said, "I hope they don't rush the soufflé. Agent Hunter's going to need a *lot* of time."

John actually spat out a little of the water he'd been drinking. He looked at her, and saw her laughing eyes and let himself laugh. Soon she was laughing too. Finally, she drained the glass of wine, signaled for him to refill it, and said, "Okay, John. Look, I'll level with you. This is all a little too much. But you seemed—seem—like a really decent guy. Can you explain any of this to me?"

"I'll try. What do you want to know?"

"Well, for starters, who do you work for? Don't say the Coolidge Foundation. I got that. Even if that's technically true, there's no way some little library foundation has its employees packing heat. 'My name is Decimal, Dewey Decimal. Double-O 813.54.'"

John laughed out loud. Anne continued, "Also, you were able to pull strings with the FBI to get us on a plane and have Agent Hunter show up at the airport with an arsenal and drive us to a safe house. That strikes me as *very* unusual for a 'historian.'" She sat back in her chair.

"Okay, well, let's see. God's honest truth." He held up a hand as if swearing an oath. "I do work for the Coolidge Foundation, and they do make me carry a gun for reasons I can't go into but aren't unrelated to the kind of unpleasant scene we had today. I do not work for the CIA, DIA, DEA, FBI, ATF, Secret Service, NSA, NIS, or, um, Scotland Yard. I called Agent Hunter and asked him to help, because he'd spoken to both of us about Mildred's death."

"So why does he call you John, John?"

"Okay, ok, you got me. I've worked with him before. A few years ago, we had some instances of interstate fraud involving some books we thought we were acquiring. He was the Special Agent in Charge. So we're friendly. He's really not that bad, even though he's a little by-the-book."

"He seemed to enjoy my ripping into you a lot."

"He has a sense of humor. It's just, well, it's just hidden behind the whole G-Man persona."

"Well, we're definitely staying out late to make him get the book back in order."

"Oh, definitely. How's the caviar?"

"Extraordinary. Pass the brie, please."

�…

When they returned to the house, which proved to be a conventional, spacious, pleasantly furnished suburban residence, they found Agent Hunter in the basement, surrounded by stacks of thin white foam board and aluminum tubes. He was thumbtacking a page to a piece of foam board that already had four or five attached neatly, though spaced seemingly at random.

"Steve," said John.

"John. Ms. Wilkinson."

"Can I ask what this art project is?" said John, slightly sarcastically.

"No," replied Hunter.

Anne stared at all the oddities. "You're organizing all the pages to be displayed on the foam board. I'm guessing ten to a side, twenty to a board. So all the pages have a pre-ordained place, and you can view them ten at a time."

Hunter looked up, his face still deadpan, but when he spoke, appreciation was audible. "That's it exactly."

"That's very clever," said Anne. "But what are all these aluminum pieces?"

"Frame," Hunter explained. "When it's put together, you'll be able to flip the boards left and right like pages in a book."

"Oh," said John, with sudden understanding. "Like a poster rack in a store."

Hunter just nodded.

"This is great. Brilliant even, Agent Hunter. Thank you," gushed Anne.

"Don't let his monosyllabic grunts and lack of social graces fool you, Anne," said John. "Agent Hunter here is a former Navy SEAL. His IQ is probably 140 or so."

Hunter scowled at John. "I don't think we should get too familiar here, John."

"Fine, fine." John accepted the reproof with obvious annoyance. "You just cost yourself an assistant." He turned and headed back up the stairs.

"I'll stay," offered Anne.

"Thanks anyway, Ms. Wilkinson. I do better work alone. Go get some rest. You've had a terrible day."

"Are you sure, Agent Hunter? I'm feeling much better with some food in me."

He shook his head. "Really, I'll be fine. You'll have this upstairs by breakfast. It'll have casters, so you can move it from room to room."

"You're sure?"

"Good night, Ms. Wilkinson."

Anne went upstairs to the master bedroom, showered, and collapsed into a black, dreamless sleep. When she came downstairs the next morning around ten-thirty in a pair of jeans and a red cashmere sweater, he'd been as good as his word. The display looked like something a museum curator might have in his workroom.

John was sitting in the kitchen drinking coffee and working through the *Post* and *Times*. He looked up from a sports page. "Hey, Caps won last night. Ovechkin had two."

Anne furrowed her brow. "That would be … baseball?"

"Close, hockey."

"Sorry, I don't really do sports. Nothing against them, but I've been a bit career-minded, so that was a whole hunk of life I decided I could ignore. I'll still watch a football game if the Broncos are playing. But hockey? I think the last game I paid attention to was an Albuquerque Scorpions game when I was home for Christmas in college one year."

"*Nekulturnaya.*"

"Ha!" she laughed. "You speak Russian?"

"A little. I take it you do."

"Yeah, I took a couple years in college. I was a bit of a Dostoyevsky freak."

"I'm a little worried that our current predicament owes a little to *Besy.*"

"*Demons?*" she asked, referring to the great novella.

"Hi, John. What are we talking about?" came a loud voice from behind Anne. She jumped. Agent Hunter stood behind her, scowling at John, with the M16 slung over his shoulder.

John looked down at his newspaper. "Russian literature."

"Really? Enlighten me," said Hunter. "*War and Peace* didn't fit in my pocket in Afghanistan."

Anne stepped in. "John was saying that our problems reminded him of the Dostoyevsky novel *Besy*, which used to be called *The Possessed* and is now usually called *Demons* or *The Devils* or something like it. It's about a bunch of political fanatics— terrorists, really."

"Ah." Hunter still looked a little askance at John.

"Right," said John with an 'I told you so, idiot' glare at Agent Hunter. "What I was going to say is that the people we're dealing with are a little too trigger-happy for my liking. I mean, they killed Mildred out of the blue, then tried to shoot Anne and me into Swiss cheese. No threats, no warnings, straight to murder. That's fanaticism, I think."

"It's scary," said Anne.

"Yep," said Hunter, crossing to the counter. "Coffee?"

"Thank you," said Anne.

Hunter poured her a cup, then returned to the living room, where he leaned the M16 in a corner. Anne took her mug and followed him into the room.

"Thank you very much for this wonderful display, Agent Hunter. This should make our job a lot easier. I noticed you put key numbers on the sides of the boards to make it easier to find what we're looking for."

"What *are* you looking for?" the FBI man asked.

"Well, first, some oddity in the text. It's conceivable that a page here or there could have been replaced with something else—a message, a map, a code, something. Secondly, maybe something extraneous like a note in the margins or the like."

"It is fairly marked up, I noticed last night. Do you know all those languages? I recognized German, Greek, Latin, and some others."

"I do, actually. I was a little bit of a nerd."

"You hide it well."

"Thanks, Agent Hunter. What about you?" Anne hoped a little chatting might make him a little friendlier, but her question seemed to turn his face to stone again.

"Me? I'm going to go clean the shotgun. I have no idea when it was last fired."

Skimming the papers, Anne ate a bowl of cereal; then she and John got settled in the living room with the chart. They decided on a methodology of scanning all the sheets on one side of a board to see if anything struck them, then taking all ten sheets down, dividing them in half, going over them closely page by page, and finally replacing them.

After a couple hours, John rubbed his eyes and said, "You know, it'd be nice to have something to compare this to, to kind of be able to say, "None of this is relevant."

"You mean another copy of the *Brevarium dæmonologicum?*" Anne replied. "I'm sure there's probably a rare-book dealer here in town that has one. They're not *that* rare. I know Georgetown's library has one."

John stood up. "Problem solved. The Foundation has excellent relations with Georgetown. I'll be right back."

"They'll just give it to you?"

"Sure. We loan them stuff, they loan us stuff all the time. It's a little bit odd for me to call them up and say I'm on my way over to get something, but …" He waved and walked out to the garage. Anne listened to the door go up and down and then turned back to the photos.

ꡃ ꡖ ꡗ ꡖ

The control copy did help, though John made himself more work by deciding to go back to the beginning and write down all the underlined phrases in case they somehow formed a code. Sometime shortly after midnight, Anne rubbed her eyes for the umpteenth time and yawned. She took a sip of the café mocha for which she'd sent Agent Hunter out to the Chevy Chase Lake Starbucks.

Anne's cell phone rang, showing a 212 number, but not one she recognized.

A man's deep voice said, "Is this Anne Wilkinson?"

"Yes, it is."

"Ms. Wilkinson, I'm Detective Marvin Lincoln of the NYPD arson squad, and I'm calling to find out if you are all right."

Her heart began to race. "Yes, yes, I'm fine. I'm on business in Washington, D.C. Why are you calling me?"

"Well, we're not one hundred percent sure, but it looks like someone blew up your office."

"*What?!*"

"According to passers-by, there was a loud boom about a half hour ago, and your office window blew out in a fireball, showering glass all over the street. FDNY responded almost immediately, and the fire was out within a relatively short period. There was some blast, fire, and water damage to the offices adjacent to yours, but the place was empty and no one seems to have been hurt. There was no evidence of anyone being injured on the scene, and we're calling all your coworkers at home to ensure they're all right."

"Oh, thank God."

"So I'm glad to be talking to you, Ms. Wilkinson."

"And I to you, Detective."

"So, can you help me out? Why would someone blow up your office?"

"I don't know, Detective. To scare me? In which case, they've succeeded. Otherwise, perhaps to destroy something? My computer? My files? The rare books in my wall safe?"

"The wall safe was intact, though damaged, and your partner Mr. Hathaway's coming down to check out any water damage to the contents. It didn't look like anyone tried to open it, though."

"That's very strange, Detective. I'd be happy to give you the contents of my computer. H&E has an off-site backup system, so I imagine you'll have all the information as of a couple days ago at the earliest."

"Thank you, Ms. Wilkinson. Did you have any personal objects or other valuables there that might have been stolen and the bomb placed to cover up the theft?"

"No, I'm afraid not. My office isn't very personal."

"Can you think of anyone who might have done this?"

"The only one who occurs to me is a very strange man who was in my office last week." She described the man to the detective and referred him to the D.C. detectives investigating Mrs. Garrett's murder. Detective Lincoln asked her a variety of other questions, to which she had very basic answers.

"Okay. Thank you for your time, Ms. Wilkinson. I'm glad you're all right, and I'll be in touch with more questions soon, I'm sure."

"Thank you, Detective."

On the couch, John looked stricken. "What happened?"

"They blew up my office."

"Oh, dear God, are your friends ok?"

"Yes, everyone's fine, it sounds like. I've got to call them though."

"If it was a time bomb," John speculated, "that was a lousy time to try and kill you."

"I doubt they were trying to kill me. Scare me, maybe. But they must have found one of our missing pages in the conference room and realized that there was a copy on my computer, and they were trying to destroy that. Of course, now I'm scared out of my mind. Who *are* these people? What's next? My apartment?!"

"Not to unnerve you further," John said, "but chances are they've already searched it."

"Okay," Anne said, her voice tight. "I'm going to do my very best not to freak out and start screaming rhetorical questions about what the hell is going on and what the deal with this goddamn book is." She took a gulp of her mocha. "And I'm going to go call my partners, coworkers, friends, and ex-boyfriend and tell them that I'm alive and then apologize for, I don't know, attracting the attention of a mad bomber. Also that I'm on indefinite leave, as of right now."

John began, "An—"

Anne held up her hand. "No, John. I can't talk about this anymore. I'm going to go make my calls and then go to bed."

As she walked up the stairs she heard Agent Hunter come in the front door.

"They blew up her office," John told him.

"Who *are* these guys?" Hunter asked with audible exasperation.

"I wish I knew," sighed John.

�བ˚ˋˋ˗

A day later, they declared the text of the book to be identical to the control breviary. The type was consistent and within the natural variations of a print run as well. John had brought a laptop from the Coolidge Foundation with which Anne was able to download the three pages left behind in the conference room. So it came down to the underlining or the marginalia, they figured. They spent another day carefully writing down all the marginalia longhand, then entering it into the computer. John already had most of the underlined words and their position on the page written out: *salvat*, p. 132 ¶3 ln. 4 wd. 8. He explained to Anne that it was conceivable that the position on the page could be a numerical code that could then be transposed back into letters. Anne agreed that that was certainly possible given sixteenth-century cryptography and steganography. But despair crept in when she started talking about the variety of codes that could have been used: the line within the paragraph could indicate the letter in the word—here, line four would indicate the fourth letter, *v*; the initial letters might be arranged in a transposition cipher; rotating letters in the word might also be used; there might be a key word or number used to encode it that they wouldn't have at all; or a variety of other methods.

"If only we knew a cryptographer," said John.

"This is Washington. Aren't there a lot of retired NSA and military types we could consult with?" Anne asked.

"I'll ask Agent Hunter. He might be able to pull some strings. But even if he can, I'm worried about disseminating the text."

"Because we know these mystery people will try and kill anyone with a copy," Anne said.

"Exactly."

"Damn it, if we could just figure out who they *are*," Anne said, smacking the page in front of her.

"Well, I know Agent Hunter has people trying to run them down."

"Of course, if this were some crappy novel, it'd be a bunch of albino Vatican hit men trying to cover up the fact that Jesus's descendants are a family of Lithuanian shoe salesmen in Perth Amboy and the papacy is run by aliens."

John cracked up. "If only it were that simple!" He laughed. "What the heck did Mildred see in here?"

"You know what?" said Anne. "Let's put codes on the back burner. She didn't have enough time to do any elaborate code breaking. Even if this was the first and only book she looked at—which I doubt—she just wasn't in the conference room long enough. So either there's a code she recognized right off—in which case, maybe we should be looking in her library, not this book—or there's no code at all, and we're just missing something."

John looked thoughtful and didn't speak for a while. "You know what, I think you're right. What say we break for the night and go down to Mildred's house tomorrow and see what we can find?"

"Sounds good to me," Anne yawned. "I'm exhausted and just about cross-eyed from looking at all this stuff." She rubbed her eyelids.

They said their good nights and went up to their bedrooms. Anne immediately went into the bathroom and began brushing her teeth. She was looking at the Van Gogh reproduction on the wall next to the sink absently when she thought she saw something move out of the corner of her eye. She turned to look in the mirror, for that's where she'd seen it, then looked behind her. Nothing. *My eyes are tired; my brain is frazzled,* she told herself. *Maybe I should take a Unisom.*

She spat into the sink and looked at herself in the mirror as she drank a cup of water. *You're not looking so hot, honey,* she told herself. *I look like I've been pulling all-nighters at college for a week, but I don't have a nineteen-year-old's constitution (or skin) anymore.*

Suddenly, her reflection rippled in the mirror. Or she thought it did. It looked like someone had dropped a pebble onto a pond surface right at the tip of her nose and a little wave radiated outward.

Oh my God, I'm tired, she thought. *I'm hallucinating.* It had happened to her once before in college. She remembered sitting in an exam room seeing little movements out of the corner of her eye that weren't really there. Nothing as dramatic or weird as the ripple, though. She rubbed at her eyes for a while.

When she looked in the mirror again, Anne was comforted to see her face undisturbed by any sort of special effect. For a moment. Then it happened again. She started and stepped back. She stared at the toilet. No distortions. The shower, nothing. The Van Gogh print, fine. The mirror again. Ripple. Ripple. Then a slowly eddying darkness at the central point—where her nose should have been. Anne shrank back, taking a step to the left. The blackness followed her to the left, as if attached to her face. She reflexively batted at her face, but only succeeded in giving herself a sore nose.

Suddenly, the blurry, indistinct lines of a face appeared in the darkness. Anne watched, riveted, as they sharpened into the features of a boy. A little black boy of about eight, who was squinting mightily. All of a sudden, he seemed to see her, and his eyes popped open in surprise. He smiled guilelessly and started pointing at her, then turned his head to talk to someone to his right. She couldn't hear a thing, but saw his lips moving as he was excitedly describing something—probably her—to someone out of sight.

Anne didn't know what to do. She waved, and he waved back. Then with a final ripple, the picture dissipated and the face in the mirror was her own again.

Anne looked around the bathroom, somehow expecting something to be different. She thought for a moment about whether she should just write all this off to fatigue, and possibly incipient mental illness, when common sense kicked in.

She knocked at John's bedroom door. "Just a second," he called, appearing a moment later in a Redskins T-shirt and sweatpants. "What's up?" he asked, looking puzzled.

"Uh, look, I know we're both tired and overworked and stuff," Anne said, screwing up her courage. "But something very weird just happened to me. If it was fatigue, it wouldn't bother me. But I don't think it was, and it was very strange, and I thought I should tell someone."

"Fire away," he said, concern and sympathy in his eyes.

"Well, either I saw something odd, or I'm going crazy, and I'm pretty sure I'm not going crazy, even given the events of the last couple weeks."

John's eyes opened a bit wider, and his face grew graver. "Tell me and I'll believe you. We've spent enough time together that I know you're the farthest thing from crazy."

"Okay." Anne took a deep breath. "I saw a face in the bathroom mirror."

John looked startled, but not shocked. "What kind of face?"

"Well, that's the odd thing, it was a little boy. A little black boy. He seemed very friendly and when I waved at him, he waved back. Then he disappeared."

"Oh crap," said John. He quickly scanned the hallway for something, and not finding it, said, "Okay, Anne. Here's what we're going to do." He reached behind him, grabbed a little ladder-back chair from a writing desk, and placed it in the middle of the hall. "Sit here," he said, stepping out of his room and closing the door behind him. "I'm going to just close all these doors here," he said, doing just that. "And now I'm going to go get Steve."

"Should I be worried?" Anne asked after she'd sat down.

"No. Well, yes, sort of. But no, nothing's going to happen to you. You're fine and you're safe. Just trust me on this, ok?"

"Um, sure. Can I have an explanation? I mean, this—" she vaguely indicated his activity by waving her hand in a tight circle, "this isn't exactly a normal reaction. You know something."

"I do. And I'm inclined to tell you about it. But I need to talk to Steve and we've got to do something first. Sit tight. Don't worry." He walked over to the linen closet, took out a stack of sheets and towels, closed the door, and went quickly down the stairs.

Anne crossed her legs and wondered, *What the hell is going on here? Are these guys crazy? Are they in on this? Have I actually been kidnapped?* Her worries were not allayed when, after the sounds of distant conversation passed, Agent Hunter and John came up the stairs, each with some towels and sheets over his arm and a man-of-action expression on his face.

Steve went into John's room, and John went to Anne's door. "Do you mind?" he asked.

Anne shrugged and smiled, shaking her head, "Be my guest. In for a dime …"

When he went in, Anne leaned forward and peered after him. She was baffled to watch him drop a hand towel over the makeup mirror that sat on the dressing table in the room, then hang a khaki-colored bed sheet over her bathroom mirror.

Agent Hunter came out of John's room and went into the hallway bathroom, his face tight with grim duty and his hands full of the good cheer of a pink and white floral sheet. *Okay*, Anne thought, *if it weren't a cliché and didn't remind me so much of what just happened, I would say I was through the looking-glass.*

After John and Steve had checked all the other bedrooms and carefully draped every mirror with Bed Bath & Beyond's finest, they met on the landing.

"Uh, guys?" Anne started. "I know I should be concerned or something, but that was the goofiest thing I've seen in a while."

"Yeah, I guess it would be," said John, one corner of his mouth turning up. Agent Hunter just shrugged, his Joe Friday mask slipping a bit as his eyes rolled in embarrassment.

"Okay, let's go downstairs and talk about this," said John with a sigh.

"Let's," said Anne, popping out of the chair.

They sat down at the kitchen table. "I'll make some coffee," offered Agent Hunter.

"Okay, Anne," said John. "Let me preface this conversation with a job offer."

"You lost me," said Anne, who couldn't have been more surprised if he'd broken into song.

"I'd like to offer you a job with the, ah, Coolidge Foundation. Mildred was our Librarian and book expert. We need to replace her. It's a good gig. The money is good—six figures after taxes, with bonuses at irregular intervals—though surely not what you'd make with Hathaway & Edgecombe. On the other hand, D.C.'s cheaper than New York, and you won't have to worry about a mortgage. The Foundation owns the house on Linnean Avenue, as well as all the books in it, and you'd get to live there rent-free for your entire career as Librarian. Plus, you get to curate one of the most unusual collections of books in the world. What do you say?"

"I'd say I'd have to think about it for quite a while."

"Well, here's the thing," said John, his brow furrowing. "I really can't explain what's going on here unless you work for the Foundation."

"What?!" Anne pushed back from the table in surprise. "That makes *no* sense at all. And, frankly, it's a kind of blackmail. I mean, obviously I want to know what's going on, but to make me give up my job for less money, move, and work for an entity that you won't even describe to me?"

"Yep," said John. "That's exactly it. Look, I don't make this offer lightly. Frankly, I'm only doing it now because of what happened to you. I've been thinking about Mildred's replacement for a while, and I very much respect your intelligence and knowledge of books, particularly of occult works, in which our collection is particularly strong. Moreover, your bravery in the face of those lunatics with submachine guns surprised and impressed me. And all the people I talked to when we were checking up on you after Mildred died said wonderful things about your character, judgment, and decency. I think you'd be an excellent candidate for this job, which—as I've mentioned repeatedly to your frustration—is more than a little strange. I'm not saying you'll have to face gun-toting madmen every week, but I can promise you you'll never be bored."

Agent Hunter laughed. Anne turned to him. "What do you think about this, Agent Hunter? Will you tell me something, or will you do your cigar-store-Indian impression?"

Agent Hunter smiled with genuine warmth. "Take the job," he said softly with a little smile and slight nod. He handed her a coffee cup. Anne looked into it, then up at the ceiling, as if trying to find a key that would suddenly make sense of all this.

"Okay, fine. I'll be your librarian," Anne said, thinking, *I can always quit when this is over and go back to H&E.*

"Very well," said John. "I know you can't really know what you're committing to, but I'm going to take that as a serious acceptance." He offered his hand and Anne shook it, resignedly.

"Now can you tell me what's going on?" asked Anne.

"Well, what happened to you is good, in a way. We have some idea what we're up against. Not who specifically, but what kind of person."

"I'm just as baffled as I was a few minutes ago," said Anne.

"Okay, let me ask you something that'll sound random but will eventually make sense. Do you know what *The Key of Solomon* is?"

"Ha!" Anne laughed. "Of course I do. *Clavis Solomonis*. It's the most important and complete early-modern grimoire available. The oldest known copy is fifteenth-century, in Greek, and it shows up in at least Latin, Italian, and English as early as the sixteenth century, and by the seventeenth it'd even been translated into Hebrew. It was probably extant in French and German as well, though we only have exemplars of the former from the eighteenth century and after and none of the latter. I once brokered a sale of a particularly nice eighteenth-century Latin edition printed in Cracow."

"Did you read it?" John asked.

"Of course!" said Anne. "I love that kind of stuff. And I'd read sections of it in college for a History of Magic class."

"What did you think?"

"It's fascinating and provides amazing insight into the mentality of the world of the day. It's the dark side of the religiosity of the Middle Ages."

"What about the content *qua* content?"

"What do you mean?" Anne asked. "The theory of magic or the spells themselves?"

"Either."

"Uh, kind of fun, but I wasn't exactly worried that reading one out loud would, you know, summon the demon Caacrinolaas who cometh forth like a dog and hath wings like a griffin."

John laughed. "Nice. That from *The Key of Solomon?*"

Anne felt herself smirking a little. "No, Wierus's *Pseudomonarchia dæmonum*. You might be confusing *The Key of Solomon* with the so-called *Lesser Key of Solomon* or *Lemegeton*, which largely reproduces Wierus's hierarchy of demons but adds some neat-o symbols for each of them."

John laughed again. "Okay, ok, you know *way* more about these books than I do. But do you think there's anything there?"

"What do you mean?" Anne asked, puzzled. "Do I think there's any real magic in there? No. I mean, you could change your psychological state pretty dramatically with auto-suggestion, and you could easily get other medievals to believe that you were a magician and then affect them by suggestion as well."

"I remember your saying that you were interested in monsters as well as magic, right? Vampires, werewolves, and so forth." Anne nodded. "Now, even if you don't believe in vampires and werewolves, you do believe there's a kernel of truth somewhere behind the myths, right?"

"Sure. There are a whole range of theo—"

John cut her off. "But you dismiss the possibility of a kernel of truth behind magic."

"No, I just told you—"

"Not a subjective psychological reality. An objective, physical reality."

"Yes, I dismiss that." Suddenly the penny dropped. "Wait a second, are you telling me that what happened in the bathroom upstairs was *magic?*"

John leaned back. "Yes. It was magic."

"There's no such thing."

"Well, then, congratulations. You've either got a sizable brain tumor or you've had a psychotic break."

Anne stared at John, then turned to Agent Hunter. "Are you buying this, Agent Hunter?" Hunter just nodded. "Okay, you guys are nuts. I'm out of here." She stood up.

"Anne, please. Look, let me ask you an academic question. In medieval necromancy, what sort of spell requires a mirror of some sort and a sinless, innocent child to look into it and report what he sees?"

Anne sat back down, crossed her arms, and chewed on her left little finger's nail. After a long minute, she growled, "A scrying spell."

"Which you use to ..."

"Spy on someone. Find someone."

"And we know—"

She cut him off. "That there's someone after me who's a little too interested in a book with exorcism rituals. Which are the Godly converse of necromantic demon-summoning rituals."

John just nodded.

"You've got to be kidding me," Anne said, rhetorically. John and Agent Hunter shook their heads.

"Okay, playing along here … because I'm temporarily at a loss to think of a different scenario. How does the scrying spell lock in on me?" Anne asked.

John said, "Usually they've got to have a connection to you. We know they were in your office. Do you ever, say, clip your fingernails at your desk?"

"Eww, no." She thought for a second. "But I had a hairbrush in the bottom drawer."

"Aha," said John.

"Sue me, I'm a girl."

"Manifestly."

"A girl with, what, a necromancer problem?" Anne asked with a mixture of sarcasm and bafflement.

"I'd say so."

"So, what, I can't look in a mirror ever again? How am I supposed to comb my hair—well, I guess the lesson is you never brush your hair lest a black-magician gets ahold of it."

"You can use the toaster or a computer screen or something. Just nothing glass with a silvered backing. Until we find the guy."

"You seem awfully familiar with this," Anne said with a hint of accusation.

John shrugged. "I heard about it happening once before."

"So, how do we find the guy?" she asked.

"Well, we know three things. One, he's using a little black boy as his scryer. So he's probably not in North Dakota. More likely a big city or the rural South. Two, he's got access to significant amounts of money. Machine guns aren't cheap, nor are hit men—unless they're his partners in hoodoo. And three?" he pointed to Anne.

"What? I'm supposed to know?"

"Who were necromancers in the Middle Ages?"

"Well, strictly speaking—avoiding the case of natural magicians, like herbalists and witches and alchemists and the like—it was usually someone literate, often familiar with Latin as well as religious rites. Which means weirdo fringy priests, deacons, and other minor clergy." John nodded approvingly. "Wait a second," Anne objected. "Are you saying we're looking for a Catholic priest? That's nuts."

"Nope. Look, necromancy is like any other secret society. Initiates learn from other initiates, and the sources and methods are kept as hidden as possible from the public," John explained.

"And the Catholic Church has been disseminating demonic magic for a thousand years?!" Anne asked incredulously. "Look, I'm not Catholic; I'm not even particularly religious, but that's a lurid slander."

"You misunderstand me—and I'm Catholic. It's not the institutional Church, which as you'll remember, spent a lot of time and energy burning necromantic texts and imprisoning and executing necromancers. According to the theory, it would be a tiny subgroup of priests. God knows what their motivations may be, or if there are more than one or two of them, but the story goes that there are some corrupt priests who have passed down some sort of necromantic knowledge. I mean, okay, magic is an outré idea, but barring that, if I'd told you ten years ago that it was more likely that the Church contained some priests in an order—or freelancing—who were guarding some very old secret, historical rites or that there were groups of priests covering for each other's practicing pedophilia and homosexuality, which would you have thought more likely? Or a worse slander?"

"Point taken. So what do we do?"

"We hunt the bastard down," said Agent Hunter.

"Wait, what, what's the 'we'? The FBI hunts sorcerers?" Anne felt totally at sea, utterly unmoored by the surreal conversations they'd been having.

"Look, let's leave that for the morning, Anne. We'll go down to the Coolidge Foundation, and I'll try and explain."

"Okay, fine. But I'm not going back in that bathroom."

"I wouldn't ask you to," said John.

As they said their good nights upstairs, Anne turned to John and said, "Um, it occurs to me that if this is all really some black-magic thing, they might have more of my hair. Could they do something to me with that?"

John looked thoughtful for a long moment that terrified Anne, then he said, "I doubt it. Because they would have already done it. I mean, they tried to kill you with guns, not voodoo, right? So I think we can assume they're trying to locate you in order to get the rest of the manuscript photos or, conceivably, to shoot you right this time. Fortunately, since you were in the bathroom, all they could have seen was the bathroom wall behind you. Not too many clues there. But we don't want to give them any more."

"Hence the covered mirrors. Okay. Look, John, I've been trusting you with my life and now my sanity. If this is all some crazy con job or you're screwing with me, I will get you. I don't know how, but I'll come up with some crazy wronged-woman revenge, I promise. Seriously, someone or something will end up shot or on fire."

John's face fell. "Anne, I couldn't be more sorry this happened to you. I like you very much, to tell the truth, and I would love to have kept you on the outside, if only because I could come to New York and have dinner with you and talk about things that aren't this and maybe we could be ... um ... friends ... or.... What I'm trying to say is just, I'm sorry. I thought we could figure this book puzzle out quickly enough to keep something like this from happening. But now, we're still stuck with the book as our only significant clue, and you're suddenly in a very strange, scary world. I am just abjectly, profoundly sorry."

"I used to like you, too, John," Anne said flatly, walked into her room, and closed the door behind her.

6

When Anne got up, Agent Hunter was gone. She arrived in the kitchen in a new business suit to find John there with two travel mugs of coffee in hand. "Ready to go to work?" he asked.

She took a mug and headed to the garage. As he turned onto Saul Road, she said, "Okay, I'm a little more collected now, and honestly, I'm a little more inclined toward a brain tumor or psychosis. I just can't accept that here in the twenty-first century we're talking about *necromancy*. I mean, that's just ridiculous."

"Okay, let's not call it necromancy," John said reasonably. "A paranormal phenomenon?"

"Meaningless term."

"Science is the way we moderns view the physical world," John proposed. "Can we call it a phenomenon which science might be able to account for at some point but can't at the moment?"

"Well, if you want to," Anne said, annoyed. "But parsimony demands that my mental state is *far* more likely to be the issue. Fatigue, stress, isolation. Who wouldn't start to crack up a little?"

"Well, you, for one. Your breathing is even, your affect appropriate, your emotions not abnormal given the circumstances and admirably under control, you're not drinking excessively or on medication, and you've been doing intellectual work at a very high level. With all due respect to William of Occam, I think we can rule out mental illness on your part." He turned the car left onto Connecticut Avenue, heading towards the District. "You look very nice this morning, incidentally."

Anne threw her hand without a coffee mug up in the air. "How can you be so low-key about this? Look, here's the thing. Pardon my bluntness, but necromancy is bullshit."

"On what basis do you say that?" John asked.

"On the basis of being incredibly familiar with the stuff. I spent half my undergrad years, all of grad school, and much of my career and free time digging through old esoteric books. Grimoires, necromantic manuals, the whole deal. And it's all ridiculous. I mean, if it worked, *we'd know*. I mean, there'd be people conjuring illusory feasts and castles out of thin air. You'd think that would have shown up in the history books. The way to a woman's heart would be through a voodoo doll. People would be riding magical spirit horses from continent to continent in an hour. It's all crap! There's an enormous amount of academic literature which concludes that a lot of this stuff was written as *entertainment*. Hell, a bunch of my college friends and I actually tried a ritual to make two people whom we thought would make a great couple fall in love, sort of as a joke, and sort of curious as to what would happen. We did everything exactly as it was written—magic circles, effigies, etc.—and ... nothing! *Of course!*"

"Okay, look, I'm really not arguing with you here," John countered, "but, to borrow a couple terms from Catholic theology, what you're arguing is that magic works *ex opere operato*, by means of the ritual itself. It might work *ex opere operantis*, though, by means of the performers. You and your friends might have had to believe in it, or have some special power to get it to work."

"I see the distinction, but it's meaningless. It can't ever work!" Anne objected.

"You're probably right. I'm not an expert, but I'm guessing ninety-nine percent of all the necromantic stuff was nonsense. Entertainment, fakery, wish-fulfillment, pseudo-religion. But what if some tiny fraction of it *did* work? It might be hidden in plain sight in those books with some secret never-written key which made it work. Maybe it required a specially initiated adept. I mean, again, to go back to the Catholic context, you have to become a priest before you can perform the sacraments. Who's to say whatever changed in you then, didn't change you in a way that made these things *work*?"

"But they don't! And nothing happens to Catholic priests when they take orders! Then or now! It's all just premodern mystagogy."

"Well, as a Catholic, I'm required to politely disagree with you on that one," said John, changing lanes. "But, look, let's get back to what happened to you. You saw a young boy's face appear in your mirror, interact with you, and then disappear. You're not mentally ill, and say it's not magic—whatever 'magic' is. Then what was it?"

"I don't know," Anne said quietly.

"Can we call it 'magic,' if we definite 'magic' as some mechanism not yet explained by science but which appears to affect the physical world?"

"So you're saying that bumblebees fly by magic?" Anne squinted as she took a drink of coffee.

"No, that's actually a myth, according to a physicist I know. It's some property called 'dynamic stall.'" John looked like he was going to expound on the topic but thought better of it. "But, no, I don't just mean any unexplained phenomenon is magical, in that sense. I mean whatever happened to you used some sort of physical force or power or mechanism that we have no idea about, in order to be able to see you through a mirror from ... well, from wherever he is."

"And therefore it's necromancy?" Anne asked. "That's a big leap."

"No, I think it's necromancy because it fits exactly with descriptions of necromantic scrying rituals," John said, matter-of-factly. "And I'm drawing the conclusion that it's most likely some rogue Catholic priest based on what little we know of the medieval context of necromancy and the fragmentary reports of its survival. I could be wrong, though."

"Wait, where do you get these reports on necromancy in the modern world?" Anne asked.

"Here we are," John said, pulling into an underground Colonial Parking lot beneath a building on Farragut Square.

They took a dedicated elevator to the lobby, then switched to a different bank of elevators. As they rode up to the sixth floor, John said, "This is kind of an odd office."

They got off at the sixth floor and walked down a hall to a door with a sign saying COOLIDGE FOUNDATION. John took a key card out of his pocket and unlocked the door. Inside was a pleasant, if bland, reception area with the Foundation's name over a desk. At the desk, a black man in a security guard's uniform with a Coolidge Foundation shoulder patch looked up at them.

"Morning, Carl," said John, signing them in on a piece of paper. "This is Anne Wilkinson. She's going to be joining the Foundation, so you'll probably be seeing a lot of her. Today's her first day."

"Welcome to you," said Carl with a smile. He stood up and offered his hand. As Anne took it and thanked him, she noticed he had a gun on his hip.

John walked to the sole door out of the reception area, unlocked it with a key on a ring, and ushered Anne through. As he locked it behind her, she looked around at the unexceptional hallway behind it. There were no side doors, merely a single elevator at the end.

"Are we in an episode of *Get Smart?*" asked Anne.

"Would you believe … *The X-Files?*" John said in a reasonably good Don Adams drone, typing a code on the keypad it had instead of buttons. The elevator opened and he held out an arm. "After you, 99."

They stepped inside and Anne was surprised to see there were only two main buttons on the elevator panel, though there were a number of odd switches and smaller buttons arrayed behind a Lucite panel. John pressed the lower of the two control buttons, the door closed, and they went down. And down. And down. Anne was surprised. The elevator felt like it was moving fairly quickly, but it seemed to take them longer to reach the bottom than it had to come up to the sixth floor. As the chime sounded, she asked, "Basement?"

"Sub-sub-sub-basement. Actually we're about five stories below street level." The doors opened on a concrete tunnel about ten feet wide. There was a wide double door across from them. John placed his hand on a plastic surface and his eye up to what looked like a keyhole.

"Scanners?" Anne asked.

"Yep. Can't be too careful these days." John smiled. "We used to have a big raccoon problem."

They walked through the door into another wide tunnel. There was a zippy-looking golf cart sitting against one wall. "Want to ride or walk?" asked John. "It's a little ways."

"Let's ride," said Anne, climbing into the passenger seat. "It'll minimize the amount of time I have to freak out that a strange man whom I barely know has me in some undetectable subterranean labyrinth."

"Hey, you work here now!" John laughed as he unplugged the cart from a large wall outlet. He hopped in and soon they were speeding down the featureless tunnel. Around the time Anne could see a wall appear at the far end, she was surprised to see the tunnel's walls change from concrete to old, skillfully laid brick, and a few side tunnels open up. John parked the golf cart and Anne looked at the door at the end of the tunnel. It was not what she expected. Rather than some sort of missile-silo blast-shield door, it was an old-fashioned set of double doors, each door a six-panel door in heavy, dark oak. The fittings were all brass, as was the small plaque on the door that said NO ADMITTANCE.

John slid a large brass key with a complicated tooth out of his pocket and turned it in the door's keyhole. From the door came a number of surprisingly loud mechanical noises—bolts sliding, parts clicking. Then, rather anticlimactically, it opened about an inch. John held the door for Anne, who unconsciously held her breath. When she walked through and saw what lay beyond, she gasped.

ㅁᄀ˒ᄀ

"It's *beautiful*," she whispered to John. The room in front of them was paneled in cherrywood and mahogany, and lit with brass-and-frosted-glass sconces on the walls and a large, circular white fixture in the ceiling above a mosaic in the center of the floor. The insignia was of a raven atop two crossed keys, ringed by the motto *ntia immo multiplicant*, "entities do indeed multiply," a wry inversion of Occam's Razor.

Twelve six-panel oak doors with brass nameplates led out from the side walls, six to her left, six to her right. Against the walls separating the doors sat ten gorgeous, heavy writing desks from, she guessed, the first couple decades of the last century. The five on her left faced this door, the five to her right faced the far wall. They looked almost brand new, despite their obvious age. Each had a large, green felt blotter and a heavy brass desk set, with a letter opener, magnifying glass, etc. Modern paraphernalia—computers, cell phones, newspapers—lay incongruously upon them.

On the left side of the opposite wall stood a small sliding door next to a little brass panel around a black Bakelite button, apparently an elevator of some sort. On the right-hand side of the wall hung a large, life-sized oil painting of—Anne did a double take—Calvin Coolidge, next to a flagpole with a raven-and-keys finial.

Most spectacular were the wide, arched floor-to-ceiling windows in the room. At first glance, Anne thought she was looking out over the D.C. skyline, but then she remembered that she was five stories underground. She squinted a little and realized that they were *trompe l'oeil* paintings, and that they couldn't have been more recent than the 1920s or '30s, given the distinctly smaller Washington they depicted. Through some trick of lighting, they gave the appearance of sunny daylight. Anne was impressed.

Five of the desks had occupants, all of whom looked up at Anne and John as they came through the door. A fiftyish black woman in a bright pink suit smiled at them, and a fair, youngish man whose blond hairline was well receded peered over a yellow legal pad with a half scowl. A lithe woman with shoulder-length curly brown hair and a regal Semitic nose was speaking into a phone but raised an eyebrow in their direction in aristocratic acknowledgement. A tall, barrel-chested, brown-haired white guy peeked around a large computer monitor with evident curiosity. And last, sitting at a desk, moving papers was—

"Special Agent Hunter!" Anne burst out.

"Call me Steve," he said, deadpan. "I'm not a special agent and my name's not Hunter."

Anne looked open-mouthed at John, who put a hand on her shoulder. "I'll explain in a minute. Let me introduce you around." He guided her to the closest occupied desk. "This is Wilhelmina Chase. Wilhelmina is the most important person in the office. She's been here the longest, knows where all the bodies are buried—"

"Mostly metaphorically," Wilhelmina cut in with a big smile.

"—and keeps track of the physical plant and all of our finances." John gestured towards an enormous spreadsheet on Wilhelmina's computer. Wilhelmina took Anne's hand, and said warmly, "Welcome, dear. This place takes a little getting used to, but once you get your feet under you, there's no place you'll rather be."

"Thank you," said Anne, feeling oddly comforted.

"Next, this is Michael Himmelberg, our chief—indeed, sole—legal Counsel, as well as one of our best investigators."

Himmelberg was already rising when John started speaking, and offered his hand. "It's a pleasure to meet you, Ms. Wilkinson," he said very formally. "Please call me Mike."

"Anne. Thank you," she countered.

"You know Steve," John said, pointing in his direction. "His last name is actually McCormack. He's an investigator, our Armorer and our Hunter. Which is why he thinks it's funny to use that as an alias."

"It is funny, John," said Steve.

"It was the name of the *Post*'s film critic. You don't think that's eventually going to tip someone off?" John asked, half-heartedly, clearly revisiting the site of a long-ago defeat.

"It's a common name and it makes me happy," said Steve, though it was hard to discern any happiness in his poker face.

"Right," said John fatalistically. "On the phone here is Claire Krakauer."

Claire held out a hand, flashed a brilliant smile, and mouthed, "Hi," and rolled her eyes toward the phone to indicate she couldn't get off right now.

"Claire's our minister of propaganda, if you will. She's in charge of making sure we don't appear on anyone's radar, as our Liaison to other bureaus and agencies—usually in the guise of someone from a different agency. She works the government, is an investigator, and will outfit you with the credentials you'll need from time to time."

"Okay," said Anne, still overwhelmed.

"Last, and never least," said John, walking her down the aisle, "this is Joe McManus."

Joe stood, drawing himself up to six-two by Anne's guess, looking even bigger because of his broad build. "Hi, Anne. I'm Joe," he said in a soft voice with a kind smile. "Since John doesn't really understand what I do, I'll save him a minute. I'm the Telegrapher. What that means these days is: I run all of our computer systems, and ensure that we're properly networked into all the law-enforcement, intelligence, and other agencies' machines so that when we dig around in their computers it looks unremarkable. I also gain access to other systems as necessary. Phones, satellites, that kind of stuff."

"I could have said that," objected John, laughing.

"Yeah, but not as well," said Joe.

"True enough," conceded John. "Joe's also an investigator, so you'll work with him from time to time."

Anne said to John, "I don't quite understand. I thought I was being hired as a librarian. For a foundation. You're telling me that this is the government? And that I will be doing some sort of investigation? Investigating what?"

Joe and John looked at each other with a knowing smile. "Let's go into my office, Anne," said John. "Joe, could you bring Anne some coffee?"

"Sure," said Joe, smiling that winning smile again. "Or would you rather have espresso or tea or hot chocolate or something, Anne? We've got all sorts of stuff in the galley."

"Coffee's great, thank you," said Anne. "Just black."

"Black it is," said Joe. "And welcome to the Black Chamber."

ༀ༵ཀྱི

John took Anne through one of the twelve doors. The brass plate on the door read HISTORIAN. His office could have been in any university, with floor-to-ceiling shelves covered with books of all ages, only the furniture was of a piece with the rest of the building: heavy, dark antiques. They sat, John behind the desk, Anne in the one guest chair. Joe brought in the coffee and excused himself, closing the door behind him.

John let Anne drink a little coffee in silence.

"Wow, that's good," said Anne.

"We tend to splurge on luxuries. We're not like the rest of the government in that, or many other respects."

"The government? What did Joe mean when he said, 'Welcome to the Black Chamber?'" Anne asked.

"That's what we call ourselves," Joe explained.

"Why?" asked Anne

"Have you heard of 'the Black Chamber' before?"

Anne shook her head. "Should I have?"

"No, it's mostly a trivia question. The Black Chamber was the first American code-breaking body, sort of a proto-NSA. It was founded by this brilliant but weird guy named Herbert Yardley who, years later, ended up breaking codes for the Republic of China, reporting at one remove to a charming guy named Tai Li, also known as 'Chiang Kai-Shek's Hatchet Man,' 'the Killer,' and most charmingly, 'China's Himmler.'"

"Wow. That must be a story."

"It is. Yardley actually wrote a book about it. But I'm getting ahead of myself. Yardley started off as a code clerk in the State Department. Around 1910, he realized that the U.S. had no facility whatsoever for breaking codes."

"They didn't? Wasn't that a problem?" Anne furrowed her brow.

"Nope. Yep. So Yardley basically reads every book on cryptography in the Library of Congress. Even though they're quite outdated, he gets the basics. He then starts breaking the codes in the messages that he handles in the code room at State and tells his superiors that the U.S. really needs some code-breaking ability. They agree, and by the time we're into World War I, he's running a code-breaking shop and is reading all sorts of German, British, Italian, and French cable traffic."

"Wow. Good for him." Anne nodded for him to keep telling the story while she took another sip of coffee.

"And good for the country," John continued. "Yardley catches German spies and saboteurs and proves the government of Mexico is colluding with the Germans. Once we're into the war, he's able to learn where and when various German offensives are going to take place. After the war, however, there's some controversy over keeping the Black Chamber up and running. The Navy is willing to pony up some money because it's of obvious use to them, plus their own short-lived, World War I code-breaking shop managed to break exactly zero codes. The State Department begrudgingly kicks in the majority of the funds, but insists they can't operate in the District of Columbia."

"Why not?" Anne asked.

John rolled his eyes as if to say, 'government,' then explained, "Probably to lessen the chance of a diplomatic incident. And maybe to keep some psychological space between State—mostly striped-suit-wearing, upper-class, Europeanized, wealthy WASPs—and the motley crew of academics and oddballs Yardley had put together to do what State saw as dirty work. Anyway, Yardley keeps on keeping on up in New York, breaking Japanese and Russian codes—of which he's frankly admiring, incidentally—until one day he gets the news that the new Secretary of State, Henry Stimson, has learned of the Black Chamber's allegedly nefarious doings and pulled his budget."

"Oh, wait," Anne said, with the eagerness of a student who's suddenly recalled an answer. "I do remember something about this. 'Gentlemen don't read each other's mail,' right?"

"Right," said John. "That was Stimson in his memoirs, years later. He later became Secretary of War during World War II and did a one-eighty on the desirability of reading your enemies' mail."

"Hitler was no gentleman?" joked Anne.

John laughed. "I've never understood Stimson's original thinking, myself, given that he must have known that other 'gentlemen' were reading each other's mail. The British required every telegraph company operating on their transatlantic cables to provide the Admiralty with a copy of every telegram sent over the cables within ten days. Not coincidentally, the Admiralty is where the British code-breaking section was located."

Anne took another drink of coffee, then said, "I still don't understand what that Black Chamber has to do with this Black Chamber. You said their headquarters was in New York."

"For that, you need to know a little something about our patron saint." He pointed in the direction of the Coolidge portrait. "Do you know anything about Silent Cal?"

"Dorothy Parker's line on the occasion of his death."

"'How could they tell?' Right." He laughed. "Well, Coolidge was one of those presidents who were massively underrated at the time, like Eisenhower or Reagan. Most of the smart set saw them as incompetent provincial boobs. Silent Cal supposedly did nothing; Eisenhower played golf; Reagan napped. Or so we believed. When you look at the historical record, though, all of those guys had depths and smarts way beyond what they ever let show in public."

"Not that I don't believe you," said Anne, with a skeptical moue, "but, well, I'll withhold my judgment until I see some proof. At least in the case of Reagan. And thank God you didn't include George W."

John laughed. "Just don't believe everything you read in the papers, is all I'm saying." His face grew solemn as he continued, "Right before Coolidge is re-elected, his younger son Calvin is playing tennis on the White House courts and gets a blister on his foot. It pops, goes septic, and he dies. He was sixteen."

"Oh my God." The thought of parents watching their teenaged son die constricted Anne's throat and turned her stomach.

"Exactly." John nodded in sympathy. "Coolidge is just crushed, and most historians agree that he's never the same man after that. His 1924 campaign is subdued, though he's popular enough that he wins the entire country outside of the Deep South and Wisconsin."

"Wisconsin?" Anne asked, grateful for the distraction of an intellectual quandary.

"Bob La Follette, the third-party, Progressive candidate was from Wisconsin."

Anne nodded understanding. "So what does Coolidge have to do with the Black Chamber?"

"As President, Coolidge was aware of Yardley's shop, which was the most secret and secretive part of the government. One day, Coolidge shows up unannounced at their brownstone at Three East Thirty-Eighth Street and asks to speak to Yardley alone. Coolidge tells Yardley he very much respects his work and his genius for codes and secrecy, and wonders if he'd be interested in doing some further outré research. Yardley says, in so many words, 'Sure, Mr. President, whaddya got?' And granite-countenanced John Calvin Coolidge, Jr., thirtieth President of the United States, whispers, 'I've seen a ghost.'"

"You're kidding me," Anne said.

"Not in the slightest. Coolidge tells Yardley that, no, he is not mad. No, he is not deranged by grief. Yes, he has an excellent bill of health from his doctors. And yet, one day, staring out the window, as was his wont, he saw his son Calvin, still in tennis whites, walking across the White House lawn. Calvin stopped, turned, caught his father's eye, smiled and waved. Then he walked around the corner of the building and out of sight. When Coolidge got over the shock, his first thought was that it must have been a cruel prank. But after that, he saw Calvin twice more. Once in a deserted hallway late at night, Calvin appeared at the opposite end, walked toward him with a big smile, seemed to laugh without sound, then disappeared. The third time, Coolidge walked into the Oval Office alone, saw Calvin seated in his chair behind his desk—which the boy would never have had the effrontery to do— patted the desk, blew his father a kiss, and vanished."

"He was obviously just seeing things," Anne said, though with a bit of doubt in her voice.

"Like you, that was his first thought," John recounted. "He confided in his wife, Grace, he told Yardley, who confessed that she hadn't seen Calvin, but her reaction was that Calvin was trying to comfort his father from beyond. Coolidge told Yardley, 'I would love nothing more than to have this consolation, and indeed I shall go to my grave hoping it is so and cheered by the memory of seeing my boy laughing a few final times, but I conclude I cannot credit my eyes. I would have you find some sober, unconventional intellects and report to me on the reality or unreality of the so-called 'spirit world' and similar phenomena. I have always assumed it is bunk, and that the Lord's plan does not allow for such things. However, given the evidence, however subjective, of these apparent visitations, I must call my preconceptions into question.'"

"Wait a minute," Anne interjected. "This was all a ghost-hunting, spiritualist-busting sort of deal? Wasn't Houdini doing that on his own?"

"Yes and no. We don't have any records of what Yardley's first investigators found, but there must have been something that interested them because they stayed on the payroll."

"Or they just liked the easy money," said Anne.

"Maybe," John said dubiously, "Though that doesn't explain all this." He gestured at the office around them.

"No, it doesn't. So what does?"

John's eyes lit up and his eyebrows shot up. "The Innsmouth Incident."

"The what?" Anne said.

"Good question. We're not actually sure ourselves. Coolidge visited Yardley in 1925. Yardley set up what he called 'Section 6' of MI-8—MI-8 was the real name of 'the Black Chamber'—on a very informal basis under his personal supervision. He declined to record the results of the investigation of the White House haunting, noting that he had reported them orally to the President. Then, in 1927, something big happened in a little town called Innsmouth in Massachusetts."

"Never heard of it."

"It's not there anymore," John said significantly. "It was a ghost town by the late 1930s and sometime in the '50s, it was just razed to the ground and made into a state park and beach. Not even the name survived. But in 1927 and 1928 it was fairly big news. The newspapers reported some very substantial police or military action, complete with dynamiting of buildings, gun battles, and so forth."

"Sort of a Waco thing?"

"That was the initial impression, except that it was assumed to have something to do with bootlegging or rum-running. Innsmouth was a very old port town: run-down, isolated, and poor. So it made perfect sense that rum-runners would be landing liquor there. There were scores of arrests, and people were held without trial in military prisons, which was a huge scandal for a while, until, apparently, the critics were actually taken to see the prisoners, after which time, they seem to have clammed up. In fact, that's the amazing thing about the whole story: everyone involved just seems to have refused to talk about it for the rest of their natural lives."

"Weird," said Anne, somewhat impressed.

"Very. And it only gets weirder. One tabloid, to be fair a very untrustworthy one, reported a submarine was concurrently firing torpedoes into an underwater trench behind a large reef a mile or two off the coast."

"Huh?"

"Right," John agreed. "Makes no sense. The story came from a drunken sailor who could never be re-located. Well, whatever happened in Innsmouth led to all of this. In the wake of the Innsmouth Incident, MI-8 Section 6 was moved to these top-secret digs below the OEOB and buried so deep in the budgets of the White House, Coast Guard, Navy, and Weather Bureau, that it's virtually impossible to detect or defund. Not that anyone's tried, as far as we know. Our budget is so small, compared to the size of the government these days, it'd be like trying to find three particular grains of rice in China."

"We're below the Old Executive Office Building?"

John nodded. "We're below the sewers in the bedrock that the OEOB's basement is sitting on. Those brick tunnels you saw outside the door are a further sub-level of the old Washington sewer system that no longer carries water."

"Okay, go back to Innsmouth. What happened?" Anne no longer felt confused or overwhelmed, just fascinated.

"To be honest, we don't know. There exists in our archives a very, very large file on it. It is, however, sealed and can only be opened with the signature of the President of the United States. Given that Coolidge was, as far as we know, the last president with direct knowledge of us, it's unlikely that any president will be ordering the file opened anytime soon."

"Why don't you just open it?" Anne asked.

"Hey, we're law-abiding citizens … for the most part. It's actually been a bit of a hobby among various Black Chamber employees over the years to try and reconstruct what must have happened. There are lots of opinions, but no one's proved anything. Something big and bad definitely happened. One of our predecessors tracked down the Navy's records, and sure enough, there is a big lacuna in the whereabouts of U.S.S. *S-19*, an attack submarine out of the sub base in New London, Connecticut, for the dates in question. And in the '80s we managed to get a line on a few of the Marines whose units, we deduced, had gone into Innsmouth. They were all really old and presumably had nothing to lose by talking. To a man they all denied having been there and claimed the story was entirely cooked up by the New York papers in a circulation war. But our men said that they were all visibly startled to be asked the question, even though they couldn't be cajoled into spilling a word. Interestingly, veterans of those units had a very high rate of suicide and commitment for mental illness in the '30s through '50s."

"Okay, seriously, let's open the file." Anne was almost bouncing in her chair.

"Not unless you want to go to federal prison," John said flatly.

"Really?" Anne allowed a little wheedling to slip into her voice.

"Really," John said sadly.

"Damn."

"I know. So, anyway, whatever happened in Innsmouth got the Black Chamber a headquarters, a decent budget for the day, and a very broad purview to look into unusual phenomena."

"Like ghosts and vampires and Bigfoot?"

"The standard Discovery Channel trifecta? Sure. But also antique occult books and incunabula, oddball cults, et cetera."

Anne had a sudden realization. "So, wait, are you telling me these things are real? Vampires and ghosts and Bigfoot?"

"Yes and no. I'm sure you've heard the cliché that 'most myths have a basis in fact,' right? Well, it's a cliché because it's true," said John.

"Wait, I'll give you cults and maybe even old books, but ghosts and vampires having a basis in fact?! Bullshit," Anne objected and not primly.

John waved a hand. "Let's not get hung up in specifics. The reason you're here is because you know old books. Particularly old books about magic, alchemy, witchcraft, the occult—right?"

"That's my job. And my hobby. Okay, really my vocation. So, yeah, but come on."

"You told me you've read a lot of these books, right?"

"Sure." Anne nodded, then took a large drink of coffee.

"Do you think the authors are idiots?" John asked in a friendly tone.

"No," Anne answered without offense. "Just massively ignorant, pre-scientific minds misdirected by the dominant superstitions of the day. And a few genuine loons."

"So you wouldn't be surprised if somewhere in the text, there were some lost bits of historical arcana or folk wisdom or the like?" John asked.

"Of course not," Anne answered.

"That's what we're mostly talking about," John said, holding his hands up as if appealing to reason, "though they can often be startling. Also, I have to say that we post-scientific minds have to be careful not to be misdirected by the dominant superstitions of the day. Like scientism and materialism. Talk to particle physicists. They'll tell you that quantum theory is flatly incompatible with materialism."

"Whoa, whoa." Anne held up her free hand. "Are you telling me because physicists haven't nailed down the finer points of cosmology that I have to believe in Casper the Friendly Ghost and the Abominable Snowman?"

"Not at all! Just, you know, keep an open mind around here. If you don't, it can be, uh, rough."

"Okay, so you guys have the real X-Files?" Anne asked, smirking a little.

"No, no. I mean, UFOs? Conspiracies to splice in alien DNA? Not at all. In fact, one thing I can say is that we've never found a shred of proof of sentient extraterrestrial life."

"But all this other stuff?"

"Maybe. Depends what you mean." He waggled his hands.

"Okay, so like the good, monster-hunt episodes of *The X-Files*," Anne joked.

"I guess. I never watched the show. Though the redhead was awfully cute." He paused for a second, lost in a reverie of Gillian Anderson, then said, "Back to the Black Chamber."

"Oh, right."

"So, in 1927, Section 6 gets set up right here in D.C., and in 1929, Stimson abolishes MI-8. Then in 1931, ostensibly desperate for cash, Yardley writes a memoir, essentially giving away the store of America's spy secrets of World War I. There's a huge uproar."

"So he went to jail?" Anne asked.

"Curiously enough, no," John said, lightly emphasizing the last word. "There was a loophole in the espionage law through which he and his book fit rather precisely."

"He did it intentionally?" Anne was confused.

"It's hard to know, but we here in the surviving Black Chamber, what was Section 6, suspect that he did it to further conceal our existence. By totally exposing the Chamber's wartime and post-war existence, he eliminated the chance that anyone else would ever stumble on it accidentally, kicking over the traces of Section 6. In fact, he may have done too good a job. President Hoover, who appointed Stimson, may never have known of us, and consequently none of his successors."

"Wait, so you're some rogue organization?" Anne was gripped by a mild suspicion.

"Not at all." John laughed. "I mean, Oliver North and his buddies were the Agriculture Department by comparison, but we strictly abide by President Coolidge's charter and, unless we're necessitated to break them under said charter, all the laws of the United States."

"But *quis custodiet* and all?" Anne asked.

"We watch each other." His eyes darkened. "And, frankly, you can't really resign and write a tell-all book. That just doesn't happen."

"Why n—"

"It just doesn't happen," he said, very, very measuredly.

"I think I take your meaning," Anne said, a chill running up her spine.

"Good," John said, cautiously and a little sadly.

"So did Yardley face, uh, consequences for writing his book?"

John shook his head. "Oh no. We're not really sure how much Yardley knew about Section 6's workings, though it's safe to assume more rather than less. He ended up in China a few years later—again, according to another memoir—ostensibly as Chiang

Kai-Shek's cryptographer during the Second Sino-Japanese War, but in the course of examining some documents recently, we think he may have also been working on a Section 6 project. Have you ever heard of *The Seven Cryptical Books of Hsan?*"

"Oh, heck yes," said Anne, happy to be back on familiar ground. "One of the principal—and rarest—treatises on Chinese occultism. It's rare enough that I've never seen a copy. I think there's supposed to be one in a restricted collection at the University of San Francisco."

"Right. Well, near as we can tell, there was a copy dating to the first century B.C. in the Chinese Imperial Library when it was in Peking, but it never arrived in Taipei."

"That's impossible. The earliest-known copy of *Hsan* is first century A.D."

John raised his eyebrow and shook his head.

"*Wow.* That'd be priceless."

"Oh yeah," John said smiling. "Our best guess is that Chiang or Tai Li stole it for his personal library, and it's possible that Yardley stole it from him."

"He never turned it over to Section 6?"

"Eh, well, we don't exactly know."

"What? How is that possible?" she said, getting genuinely irate at the thought of a lost book.

"Okay, remember the last scene in *Raiders of the Lost Ark?*"

"Sure," Anne said, "wheeling the crate into the giant, anonymous storehouse."

"Well, our Archive," he pointed to the floor, and presumably a further sub-basement, "is kind of like that. There are a lot of sealed, plain wood boxes with file numbers on them. And a lot of those files are sealed, pending a direct need on a current case to learn the details of their contents."

"So you could have the lost Ark down there and you'd have no idea."

"Almost. I mean, I think if we had the Ark, over the years we'd have had some Librarians struck dead by God for bumping into its crate."

"You know what I mean."

John shrugged. "The short answer is yes. We do have comprehensive indexes with cross-references on hundreds of topics, but there are no details whatsoever in the indexes. It's a deliberately inefficient system designed, in some bizarre way, to keep anyone from compiling too great a knowledge about our holdings and their contents."

"Why is that?"

"I suspect because whoever designed it thought he was protecting us from some very, very dangerous things."

7

Anne and John spent several more hours discussing what, exactly, Anne would do as Librarian. She'd be asked to acquire, maintain, and index all the Black Chamber's rare books, as well as keep the Archive's indexes current. Anne thought that perhaps they might be reorganized and investigated further, but John flatly ruled it out. They were interrupted only once by Claire Krakauer, who came in with a digital camera and took a few pictures of Anne.

By noon, Anne was overwhelmed. She tried to keep her end of the conversation at a high level, but was beginning to get confused. She welcomed the knock that came at the door.

Claire strode in, wearing Armani. "Hey, John, I'm taking Anne to lunch." She put her hand on Anne's shoulder. "You guys can talk more later."

John grinned amiably. "Great idea, Claire."

Claire clipped a photo ID onto Anne's jacket's breast pocket and ushered her out of the room. "Want to see something *really* cool?" she whispered conspiratorially.

"Sure," Anne said with as much enthusiasm as her befogged wits could muster.

Claire walked her over to the little elevator door in the wall with the Coolidge portrait and pushed the Bakelite button. "It takes a second to come down," said Claire. A long minute or two later, the door slid slowly and silently open.

"Come on in," said Claire, waving her into a tiny space, only about six feet wide and no more than two feet deep. The door slid closed in front of them. "Okay, here's the drill. Do not touch the walls, and keep your feet about eighteen inches apart. How's your balance?"

"Mental or physical?"

Claire laughed. "The latter. No inner-ear imbalances or the like?"

"No, I'm good. I actually did some gymnastics in high school before a growth spurt made me the towering specimen before you. Why do you ask?"

"Because some people don't do too well in here." Claire pushed the sole button on the elevator panel, and slowly they began to rise. Anne immediately noticed that the walls didn't rise with them. Looking down, she saw that what she'd taken as the floor was a platform that didn't quite touch the walls. Looking up, she saw a long shaft, paneled in dark wood. She got a twinge of vertigo and was happy to feel Claire's hand grabbing her arm.

"Steady," Claire laughed. "It's a little weird the first couple times."

"Thanks," Anne said. "Boy, you couldn't get a fat guy in here."

"You're right. Phil Hendrickson was a heavy guy working for us few years ago, and he couldn't use this door. We sometimes like to come in through the OEOB, but he never could."

"Where's he working now?" Anne asked, wondering what kind of career path former Black Chamber people took.

Claire was quiet. Anne looked over to see her twisting a watch around her wrist unconsciously. After a moment, she said, her voice rough, "There was a thing with an, um, thing in northern Nevada. Phil didn't come back."

"I'm sorry," Anne said.

Claire said nothing.

When the platform stopped rising, they were in a small, dark wooden space with a little light leaking through a pair of double doors in front of them. Claire counted, "One, two, three ..." and a click sounded from the doors. Claire reached out and pushed them outward, revealing a lovely, nineteenth-century-style salon.

"Watch out, the first step's a big one," Claire said.

Anne looked down to see that they were a foot or two above the carpet. She stepped down onto the soft rug, watched Claire follow, then stepped back to take in the strange elevator. It was a large, ornately carved piece of cabinetry, with shelves to either side holding decorative antique books, pieces of porcelain, and a few pictures of presidents. Her mouth fell open as the platform they'd been standing on rose up further, revealing itself to be the top of a third set of shelves, lined with books. They reached the top of the surrounding cabinet, aligning with the side shelves, and stopped with another click.

"That's so—" Anne started and left off.

"What?" Claire said.

"I wish I could come up with a more articulate way of saying 'cool,'" Anne said, "but, damn, that's really cool."

Claire laughed. "It is, isn't it?" She reached forward and closed the double doors in front of the books. Claire led her out the door on the far side of the room. On the other side was a small brass plate reading:

JOHN QUINCY ADAMS SALON.
RING 333 FOR RESERVATIONS.

Claire pulled the door shut and a very modern electronic pass-card lock fired a bolt home. Anne looked around and saw that they were in an enormous Beaux Arts corridor with a ceiling that must have been twenty feet high. Men and women, mostly in dark suits, walked by purposefully, some nodding friendly acknowledgement.

Claire said, "This way," and strode down the corridor.

Anne caught up and whispered, "Where are we?"

"This is the Old Executive Office Building; didn't John tell you we were under it?"

"Yes, but ..." Anne didn't really know what to say. A sudden thought struck her and she looked down at the photo ID she was wearing. It bore her picture, name, the Presidential Seal, and the legend WHITE HOUSE—OEOB.

A few minutes later, they'd come out the back of the OEOB and were walking up a path towards the White House past reporters and cameramen who were set up under little semi-permanent tents at ten-foot intervals. Anne feared she was fairly wide-eyed when Claire led her into the White House Briefing Room—which was a tiny little dump of a place in person—and down a few hallways.

"Is the White House Mess all right?" Claire asked with a slightly ironic grin.

"Lovely!" Anne replied in her best cheery-ditz tone.

They got a table. Anne leaned over and said, "Okay, this is incredible, but, seriously, what are we doing here?"

Claire said softly, "We work here, so we're entitled to dine here. We don't do it too much as a rule, as we try not to get too familiar with anyone else who works around here, but once in a while, it's fun. And the food's surprisingly good."

They ordered food in the small dining room and it was, in fact, tasty. Eventually Claire said, "Okay, Anne, let me level with you. This is a hard, hard job. It's more interesting and more fun and more terrifying than anything you'll ever do. But you need to commit to it completely. There aren't many of us, and our lives will inevitably end up in your hands on more than one occasion. You've got to be ready for that, and you'll have to trust that when yours is in our hands, we won't let you down." She lowered her voice. "Also, there's a chance that you'll get killed. Maybe in some genuinely awful way."

"You're serious," Anne said.

"Completely."

"I have to admit, I'm intrigued. But at the same time, the life expectancy and income in the auction world is pretty good."

"I won't argue with you. However, we do pretty well, income-wise. By whatever bizarre means we're budgeted, we have great salaries. Probably because there are so few of us. And usually get a pretty hefty yearly bonus."

"Bonus?"

"Yep," Claire nodded. "Not exactly usual for the government, but we tend to confiscate a lot of stuff, including money. The Chamber puts aside much of it in a general-use fund, but a portion of it gets divided up among the rest of us, and the next of kin of anyone killed that year."

"Do people really get killed that often?" Anne asked, putting her utensils down.

Claire looked away, fighting off a scowl, and unconsciously twisting her watchband around a finger. "Don't get the wrong impression. It's not like we drop like flies. But it happens. Too often."

"So you're saying I need to consider this before I sign up."

"No," Claire said, locking eyes with Anne. "You've already signed up. And we don't take resignations. What I'm telling you is that you have to commit to this completely, every day, or you'll get yourself or someone else killed."

ᡃᡥᠬᡥ

After lunch, John said, "Okay, Anne, time to take a ride." They retraced their vaguely fantastic route back to John's car, and he took K Street to Fourteenth, then down across the Fourteenth Street Bridge to the George Washington Parkway. When the Parkway turned from a scenic, limited-access highway to a street in a charming little downtown, Anne asked where they were.

"Alexandria, Virginia. The home of the Coolidge Foundation."

"Wait, I thought you just made that up as a cover."

"Oh, it's a cover, all right," John said, nodding, "but it's a real foundation with actual assets and so forth. Heck, you can donate to it and write it off on your taxes, if you want. It's a very, very *good* cover. We're headed to its library. It's closed. Our last small-l librarian resigned when Mildred died. He was her grandson, so we closed the Foundation while he was mourning. Turns out Mildred left him quite a lot of money, and he decided he'd rather be a freelance expert on rare books. He was quite smart, so I expect he'll do well. Whenever you feel like getting around to it, you'll have to hire a new librarian. Let me mention right out that the Foundation's librarian never knows that the Foundation is a cover. It's a small, well-funded, slightly eccentric foundation dedicated to the preservation of rare and strange books. You, as the Black Chamber's Librarian, are *ex officio* president and CEO of the Foundation. As the Chamber's Historian, I'm vice president. The Foundation's librarian should be a smart pro who loves books. That's really all we're looking for. The Foundation's library has all state-of-the-art climate and humidity control, lighting, and so forth. We hire outside contractors for maintenance. If the librarian is a conservator, great, they can do some conservation, otherwise, we've got a budget to fly in conservators or to ship books around the world for repair and conservation. Oh, and we have a bonded cleaning company which comes in and has special instructions how to clean around rare books. So that's really it. Staff of three. Minimal paperwork. A nice additional salary for you, and you stay in rare-book circles."

They drove down to an unusual, three-story, octagonal stone building across a street from the Potomac. Its architecture might have been characterized as Gothic Deco. There were five parking spaces in a tiny lot next to it. Signs indicated three were reserved for employees and two were marked GUEST.

John unlocked the heavy, bronze double doors and ushered Anne inside. He flipped some light switches and Anne gasped. The interior was a single large atrium under a filtered-glass skylight. The perimeter of each upper floor was a balcony with old-fashioned built-in bookcases with rolling library ladders. Their dark, lacquered hardwood glowed with reflected light. On the enormous Persian rug in the center of the ground floor sat two huge desks, each with a couple comfortable-looking padded-leather chairs pulled up. Brass-and-mahogany spiral staircases ran up in the corners of the side walls perpendicular to the front door. On the right-hand wall, a spiral staircase rose along the near corner, on the second floor, the farther. On the left-hand wall, the arrangement was reversed, providing a nice sense of balance.

On the second-floor balcony rail facing the door hung a picture of President Coolidge, looking on impassively.

"This is … amazing," said Anne.

"Most book people have that reaction. It's sort of a dream library, isn't it?"

"Oh yes," Anne said. "I've had sex dreams that weren't this good."

John led Anne up the right-hand staircases to the third floor. Anne instinctively scanned the shelves for titles. He led her to a small three-room office above the front door. Windows looked out over the Potomac and the Jefferson Memorial on the other side.

"You should see the view when the cherry blossoms are out," said John. Anne just nodded. "Okay, these are the three offices. There's only this one entrance, so you have to walk through, like a shotgun apartment. Yours is the farthest back there, mine's in the middle, and the librarian's up here. Nice old-fashioned furniture, Silent Cal on the walls, phones, new Macs." He took a book off a low bookcase. "Here are the complete holdings."

Anne skimmed it and raised her eyebrows. "This is very nice. I mean, this must run into the millions of dollars."

"We've had good people running it for almost a hundred years," John said humbly. "And we have a good alarm system."

"So what about the occult volumes?" Anne asked. "I don't see many unusual ones in here."

"Excellent point. Those, especially the really weird ones, are kept in the Chamber's archive in the basement below the office. If, as occasionally happens, some library or scholar wants a look at one, you make an appointment and hand-carry it over here for them to look at. The excuse you tell the librarian is that you've either got them at home or in a special storage unit, or something. We don't advertise those holdings, though, so it's usually a book we've acquired at a public auction that someone was following."

"So why did the bad guys kill Mrs. Garrett at her house, rather than just make an appointment and steal the book here? Or try and break in here some night?" Anne asked.

"I don't know. Maybe they were in a hurry?" John said, frustration in his voice. "On a cheerier note, do you know anyone who knows rare books and might like a quiet, very well-paid job?"

"Do you require any credentials? Master's in library science?" Anne asked.

"What do you mean 'you'? You're the Foundation now, Anne."

"So I am. Well, I do have a friend, sort of a former colleague, who knows a hell of a lot about rare books, because she's the daughter of a senior partner in my firm, so she grew up around them. She's quite young, though, just out of college, and hasn't got much of a résumé yet. B.A. in English Literature from Yale, though. Spenser, Chaucer, Marlowe, Shakespeare. Knows Latin, French, and I think some Old Norse."

"Hey, if you think she's up to it, it's entirely your call," John said amiably.

"Okay," said Anne, and picked up the phone on the desk. She dialed H&E and when the receptionist answered, she smiled involuntarily and said, "Hey, Linds, it's Anne. Want an awesome job?"

�ད᠋ᠵ᠋

Late that afternoon, returning to the Black Chamber, as Anne now thought of the subterranean offices, John told Anne, "Okay, now you get to spend an hour or so with Steve. Try not to hold his laconic manner against him. He's actually pretty hilarious and kind, although very, very dry." He walked her down a side hall to a staircase leading down. It was secured by a very impressive electronic lock on a heavy steel door. At its foot was another seriously locked, impregnable-looking door. "This, incidentally, is where we all run to make our last stand, if anyone ever invades the office," John explained. "Not that that's ever happened, but just FYI. I'll give you a list of combinations when you get back. You can start memorizing them—but you can't take the list out of the office."

Upon passing through the door, Anne realized why this was the stronghold. It was one long concrete room, with a two-lane, one-hundred-foot shooting range running down one side. The rest of the room was given over to racks and racks of weaponry, from pistols, through submachine guns, combat shotguns, and assault rifles, to—although Anne was no expert—some elaborate-looking ones she thought she'd seen in movies as grenade and rocket launchers.

"Hi, Anne," said Steve McCormack, standing at a workbench, cleaning some pistols, grinning uncharacteristically. "Ready for some fun?"

"I guess so," Anne said, thinking that this would probably be the least weird thing she'd done all day.

"I'll leave you crazy kids alone. I've got some breviary pages to look through," John said.

"Any excuse to stay off the range," said Steve. "No wonder you didn't take out those guys in New York."

John gave a sarcastic wave and headed up the stairs.

Steve turned to Anne. "I'll kill you if you ever tell him, but he's actually a good, natural shot. He just doesn't like practicing, so I take it on myself to force him to every week. Okay, look around you, welcome to Steve's Basement of Fun."

Anne laughed. "You're a lot funnier than Agent Hunter."

"Yeah, I know. When I'm posing as a lawman, I tend to overdo the Joe Friday bit, but it keeps people at arm's length, and they don't ask too many questions of me. So it has its uses. And, of course, we never expected you to get professionally involved with the Chamber. You were just an expert John was hoping to add to his Rolodex. But congratulations and welcome." He offered his hand and Anne shook it.

"Thank you. Um, everyone else seems to have a warning for me when they welcome me. I'd have thought you'd be the first one to tell me that I'd probably die in the line of duty or whatever."

"We're all going to die, Anne," he said softly but plainly. "What we're doing here is serving our country. There are worse ways to die." He paused, then saw something in her face and felt compelled to add, "But you're the Librarian. Mostly, you'll have to worry about putting Neosporin on your paper cuts."

Anne laughed. "Okay, that I can do."

"Safety first, Miss Wilkinson," Steve joked. "But now, let's work on your personal safety. These are Glock handguns. We use them because they're ridiculously reliable under the most extreme conditions. And we occasionally find ourselves in quite extreme situations. Once I get you up to speed on the weapon, you should carry this at all times. You'll never lack identification establishing you as law enforcement of some stripe, so you can carry anywhere in the country, on airplanes, et cetera. Now, have you ever shot a gun before?"

"Yep," Anne said. "I'm from New Mexico. Big-time gun country."

"Excellent," said Steve. "I'm from Colorado."

"Hey! Go, Broncos," Anne said.

"Your mouth to God's ear." Steve smiled. "I was worried that you were a native New Yorker. So, I don't have to worry about your being afraid of them, or being taken aback by the big bang?"

"Nope. Dad and I used to shoot targets and varmints with .22s and later .223s. I've fired a couple pistols: my grandfather's old .45 from Korea, a nine-millimeter Beretta that a boyfriend brought back from the Marines, and a .357 revolver of some sort one time. *That* was a big bang. Almost broke my wrists, too." McCormack laughed. "But I shot the whole cylinder, popped in a speedloader and fired another six."

"Were you any good?" he asked.

"Pretty," Anne said.

"Great. So, all I have to do is get rid of the bad habits you picked up as a recreational shooter. And get you used to the idea of shooting someone, rather than something."

"I can't say that sounds fun," said Anne.

"Getting rid of the bad habits is, because you become a better shooter," Steve said philosophically. "Shooting at people is never fun, even if you do it perfectly. Maybe especially if you do it perfectly."

"I take it you're the voice of experience there."

Steve nodded and the impassive Agent Hunter mask slipped over his face for a moment. He relaxed again and said, "Okay, well, that answers my question about what caliber to give you. We'll go with a .45 GAP that'll give you the stopping power of Grandpa Wilkinson's .45 with a lot more control."

He picked up one of the Glocks on the bench, and handed it and a full magazine to Anne. The Glock's slide was back, so Anne pointed it at the floor, and pushed the magazine home. The slide snapped forward, chambering a bullet with a quiet click.

Anne spent the next hour on the firing line, shooting at targets at various distances, trying to learn the new two-handed grip Steve recommended and, eventually, trying to eject and reload magazines smoothly and quickly. When she finally fumbled one completely and it went skittering across the floor, Steve took off his ear protectors and signaled for her to follow suit.

"Okay, great, Anne. I think that'll do it for now. You've been tired for the last fifteen minutes, but I wanted to see how you did tired. And mostly, you did very well for someone who's inexperienced. You're a pretty good shot out of the box, and you'll only get better. I'm available for tips anytime I'm around here, and the range is yours to use anytime."

Anne was, in fact, exhausted, both physically and mentally. Her muscles had been trying hard to pick up the new positions, and she'd been concentrating so intently she only realized how tired she was when she stopped. "Okay, thanks, Steve," she said, wiping her brow. She held out the gun to him.

"Nope, that's yours," he said. "I'll give you the case and cleaning kit, although frankly, you can just bring it to me for maintenance. That's my job. For now, just keep it in a purse or a coat pocket or someplace fairly handy. Sometime this week, I'll give you a holster and we'll practice drawing. I'd rather you didn't shoot yourself in the spleen trying to draw and shoot."

"Sounds like a plan. And I don't have to worry if I drop it?"

"Well, you should never drop a gun, period, but the Glock is very, very safe in that regard. There's *almost* no chance it would go off. But I wouldn't try playing the percentages."

"*Comprendo*," said Anne, involuntarily recalling her New Mexican roots. "So, do I get to play with these sometime?" she asked, indicating the racks of small arms.

Steve's eyebrows shot up in surprise. "You want to?"

"Sure. It'd be fun. And this is the Basement of Fun, right?"

"Hey, anytime you want, Anne. I'll give you as much weapon training as you like on anything you see here. Most of them," he gestured upstairs, "do it once or twice, but lose interest because it's a skill that takes practice. But if you want to, I'll make you as good as an average SWAT team officer within a year."

"Wow, well, let's see how it goes," said Anne. "But I am definitely interested, after what happened in the Marriott with John. I'd much rather find myself behind one of those than in front of one again."

"Amen, sister." Steve grinned. "And going back to what I said about John earlier: what he did there, as I understand it, was some terrific gunfighting. He was massively outgunned and had an unarmed civilian to protect, and he managed to pin those two guys down long enough for you to escape with almost all of your printouts. Of course, if the guys he'd been up against had been real professionals," *Like you*, Anne thought, "there's no way either of you would still be alive. So we'll have that in our favor when we run up against them again."

Steve gave Anne the combinations to the stair locks, and she let herself out.

She arrived back at the bullpen-style office to find people still working hard at their desks. She sat down at an unoccupied one and stared off into space, not really thinking about much but struck by the immense oddity of what she'd been drawn into.

"John!" said Mike Himmelberg in a loud baritone. "John!" Anne looked lazily at John's open office door. He stuck his head out.

"What's up, Mike?"

"Anne here is obviously wiped out," he said, concern in his voice. "Take her home and let her sit in a tub or something."

"Just don't forget to cover your mirrors for modesty," Claire chuckled over her computer. *She must have been the one to have covered the ladies' room mirror pre-emptively*, Anne thought.

"No, really, I'm ok," Anne objected weakly to John.

"Nope," John said cheerily. "Mike's right. This place can be overwhelming even after you've been here a while. Let's go!"

On the car ride up Rock Creek Park, John was mercifully quiet, and just put in a New Order CD, which made a pleasant aural backdrop to the ride, its electronic ambiance contrasting pleasingly with the natural beauty of the park. Anne thought she saw a deer walking through an old cemetery up the side of a hill, and suddenly they were pulling into the garage of the safe house in Kensington.

"I think I fell asleep," Anne said, running her fingers through her hair and reaching for the visor. John pushed the visor back up to the ceiling. "Ah, ah. Mirror," he said.

"Oh geez."

John turned in the driver's seat. "You look great. Wait, wipe the corner of your mouth. No, the other one. Just a little drool."

Anne rolled her eyes and groaned. "Dignity, dignity, my kingdom for some dignity!"

"Tell you what," said John. "You go inside and take a nice hot bath. I'll run up to the China Gourmet on Connecticut and get us some dinner and bring it back. There's a liquor store right there, too, so I'll grab a bottle of wine. And we can skip the breviary tonight. I don't know that we'll be all that productive."

"Get two bottles," said Anne imperatively. "And, no, I think with a bath and some food—how's their kung pao chicken?"

"Great."

"Okay, get me some hot and sour soup, some pot stickers, and some kung pao chicken."

"Pot stickers?"

"You know, the little dumpling things?"

"Oh, sure. Steamed or fried?"

"I'll leave that up to you." Anne smiled and climbed out of the car.

8

The bath was heaven, and Anne fell asleep in it. She woke feeling terrific, aside from the bathwater in her mouth. She dried off, enjoying the thick, fluffy towels someone had outfitted the place with (Claire? Wilhelmina? Mrs. Garrett?), and got dressed in some Redskins sweats she'd picked up at the mall. It felt disloyal to the Broncos, but they were thick and warm and they hadn't had any Broncos gear. She pulled on a pair of thick socks and padded down the stairs. She wasn't halfway to the bottom when the smell of Chinese food hit her, and she went down the rest of the way double-time.

"I am *famished*," Anne said, moving very quickly to the table. John was pouring white wine. "I hope you like it."

"I think I would like fiberglass insulation at this point."

They had a very pleasant dinner, chatting casually, but mostly Anne enjoyed the tasty food and the wine, which John had chosen well. After dinner, Anne opened a bottle of red wine and poured them each a glass. "Okay," she said, not tipsy but mildly euphoric, "Let's talk about the breviary."

"You sure you wanna talk shop?" John asked.

"Well, it's that or watch some TV." Anne got up and sprawled her long body on a couch, wineglass in hand.

"Honestly, I wouldn't mind some TV," shrugged John, following her into the living room.

"No, no, no. I'm feeling good and I'd really love to see what we can do with the breviary. Let's just talk a bit about it without getting into the weeds. What's in the book?"

John plopped down into an armchair, closed his eyes, and thought. "Well, the text, of course, the marginalia, and that doodling and laundry list and stuff in the back."

"Right. And outside?"

"Binding, glue, no lettering or design on the cover."

"Now, we've verified the text, right?" Anne asked.

"Yep. And most of the marginalia we've seen is pretty pedestrian and doesn't have any of the oddness you sometimes see in encoded messages," John said. "Although we're not experts."

Anne was curious. "Does the Black Chamber have a code expert?"

"No," John said. "Joe McManus is probably pretty knowledgeable about them, I'd guess, though electronic encryption is more his thing; but he's not a cryptographer. And I don't think he can read Latin."

"But if we gave him some words we suspected were code, he might be able to discern some sort of pattern that'd indicate there was a text to decipher?"

"That hadn't occurred to me," said John, opening his eyes. "He well might be able to. It's math at bottom, right? We could get him a frequency distribution of letters in Latin from somewhere—hell, it's probably on the Internet."

"Now, what about that stuff on the endpapers? Do you think that list of sundries he scribbled in there could be a cipher? Or the prayers? Or the names of people and their addresses?"

"It could be," said John. "I mean, there's no weird capitalization or underlining or odd words interpolated, but you never know. Maybe we can transcribe that tomorrow and give it to Joe."

"Why not tonight?" Anne asked. "I mean, there are guys with machine guns and creepy magic spells out there looking for us—looking for me, really. We really shouldn't give them more time to find us—me."

"I agree, Anne," said John, "but look, it's late in the evening, Joe's a family man, and I don't think a few hours will make a difference. Let's let him rest, we'll rest, and we'll all attack it fresh in the morning. We can also run it by our scientists. You didn't meet them today. I think they were working on something in their lab. Or playing Halo over the LAN, knowing them. They're very, very smart. We've got Raphael Stoll, a physicist, and Eulalia Park, a biologist—and medical doctor, as well. They sort of overlap on chemistry. Lily takes the organic, I guess, and Rafe the inorganic."

Anne took a big sip of wine. "Eulalia?" She found herself almost giggling.

John gave an amused snort. "I know. I guess it sounded American to her parents when they came over from Pusan. She's from Portland and is probably a genius, so don't hold her name against her."

"I take it she uses Lily."

"Yes, indeed. And she's E.S.S. Park in the medical literature. Eulalia Sun-Sook Park."

"How did she get involved with the Black Chamber?"

"Long, long story. Short version: pretty much like you. The incumbent Doctor had died—of natural causes, I hasten to add—and she had come to our attention a couple years earlier when she had been involved in something strange. We convinced her to join us and help keep a lid on the Weird." John rubbed his neck. "I imagine she probably could have become world-famous by publishing scientific papers on what happened, but she was more than eager to help us cover it up."

"Cover it up?" Anne asked.

"That's part of the job. You'll see in the Presidential Charter. Basically, we're to keep tabs on weirdness, stamp it out where we can, and keep too many people from finding out about it."

"So we're the Men in Black?" Anne asked.

"I wish I were as good looking as Will Smith, if that's what you mean."

"Ha."

"To answer your question: sort of. Honestly, most everything we run into ends up so ambiguous and odd that it's not all that hard to keep a lid on it."

"But doesn't that impede science and people's right to know what's out there?" Anne frowned and took another sip of wine.

"Remind me of where in the Constitution the Right to Know is?" John joked. "No, this isn't about cover-up for the sake of cover-up, or trying to keep a monopoly on occult knowledge in the government's hands. It's trying to keep the Weird at bay and its existence a secret, insofar as it's possible, lest someone discover it and try to do bad things with it. Like our necromancer friend. If whack-jobs out there knew that you could do that kind of creepy shit, you don't think you'd get a bunch of loons getting ordained as priests, quitting, downloading the spells from the Internet, peeping in girls' locker rooms, or worse?"

"Speaking of the Internet, doesn't it complicate your life a lot?" Anne asked.

John waggled his hand. "Well, we worry about it a lot, and Rafe and Joe and Lily have spent a ton of time working on programs for scanning for material, others for scrubbing servers of specified code, and even more for breaking into secure sites that we think might be hiding something. But to tell the truth, we haven't had a single really worrisome incident on the Internet. In general, those who desire this kind of knowledge also want to keep it all for themselves, so their paranoia and secrecy work for us. But we assume something bad on the Internet is inevitable, and we hope that our preparations are at least partially adequate."

Anne crossed her arms. "If I accept the lawfulness and desirability of your, er, our cover-ups—and I can't say that I yet do—isn't it really hard to do?"

"Not really," John said. "First, the culture doesn't accept weird occurrences. We're all science, all the time. Oddball stuff gets shoved onto sketchy cable documentaries and is considered the province of eccentrics. Second, really explicit encounters are very, very rare. You'd be amazed what most people can rationalize. Third, some combination of legal threats, large sums of cash, and/or assurances that they're part of a secret elect, will generally obtain most people's silence, especially given that they know they're likely to be mocked and treated like a lunatic if they tell the truth anyway. And, honestly, I think most people want a reason to forget. Tell me you wouldn't rather forget that face in the mirror."

Anne tapped her wineglass in thought. "You're probably right. I've lain in bed wondering how I could ever tell a friend or even my parents what had happened to me. And I don't think I could. They'd immediately conclude I was mentally ill. Heck, I was ninety percent of the way towards convincing myself that I was mentally ill."

John smiled. "Yep, but I'm glad that the offer of a sizable salary, my insistence on the classified nature of our work, and your initiation into the most secret organization in the U.S. government have bought *your* silence."

Anne laughed and drained her glass. "On that note, sir, good night."

ᘔᠵ᠊ᠵ

Two weeks passed, during which Anne almost got used to never seeing her own reflection. On her fourth day, she'd been trying to do something with her hair in the ladies' room, and Wilhelmina had come in. Anne shrugged helplessly, and Wilhelmina immediately came over and began coiffing her, saying, "Oh, let me help you, sweetheart. This has got to be hard on you. I know you're young and you've got your looks, but I remember those days and I'd have gone crazy without a mirror. Girls have to know they look good to feel good, am I right? Tell you what, you bring in whatever you normally use on yourself and first thing, I'll make you up." Anne had tried to demur, but Wilhelmina was insistent. Anne thanked her—feeling so grateful she wondered if she were vainer than she thought—and told herself that, well, she didn't really wear much more than a little eyeliner and lipstick, so it wouldn't really be too much of an imposition.

Anne came to like her other coworkers as well. Rafe Stoll, the Scientist, turned out to be a quiet, funny guy of about six feet with black hair and startling blue eyes. She'd broached the topic of how magic could be reconciled with science. He'd laughed. "Well, if you held a gun to my head, I'd posit that it was some sort of means for causing a large-scale quantum entanglement or quantum teleportation, since it's clearly a violation of the principle of locality—and of course it fits perfectly with Einstein's description of *spukhafte Fernwirkung*, 'spooky action at a distance.'" She'd laughed at that. He'd continued, "Of course, translated from the Physickish, that means, 'Uh, it's magic?'" and they'd both laughed.

Lily Park was a little tougher to warm up to. Maybe five-one in heels, wearing a white lab coat over a series of interchangeable dark suits, she had sharp, excellent features set in a wide, flat, Hangukin countenance. Her eyes were often a bit red, as if from fatigue, and her manner could be distant and self-contained, which after a while Anne ceased ascribing to hauteur or aloofness, but rather to the fact that she constantly seemed to be preoccupied with some sort of complex mental gymnastics. If she was the genius John said she was, she was living proof of the maxim that the brilliant are never bored.

Every day, they'd all meet in the morning for an hour or so to kick around ideas for finding the necromancer, as they decided to call him. Given the historical association of necromancy with Catholic clergy, Mike Himmelberg had suggested asking some of the Black Chamber's contacts within the Church. Anne was a little surprised that they had multiple sources in the Catholic hierarchy around the country. "There's a surprising amount of overlap between our bailiwick and theirs," Mike had explained. "And when you've seen some of the same strange things, you tend to trust each other."

The problem had been, however, trying to figure out how to find the necromancer, who—even if their guess was correct—was, as Mike said, "a beadle in an abbé stack." Lily had suggested that an element of the FBI's profiling practices might help: identify those clerics whose background indicates that they'd be inclined to evil practices. Mike said, "Hmm, so we just have to get a list of all the Catholic clergy in the country, then do background checks on all of them to see if they tortured animals as a kid. Ay yi yi."

"Poor you," joked John. "Mike already owes the Archdiocese's official exorcist a slew of favors," he explained to Anne.

"Worse, I owe him two hundred bucks from poker," Mike mumbled.

"There's an official Washington exorcist?" Anne asked, surprised.

"Sure," said Mike. "A few of the big archdioceses have them. Although they don't admit it. I want to say New York and Chicago admit they do, but they won't reveal the exorcists' identities. D.C. portrays itself as more 'modern,' so they've never announced they have one. Too medieval, you see. But they do. I met him investigating an incident in West Virginia one time. He'd gotten there independently."

"An incident?" Anne asked. "Like a demonic possession? Linda Blair, pea soup? 'Your mother sews socks in Hell?' That kind of stuff?"

"Sort of," said Mike, screwing up his face as if trying to think how to describe it. "Yeah, sure. Okay. That kind of stuff. The four marks of possession, just for future reference, are a strong aversion to holy objects, supernatural strength, knowledge impossible for the possessed to have, and speaking in identifiable languages that the possessed doesn't know." He ticked them off on the fingers of his left hand. "Aversion, Strength, knowing Stuff, and Speaking. Or as I like to call them, ASSS. The extra S is for 'extra scary.'"

Wilhelmina scowled and shook her head. Claire rolled her eyes. Rafe laughed. Joe McManus swatted Mike on the head with a three-ring binder. To Anne, he said, "Unfortunately, you'll get used to Mike's sense of humor."

"No offense taken. And, sadly, I will remember that mnemonic," Anne said.

"See?" said Mike to Joe triumphantly.

"Back to the problem, though," said Anne. "If you're trying to find out who tortured animals as a kid ... aren't those all sealed court and psychiatric records?"

Joe laughed silently, his head going back. "Yeah, that's not a problem. Sealed or not, they keep those records on computers. And the computers are on networks."

"This is going to be a ton of work," said John. And time proved him right. Mike had obtained a thick computer printout from his exorcist contact, and they'd begun the laborious work of trying to identify juvenile-court records or newspaper stories that matched the names and ages of the priests, in hope that something would jump out. Very little did. It was slow, painstaking, frustrating work, and after a few days of it, no one was in a particularly good mood. Anne was particularly frustrated that she didn't seem to have any extra brainpower to devote to the riddle of the book. They'd moved the rack with the scans of the book into their headquarters, though, to give everyone a chance to look it over.

One afternoon, John, Claire Krakauer, Rafe Stoll, Anne, and Steve McCormack were sitting at the long table in the conference room, which doubled as a general reference library, sorting through stacks of documents they'd dug up. They'd stopped for a moment, and Claire was telling a funny story about running into the character actor Ben Stein in Georgetown a few months back when Mike Himmelberg knocked on the doorframe and said, "Hey, can I ask a question of the Book Lady?"

"The Book Lady is in," said Anne.

"Okay," he said, holding a piece of paper in his hands. "I've had my computer monitoring various news feeds, law-enforcement systems, and so forth. Since this all started with rare books, I set it to alert me to anything involving rare books, book thefts, and the like. I really haven't gotten anything significant. But all of a sudden, I'm getting a whole bunch of stuff revolving around Yale. Near as I can figure, they've had a very valuable book stolen, but they're doing their best to cover it up and keep it out of the papers."

"That's pretty common," said Anne. "You tell people the book's being restored or on loan to another institution while the insurance company pays whatever fraction of the insured value the thieves will take as ransom."

"Ah, like art theft," Mike said, nodding. "Well, here's the thing, they've brought in the Connecticut State Police, they've talked to the insurance companies, and they're calling lawyers, private eyes, auction houses, and people all over the world. They seem to be more than slightly worked up. Do you think we should go up there and find out what's going on?"

Steve said, "We'd have to be very careful. The FBI has an office in New Haven and it's not that big a town."

"Where was the book stolen from?" asked Anne.

Mike looked down at the paper. "Looks like the Beinecke Rare Book & Manuscript Library."

Anne perked up, having spent many hours of research there. "That could be a very valuable book. They've got an original Gutenberg Bible and an Audubon folio. Do they say what book was stolen?"

"No. Even with the police, they're just using some code number. MS 408." Anne did a double take and almost spat coffee all over the table. Mike went on, "Sounds like a second-tier Central American gang. 'Hey, *ese*, you in MS-13?' 'No, man, I couldn't get in. I'm in MS Four Hundred *Ocho*.'"

Now able to speak, Anne asked, "MS 408?! Are you sure?"

Mike checked the paper. "Yep. Mike Sierra four zero eight."

"That means 'manuscript number 408.' And that's *huge.* That's the Voynich Manuscript!"

"Holy crap," said Rafe, his eyes wide.

"Wow," John said, pushing back from the table.

Claire, Steve, and Mike looked at each other. "Anybody going to explain?" asked Claire after a moment.

"You're the Book Lady," said John to Anne.

"Ah, okay.." She took a deep breath and started in. "The Voynich Manuscript is a totally unique text, not least because no one has any idea what it is. It's named after Wilfrid Voynich, an English book dealer who bought it from the Jesuits in Italy in 1912 and eventually gave it to Yale. It's written in a language no one understands in an alphabet that no one understands. It's got pictures of people and plants and astronomical charts and all sorts of crazy stuff—like the pictures of little nude women, some wearing crowns, who appear to be bathing inside bodily organs—but no one has ever been able to make heads or tails of the thing. It first surfaced in Prague during the reign of Rudolf II, who was a famous patron of alchemists, mages, and the like. One very popular solution to the problem of what it means is simply dismissing it as meaningless, a hoax to be sold to some gullible rich guy as a mysterious book of occult wisdom. And it'd have to have been a rich guy because the thing isn't a slapped-together job. It's got 240 pages and originally had 272, all of which are pretty much covered in text and pictures. It's got a strange, but reasonable-looking alphabet, which probably has twenty or thirty underlying letters, though there are what appear to be ligatures and combinatory glyphs."

Claire said, "Hmm. Could we get a facsimile and have Joe run it through some computer algorithm or other to try and figure out the code?"

"No, no way," said Rafe. "The Voynich Manuscript is legendary among cryptographers. Some of the best cryptanalysts in the world have gone to town on it for decades, and no one's figured out a thing. Which is why so many are convinced of the hoax theory that Anne mentioned."

John spoke up. "Right, I think they've ruled out that it's Latin or German or English or most European languages. If I'm remembering right, someone did a frequency-of-letters or structural analysis and the ones it came up closest to were East Asian: Chinese, Burmese, Vietnamese, Thai. So that theory is that it's just one of those languages written in a made-up phonetic alphabet. Which, oddly enough, tracks closely with a purely hoaxed theory that a guy put forward a couple years prior, saying that it was written by a couple Chinese visitors to Venice in the 1400s, using a Roman-looking alphabet of their own invention. The hoax guy was as shocked as anyone else to find that the structural analysis made Mandarin a plausible idea."

"But, wait, what would be the point of such a book?" asked Steve.

John held up his hands in helpless ignorance. "Got me. A private code? There's an Englishman who makes a very persuasive, very clever argument that it's the private technical diary of a fifteenth-century Italian architect/engineer who was heading off to the Ottoman Empire to build some buildings and wanted to take his technical secrets with him, so he encoded them and camouflaged his technical drawings by making them fantastical plants, and so forth."

"Really?" said Anne.

"Yeah," said John, "it's a great book. I'll loan it to you."

"Thanks. Returning to what Rafe said ..." said Anne, looking over at him. He seemed to be trying very hard to remember something, looking into the middle distance, his eyes moving back and forth, "... the other main theory—which jibes with the architect story—is that it *is* something meaningful in a European language, just encoded a number of times, the last of the encodings being the secret alphabet. And, last but not least, there's a theory that it's written in an artificial language someone made up. Like Esperanto."

"Or Klingon," Mike deadpanned.

"That's an excellent point, Mike," Anne humored him. "The academy has been terribly remiss in not checking it against Klingon, Esperanto, Volapük, and Tolkien's elvish languages."

"Hey, Rafe, you know Kli—" Mike started to joke, but Rafe leapt out of his seat without having heard them and ran out the door. "Was it something I said?" Mike said sarcastically.

"You just have that effect on people," said John.

Rafe came bursting back in, holding a piece of paper with something printed on it in color. He started at it intently. "I *knew* it! There you are, motherfucker. Look, look here." He put the paper down in the middle of the table, and everyone was drawn to it like a magnet. It was a printout of one of the pages of the *Brevarium dæmonologicum* from the back of the book, with mundane notes and doodles they'd ruled out as meaningless.

"Here, right here. See that?" Rafe stabbed his index finger at a series of unassuming doodles on the left-hand edge of the page next to the binding that looked like:

cgHg

"That," Rafe said, "is Voynich. Voynichish? Voynichese? Whatever."

"Are you sure?" asked John.

"Pretty damn sure," said Rafe.

"I think he's right," said Anne. "It's been years since I looked at it, but now that he says it, it seems exactly like it could be. I'd dismissed it as just practicing with a new pen nib or something— trying some ligatures or ampersands or something. But—I'll be damned. I think that is a Voynich word. We'd have to look to see if it actually occurs in the manuscript. But, wow, that's a huge scholarly coup, finding some evidence of it outside the book itself."

"Woo!" said Rafe, still adrenalized.

"Wait," said Mike. "Correct me if I'm wrong, but you guys said that this language—if it is a language—has defied generations of cryptographers and linguists. What good does having one more word do? I mean, as Anne says, I'm sure this is a huge historical clue to its origins, but … it doesn't really help us, does it?"

"No, not really," said John. "But it can't be a coincidence that someone's stolen Beinecke MS 408 and Mildred was killed for this book with the only known sample of Voynich … ish outside the book."

Claire hadn't taken her eyes off the page since Rafe set it down. "Okay guys, wait. Look here. See these squiggles right under the Voynich-ish? What if that's a translation or transliteration?" She pointed at a group of doodles or practice marks that looked like:

zhæh

"I mean," Claire suddenly seemed less certain, "I know it's a long shot, but it kind of looks like there are four letters in the Voynich word, and there are four marks here."

They all squinted at the page for two full minutes in silence.

"It doesn't really look like anything, does it?" asked Anne.

"I don't know," said John.

"Sorry—" began Claire.

"No, no, hold on," interrupted Rafe. "Here's one thing for your theory. The first Voynichy word has what looks like four letters, and two of them—the sort of ampersands with tails—are the same. What we've got here is four marks, two of which are the same. Now, if we're to read left to right, we know the first 'letter' is not the one that's used again. And that's true in the second one as well. Similarly, the right-most 'letter' in both is one that's redoubled. But … of course, that leaves out the possibility that the final 'letter' in that second series of marks is actually the bottom-most squiggle."

Mike walked out of the office for a minute. The rest of the crew stared in silence. Not long after, he came back with Lily, Wilhelmina, and Joe. "Okay, first question is to Lily. Lily, is that Korean?"

She squinted. "No. It's not. It looks kind of like Korean, but that Nike swoosh at the bottom can't be Korean. First, it's swoopy; second, it looks like it starts on the right and then comes left. All lines in Hangul are written top-down or left-right. No exceptions. If it were illiterate Korean, it would say something like *ae* or *i-i* or *e* or maybe *mae, me, mi-i* or something. And maybe the swoosh would be a final *eu*, just written poorly. But, no, I can't think of a Korean word that would look anything like that, even copied by someone who doesn't know the language."

"Thanks, Lily," said Mike. "The next question is for all of you guys. You have any clue what that might be?"

"Hmm. Zero-one-one is three in binary," suggested Joe.

"It kind of looks like a smiley face with the right eye closed or covered or scratched out. Maybe a pirate eyepatch?" said Wilhelmina.

"Good point. Maybe it's an ideogram," said John. "I hadn't thought about it as a whole; we've just been looking at the elements."

"Anyone know any Chinese?" asked Claire.

Lily said, "A little. Mostly through Hanja in Korean. It doesn't look like anything to me, but I'm not an expert. What about another script? Something like Demotic Egyptian. Didn't they simplify the hieroglyphs down to strokes?"

John said, "Great thought. Wait a second, I have some books on Egyptian in my office." He returned a moment later with an armful of books, including Gardiner's big blue *Egyptian Grammar*. He flipped through one book and said, "Okay, here's the demotic alphabet. It's pretty much just squiggles to my eye. But it does have a double-vertical-line letter and a swoop. No real circle, though. But still. Could be. You know, what we'll have to do is send this to some experts and see if they can make any sense of it. But for once … I think we're onto something. Excellent job, guys. Anyone who doesn't have plans, dinner's on Grandpa Cal."

9

"Hey, I got it!" Claire shouted, hanging up the phone. It was two days later, and faxes and e-mail with the mysterious markings had sped around the world to various trusted academics who were part of the larger circle of individuals whom, to Anne's amusement, the Chamber traditionally called Collaborators. Everyone in the room turned to look, and John, Mike, and Anne came quickly out of the conference room.

"An old professor of mine at Oxford recognized it," Claire explained. "He said it's a Tibetan script."

"Tibetan?" asked Mike. "Don't tell me, it's a cryptic yak-butter recipe."

"No," Claire said with a mixture of triumph and trepidation, "apparently it says 'demon.'"

"Of course it does," said Mike.

"Jesus," said Steve.

"Okay, so what next?" asked John.

"We have to leverage this into some sort of knowledge about the Voynich Manuscript," said Joe. "That'll let us know what our bad guy is up to."

"Okay," said Rafe. "Here's what we'll do. Lily, Joe, and I will go through as many images of the manuscript as we can find, looking for that sequence of letters. We'll send that to Claire's guy, and see what he can make of it. Then we send him a bigger piece to see if he can do that."

"But we don't want to let him know it's the Voynich Manuscript," Steve objected.

"That's probably true," said John.

"We can trust him," objected Claire. "He's wonderful and completely reliable."

"I'm sure," countered John, "but we really should do this need-to-know."

"All right," Claire conceded. "So how?"

"I've got it," said Joe. "We convert the Voynich text into a secondary substitution cipher."

"English, please?" said Mike, to Anne's relief.

"We just change the funny Voynich letters to regular letters or numbers." Joe looked off into space for a moment. "Maybe numbers would be clearer. Yeah, I think numbers."

"Okay, can you do that, Joe, while the other two get to work on finding the character sequence in the manuscript?" John asked.

"Sure," Joe said.

"I'll help Rafe and Lily," volunteered Anne. "I can navigate old books very quickly, and I'm good with scripts and their variants."

"I'll help, too," offered Wilhelmina. "Sounds a lot less depressing than trying to dig up dirt on priests. I can't think the Lord looks too kindly on that, even though our motives are good."

"*Ora pro nobis, Sancta Wilhelmina,*" joked Mike.

Wilhelmina laughed. "I'll pray for you in particular, Mike. You need it."

"Have you been talking to my wife again?" Mike grinned.

"Okay," said John. "So, Joe does the cipher. Rafe, Lily, Anne, and Wilhelmina go through the manuscript. And the rest of us get back to digging up dirt on priests."

Lily, Wilhelmina, Steve, and John, closest to the door, left to get to work.

"Hey, wait," said Joe. "What part of the text do you want enciphered?"

"I dunno," said John.

"How about the beginning?" asked Anne.

"Works for me," said Joe.

"So, Claire, this old professor of yours, were you his *special* student? Did you learn anything that you can't share with the class?" Rafe asked with a theatrical leer.

Claire rolled her eyes and left, shaking her head.

"Jesus, Rafe," said Mike, "dip her braids in your inkwell, why don't you?"

"What?"

"Dude, you *so* like her."

"Well, of course I like her, she's a great coworker."

"You liiiiiiike her."

"Shut up."

"You liiiiiiike her."

Rafe flipped Mike the bird and stalked out.

"He likes her," Mike said to Joe and Anne.

"Oh yeah," said Joe.

First thing the next morning, Joe called a meeting. "I've got the cipher. Let me explain this to everyone." He connected his laptop to a projector and displayed a section of Voynich text. It read:

> ab cdefbfd vbh cdvdjbveHl cmbebno vstH
> vohu ab gscmb go cHgbk poqxdhqgba qvbvbgba
> qHcpH qd poqfb bhhd gdeohomb cyrbv gba ⁻
> edaqdmrbvgba mbxohbrbv gba qksrbnorbvrvol
> goh cy abno voqsnol ckolqovy gdhgH zdaFd
> gdhmb rodq hHlfbqoebkbvu

Joe said, "Okay, this is the opening paragraph of the manuscript. It's got a lot of different letters, as you can see. There are twenty-seven, by my count. What I did was assign each a number, starting with the first character on the first line as number one, then the next as number two, and so on. So, for example, the first two words are…" He pushed a button and the following numbers appeared below the Voynich text.

1-2 3-4-5-6-2-6-4

"What this means is that we have six unique letters, then the second letter repeats, then the sixth, then the fourth. Everybody following me?"

Everyone nodded. "I don't know for how much longer," joked Mike.

"No, if you've got that principle, you've got the whole thing. So here's what the whole text looks like as numbers," said Joe, pushing another button, revealing:

1-2 3-4-5-6-2-6-4 7-2-8 9-4-7-4-10-2-7-5-11-12 9-13-2-5-2-13-15 7-18-19-11 7-15-8-20 1-2 21-18-9-13-2 21-15 9-11-21-2-22 16-15-23-24-4-8-23-21-2-1 23-7-2-7-2-21-2-1 23-11-9-16-11 23-4 16-15-23-6-2 2-8-8-4 21-4-5-15-8-15-13-2 9-25-17-2-7 21-2-1⁻ 5-4-1-23-4-13-17-2-7-21-2-1 13-2-24-15-8-2-17-2-7 21-2-1 23-22-18-17-2-14-15-17-2-7-17-7-15-12 21-15-8 3-25 1-2-14-15 7-15-23-18-14-15-12 9-22-15-12-23-15-7-25 21-4-8-21-11 26-4-1-27-4 21-4-8-13-2 17-15-4-23 8-11-12-6-2-23-15-5-2-22-2-7-20

"And, so, this is what we'll send to Claire's professor. I checked it out, and the letters from the breviary are 9-21-11-21. That sequence doesn't appear anywhere in my sentence, but the letters are pretty common throughout. There are six 9's and 11's, and twelve 21's. So whatever the professor decides those are, he'll have a decent head start. There are two hundred five total letters, and he'll have twenty-four off the bat. That's about twelve percent. Not great, but a lot better than nothing. And it'll be even better if Rafe's team's discovery pans out."

Rafe spoke up. "Well, we think we can maybe help him out on that. Lily, Anne, Wilhelmina, and I managed to identify multiple instances of a long phrase with that characteristic sequence. Can you put it up, Joe?" Joe pushed a key and a Voynich phrase appeared.

npocgbqqocgHg bcbggdh bfdmvdh

Rafe pointed to the end of the first word. "Okay, here's our word, though it seems to be the ending of this long word, or a suffix or a compound or something. The really cool thing about this excerpt is that it's got multiple instances of each of two of those letters. Okay, ours kind of looks like c-ampersand-t-ampersand. And you'll notice that there are one, two, three c's, and one, two, three, four, five 'ampersands.' And these two ampersands here are right next to each other. So presumably that's a double letter, which should help Claire's professor identify the word more easily. Oh, and I almost forgot, all these letters occur in Joe's section as well, and he was able to encipher them like this." Joe pushed a button and up popped two strings of numbers.

14-16-15-9-21-2-23-23-15-9-21-11-21 2-9-2-
21-21-4-8 2-6-4-13-7-4-8

Anne raised her hand. Rafe smiled and said, "This isn't school, Anne. Fire away."

"Isn't this still going to be close to impossible?" she asked.

"Absolutely. We have one, sole hope—that the underlying language is Tibetan and that the professor can solve it on that basis."

"So," Mike said. "Everybody happy with this plan? Any obvious flaws?"

The futility and frustration of the previous weeks' work was visible on the faces of everyone in the room. After a long pause, murmurs of "let's do it," "ok," "give it a shot," and the like burbled around the conference table.

Claire stood up. "Why don't you print the numbers out and I'll fax them to him. That way we can avoid electronic copies."

Anne said, "My old office's interior decorator recommends that highly. Avoids firebombings and the like." Everyone laughed quietly.

Joe said, "Okay, we're done."

�

A week later, Anne had a question for Claire and walked over to her desk. Claire, on the phone, held up a finger, and Anne walked to the empty desk across the way and leaned on it. She stared off into the middle distance, half watching Mike Himmelberg flipping through various Catholic-looking websites on his big iMac monitor. Something caught her attention, but she wasn't sure what. A moment later, her synapses reestablished the fleeting connection, and she knew. She rushed over and grabbed Mike by the shoulders.

"Oh my God, you found the guy! Why haven't you told anyone?!"

"Uh, what?" Mike looked from Anne's suddenly proximate face almost atop his left shoulder to the monitor and back.

"You found the guy. That's the tell, right there!" She pointed to a coat of arms on the computer screen. John, Joe, and Wilhelmina walked over and looked on.

"No, I'm just looking at some unofficial organizations around the Church, thinking maybe there'd be a secret necromancer club or something," Mike explained. "This is one that's sort of trying to lobby the Church to ditch all the smells and bells and become the Church of What's Happening Now, especially in terms of sex and divorce and women priests and the like. There are a bunch of these groups, but this is probably the best funded and most respectable. There's no way these guys are mixed up in medieval weirdness. Heck, I'm not sure that they're even all that keen on God."

"Well, then that's an awesome cover," Anne said loudly, "because that there is the proof that you've got a necromancer on your hands." She pointed at the arms depicting a large, crested bird with orange and black plumage and black-and-white striped wings pecking at its breast, blood dripping from the wound.

"I think you're mistaken, Anne," said John, squinting at the bird, as Joe leaned over and enlarged the image. "The pelican pecking at its breast is a common motif in Christian art. They were thought to nourish their chicks with their own blood—a sacrifice like Jesus's, if you will—and they were thought to be able to use the blood to bring dead chicks back to life—a resurrection motif, too."

"Point taken, John. But here's the thing." She paused, looked around at her expectant audience, and announced, "That ... is not ... a pelican."

"Sure it is," said John, staring at the bird. "I mean, it's all stylized and heraldic, but it's a pelican." He canted his head. "Isn't it?"

"I think it is," said Mike, though somewhat dubiously.

"Nope," said Joe. "Look at the crest and the colors. I mean, orange? And stripes?"

"The colors and crest could be additional heraldic symbolism. I'd have to look it up," said John, less and less sure.

"I'm with Anne and Joe," said Wilhelmina. "Look at the beak, it's all long and curved and pointy. Pelicans have a big pouch on their lower bill."

"Heraldic motifs are often stylized, to the point they don't really look like the real animal. Think of the lion rampant. It sometimes looks like a boxing dog-monster," John objected, though his confidence was ebbing in proportion to the width of the grin on Anne's face, which seemed to grow every time he offered an explanation. Finally, he said, "Okay, Anne, if that's not a pelican, what is it?"

"I thought you'd never ask. That, dear colleague, is a hoopoe," Anne stated.

"A what?" everyone asked simultaneously.

"A hoopoe. An hoopoe? I'm never quite sure of that rule."

"Never heard of it," said Mike.

"Me neither," chimed in Joe.

"It's an Old World bird," explained Anne. "You'd never have seen one in this hemisphere outside a zoo."

"Zoo aviaries drive me nuts," said Mike, warming to his tangent. "I mean, I go to a zoo to see animals displayed for me, the paying customer. I don't want to be wandering around staring at a bunch of trees hoping to catch a glimpse of the deep-throated Greek swall—"

"Shut up, Mike," said John, swatting the back of Mike's head. "I've heard of the hoopoe. In *The Conference of the Birds*, a Persian Sufi poem, the hoopoe's sort of the head bird. But I never bothered to find out what one looks like."

"It looks like this," said Joe, having pulled the Wikipedia "Hoopoe" page up in another window of Mike's web browser.

"That's the same bird," Wilhelmina said with finality.

John looked at the picture on the screen. "You're right. That's the same bird."

"Whoever did this slipped a hoopoe here where you'd expect a pelican?" wondered Mike aloud. "Wouldn't that sort of be blasphemous, if the pelican has all those Christ-like connotations?"

"Oh yes," said Anne. "And not just because of that. I once read a necromancer's manual in the Bavarian State Library in Munich that said, and I quote, '*Debes igitur attendere quod uppupa magne virtutis est nigromanticis et demones invocantibus, quapropter ipsa multo utimur ad nostri tutelam.'"*

Mike said, "*Uppupa* is my new favorite word."

Joe grimaced at Mike and appealed, "Now *I'm* going to have to say, 'English?'"

John said, "'*You should note that the hoopoe is possessed of great virtue for necromancers and those who invoke demons, because of which we use it much for our safekeeping.*' That about right?"

Anne was impressed. "On the nose!"

John said, "Latin rocks."

Anne said, "It does at that. But I should also add that hoopoe blood is used very frequently in necromantic rituals."

"Holy shit," said Mike. "Sorry, Wilhelmina, Anne. But so this is a black-magic bird dripping its hoodoo blood out where you're supposed to see a pelican representing Christ? This definitely must be the guy. There's no way that's a coincidence. And hanging it out here for everyone to see? What an arrogant prick. Sorry, Wilhelmina, Anne."

"Well, it might not be the same necromancer," said Joe. "For all we know there are a few."

"But I bet they'd know each other," said Wilhelmina. "Who runs this organization?"

Mike clicked a few links on the page and they found themselves looking at the biography of the organization's director, Monsignor Wystan Clairvaux. A professionally photographed black-and-white headshot of a very good-looking, clean-shaven, dark-haired man in a Roman collar looked out at them.

"I saw that guy on Fox News the other day," Wilhelmina said. "He was great. Very smart, very adept in arguing his points. I disagreed with him, in that I think you Catholics should stay Catholic, but he just about made me forget that. And he's even better-looking on TV. Richard Chamberlain used to be everyone's handsome priest, but this guy could eat his lunch."

"Jesus, Mary, and Joseph," swore Mike. "Look at this guy's CV. No wonder he can do what he does. He's totally wired within the hierarchy. North American College in Rome. Taught in Prague and Liège. Stints assisting the Cardinal Archbishops of Los Angeles and Chicago. Speaks six languages. Doesn't say what they are. Had a gig at the Vatican Secretariat of State in the Section for Relations With States. Doing China. Oh crap. What do you bet one of his languages is Tibetan?"

"The breviary came from Prague," Anne said.

"This can't be a coincidence," said John. "Where's Claire?"

"In the science lab," said Wilhelmina. "She's working with Rafe and Lily on some background stuff."

John picked up the phone on Mike's desk and got Claire to come to the main office. They explained their deductions to her evident satisfaction, and she was quickly on the phone, dialing the Manhattan offices of *Ecclesia Nova*, Monsignor Clairvaux's organization.

"*Allô?* Yes, I am Martine du Bois calling from the offices of France 2 television," Claire said in a very good, subtle French accent. "I would like please to arrange an interview with the Monsignor Clairvaux on the topic of the future of the Catholic priesthood. No? Really? Is he to be reached there? No? Do you know when he shall return? Well, I am sorry. Our story will run within the week, as there is a current scandal in the Dordogne over the shortage of priests. If you can please to have him call me at the following number …"

Claire hung up and said in pure American, "He's gone. 'On retreat.' He does this a lot, apparently, and no one really knows for how long or exactly where."

"Wanna bet he's holed up with the Voynich Manuscript somewhere?" asked Joe glumly.

"All right, this is mostly Steve and Mike's beat," said John. "I'll go downstairs and get Steve up to speed. John, you start working the property records in and around New York City—check

Connecticut and New Jersey, too. Also, maybe check L.A. and Chicago, since he lived there at one point."

"Got it," said John.

Wilhelmina walked over to her desk and picked up an overnight-letter envelope. "Claire, this came for you."

Claire looked at the return address, tore it open, and scanned the first couple of lines. She looked up and said, "Ladies and gentlemen, we have a translation."

ཨཱ ༷ཨ

Everyone packed into the conference room, fidgeting nervously and waiting for Claire and Joe. Lily looked a little bleary, and Anne thought Rafe looked hung over. They came in together a few minutes later, Claire still staring at the sheets of blinding white 30-pound bond paper in her hands, and Joe carrying an overhead projector. After Joe set it up, Claire set the papers on the projector and said, "I think this speaks for itself. By way of background, Professor Geoffrey is a wonderful, grandfatherly former professor of mine at Oxford who knows more than anyone else alive about the history of Inner Asia and China. He became a Collaborator at my invitation, as he'd once intimated he'd had an uncanny, terrifying experience in Bhutan. He knows very little about what I do, but he's just the most wonderful gentleman. His books are both scholarly and *funny*. So, anyway, without further ado ..." She switched on the overhead projector and put up the following letter, which the members of the Black Chamber read in stunned silence, broken only by the occasional gasp or profanity.

ཨཱ ༷ཨ

My dearest Claire,

Thank you very much for allowing me to provide you with some slight assistance in your duties, whatever they may be. I am delighted to have this opportunity to put my meager knowledge at your disposal.

The original facsimile you sent showed a word in a handwritten form of Tibetan. It spells བདུད. Which is to say, **bdud**, the written form of **dü**, or **demon**.

Applying them as the numbers 9-21-11-21 in the shorter cipher you provided yields:

14-16-15-**b**-**d**-2-23-23-15-**b**-**d**-**u**-**d**   2-**b**-2-**d**-**d**-4-8 2-6-4-13-7-4-8

Some thought led me to believe that the first word ending in **bdud** might well be the traditional name of one of the Four Māras (*bzhi bdud*), four traditional Tibetan demons syncretized into obstacles to enlightenment by Buddhism. And, in fact, the name ʼ**chi·bdag·gi·bdud**, the name of **Chidag Dü**, the Demon of the Lord of Death, fit perfectly. Inserting his name provided me with some further letters to fill in the code, thus:

ʼ-**č**-**i**-**b**-**d**-**a**-**g**-**g**-**i**-**b**-**d**-**u**-**d**   **a**-**b**-**a**-**d**-**d**-4-8 **a**-6-4-13-7-4-8

At this point, I was frankly stumped for several days, as the second word does not fit any Tibetan word, demotic or literary, written or spoken, that I could conceive of. My inspiration came by simply Googling the sequence. **Abaddon** is Hebrew for "destruction" and is the name of a demon—"the angel of the bottomless pit"—in the Christian Bible (Rev. 9:11).

'-č-i-b-d-a-g-g-i-b-d-u-d   a-b-a-d-d-o-n
a-6-o-13-7-o-n

Examining the beginning of Revelations 9:

1. And the fifth angel sounded, and I saw a star fall from heaven unto the earth: and to him was given the key of the bottomless pit. 2. And he opened the bottomless pit; and there arose a smoke out of the pit, as the smoke of a great furnace; and the sun and the air were darkened by reason of the smoke of the pit. 3. And there came out of the smoke locusts upon the earth: and unto them was given power, as the scorpions of the earth have power. 4. And it was commanded them that they should not hurt the grass of the earth, neither any green thing, neither any tree; but only those men which have not the seal of God in their foreheads. 5. And to them it was given that they should not kill them, but that they should be tormented five months: and their torment was as the torment of a scorpion, when he striketh a man. 6. And in those days shall men seek death, and shall not find it; and shall desire to die, and death shall flee from them. 7. And the shapes of the locusts were like unto horses prepared unto battle; and on their heads were as it were crowns like gold, and their faces were as the faces of men. 8. And they had hair as the hair of women, and their teeth were as the teeth of lions. 9. And they had breastplates, as it were breastplates of iron; and the sound of their wings was as the sound of chariots of many horses running to battle. 10. And they had tails like unto scorpions, and there were stings in their tails: and their power was to hurt men five months. 11. And they had a king over them, which is the angel of the bottomless pit, whose name in the Hebrew tongue is Abaddon, but in the Greek tongue hath his name Apollyon.

… suggested to me that **Apollyon** (Greek Απολλυω, meaning "destroyer" as well), might be the correct reading of the last word, the remaining missing letters then being **p**, **l**, and **y**, yielding:

'-č-i-b-d-a-g-g-i-b-d-u-d   a-b-a-d-d-o-n
a-p-o-l-y-o-n

Or, simply, **Chidag Dü Abaddon-Apollyon.** To be sure, a fearsome juxtaposition, or perhaps identity.

Plugging these letters into the longer cipher text, I thus had:

1-a 3-o-5-p-a-p-o y-a-n b-o-y-o-10-a-y-5-u-12 9-l-a-5-a-l-i y-18-19-u y-i-n-20 1-a d-18-b-l-a d-i b-u-d-a-22 č-i-g-24-o-n-g-d-a-1 g-y-a-y-a-d-a-1 g-u-b-č-u g-o č-i-g-p-a a-n-n-o d-o-5-i-n-i-l-a b-25-17-a-y d-a-1 ⁻ 5-o-1-g-o-l-17-a-y-d-a-1 l-a-24-i-n-a-17-a-y d-a-1 g-22-18-17-a-'-i-17-a-y-17-y-i-12 d-i-n 3-25 1-a-'-i y-i-g-18-'-i-12 b-22-i-12-g-i-y-25 d-on-d-u 26-o-1-27-4 d-o-n-l-a 17-i-o-g n-u-12-p-a-g-i-5-a-22-a-y-20

At this point, a combination of extensive knowledge of Tibetan, a fondness for acrostic and crossword puzzles, and—oddly enough—the classics, allowed me to fill in the rest of the letters thusly:

ñ-a z-o-m-p-a-p-o y-a-n b-o-y-o-h-a-y-m-u-s b-l-a-m-a-'-i y-e-š-u y-i-n-. ñ-a d-e-b-l-a d-i b-u-d-a-r č-i-g-t-o-n-g-d-a-ñ g-y-a-y-a-d-a-ñ g-u-b-č-u g-o č-i-g-p-a a-n-n-o d-o-m-i-n-i-la b-ö-k-a-y d-a-ñ ⁻ m-o-ñ-g-o-l-k-a-y-d-a-ñ l-a-t-i-n-a-k-a-y d-a-ñ g-r-e-k-a-'-i-k-a-y-k-yi-s d-i-n z-ö ñ-a-'-i y-i-g-e-'-i-s b-r-i-s-g-i-y-ö d-o-n-d-u q-o-ñ-x-o d-o-n-l-a k-l-o-g n-u-sp-a-g-i-m-a-r-a-y-.

Or, more recognizably:

nga tsom·pa·po yan bo·yo·hay·mus bla·ma'i ye·shu yin. nga deb·la di bu·da·r chig·tong·dang

gya·ya·shi·dang gub·chu go chig·pa an·no
do·mi·ni·la bö·kay·dang mong·gol·kay·dang
la·ti·na·kay·dang gre·ka'i·kay·kyis din·tsö nga'i
yi·ge·'is bris·gi·yö don·du khong·tsho don·la klog
nus·pa·gi·ma·ray.

This is clearly Tibetan—not particularly
literate Tibetan and a transliteration of the
spoken language rather than the formal written
language—but Tibetan nonetheless. In case, for
whatever reason, you require the equivalent text
in written Tibetan, it would read:

ང་རྗ་སྨ་པ་པ་ཁས་ད་ཁ་ཅྱས་སྨ་ས་ར་ད་སྨ་ད་ག་སྨ་སྨ་ཅ་སྨ་ན། ང་ད་ད་སྨ་ད་
བ་ད་ད་ར་ཆ་གྱ་ཅ་ད་ར་ད་བ་ར་ཁ་སྨ་ད་རང་ག་བ་བཅ་ག་ག་ག་པ་ས་ན་ད་ར
་སྨ་ད་ན་བ་ད་སྨ་ད་ད་རང་སྨ་ད་ག་ལ་སྨ་ད་ལ་ད་ད་ན་སྨ་ད་རང་ག་ གྱ་ང་སྨ་ད་ག
་སྨ་ཅ་ཆ་ད་ཅ་ལ་ག་ ད་ཅ་སྨ་ད་སྨ་ག་ལ་ད་ད་ན་ད་ཁ་ང་ཆ་ད་ན་ལ་ག་ ག་
ན་སྨ་པ་ག་སྨ་ར་ད།

Now, begging your pardon for the pedantic
manner in which I have reached it, I am very
gratified to present you with my translation. I
suspect it will surprise you greatly, and I hope it
is some assistance to you.

I the writer am Jan Boiohæmus, priest of
Jesus. I am writing this book in Buda in one
thousand and four hundred and ninety-one *anno
Domini* with Tibetan, Mongol, Latin, and Greek
sounds, with these my letters, so that they will not
have the power to read the meaning.

So, you appear to have a document written
by Father John the Bohemian in a mixture of
languages and a cryptic cipher, in Buda in 1491.
This is fascinating, as there's no known contact
between the West and Tibet between the journeys
of Odoric of Pordenone circa 1325 and António de

Andrade, S.J., in 1624, yet our friend Jan clearly speaks Tibetan and, apparently, Mongolian. Why do we not know anything about him? Why did he disappear? Did "they" get him? The document you have is fascinating. If it comes to the light of day before I shuffle off this mortal coil, I'd love to have a look at it. Thank you very much for allowing an old man to attack a genuinely new and interesting puzzle. I hope my solution satisfies.

In accordance with your instructions, I have discussed this with no one. I trust I will not have offended you by destroying all my notes and sending you the sole copy of this letter, which I have not saved to any computer medium. I remain eternally in your debt and thus ready to assist you in any regard in the future.

With fondest regards,

Lewis

Lewis Geoffrey

Professor Emeritus
Balliol College, Oxford University
School of Oriental & African Studies

ཨ་ཀ་ར

After a long silence, John spoke up. "Okay, what does this tell us?"

"I'm not sure, but I just crapped my pants," said Mike.

"Seriously," said Joe, "this is scary."

"I think we can all agree on that," said Rafe, rubbing his temples hard, "but what can we take away that's helpful?" He took a long draw on a water bottle.

Anne spoke up. "Well, the fact that Jan writes '1491' fits with what's known about the Voynich Manuscript as well as the breviary. No one's exactly sure, but as far as anyone can tell, the Voynich Manuscript was written between about 1450 and 1520."

"And Buda in that period makes some sense if he were a scholar," said John. "There was a university there then, and it's right around the reign of Matthias Corvinus, the great patron of art and scholarship. Maybe more importantly, it would have been a way point from Western Europe to the East, either via Russia or, more likely, the Ottoman Empire." He turned to Anne. "Is there any known connection of the Voynich Manuscript to Budapest?"

"No. The first record we have of it is in Prague in the early 1600s, in the possession of an alchemist named Georg Baresch who studied at the Jesuit Clementium in 1603. Baresch evidently had no idea what it was, as he wrote repeatedly to Athanasius Kircher—another Jesuit, incidentally—who had published a Coptic dictionary and a decipherment of Egyptian hieroglyphics."

"A famously ridiculous decipherment," interrupted John, "but that's hindsight for you. Sorry, Anne. Go on."

"No problem," nodded Anne. "We have Baresch's 1639 letter to Kircher mentioning it as a 'Sphynx' (with a y, yet!) that has been quote—'taking up space uselessly in my library for many years'—unquote. Interestingly, he asked Kircher to solve the cipher, but not the content—which is of course impossible—but apparently Baresch knew or suspected something about the content. Also, he may have acquired the book illegally."

"Nice," joked Rafe. "I like my alchemists shady."

"Now, there once was a faded signature, or inscription, on the first page of the name Jacobus de Tepenec, who's known to be a Czech doctor who received the title 'de Tepenec' in 1608. So conceivably he owned the book sometime after 1608 and before Baresch, but there's no direct proof of that. One leading theory is that since he got his title from Rudolf II for curing the Emperor of a disease, perhaps Rudolf gave him the book. Or, since it doesn't seem to match de Tepenec's handwriting, maybe someone else wrote his name there at some undetermined later date."

"My head hurts," joked John.

"Sorry it's so vague, but that's history," said Anne. "So Baresch dies, sometime before 1662, leaving the book to one Johannes Marcus Marci, another doctor. The last written document we have from Marci is a letter to Athanasius Kircher dated 1666, which seems to be a cover letter sending Kircher the manuscript along with Baresch's copious notes on the thing. And at this point, the book disappears. Wilfrid Voynich said he found the Marci letter with the manuscript in the library of Villa Mondragone in Italy in 1912."

Lily tapped her nails on the conference table and said, "So its provenance is almost entirely mysterious. No wonder it has so frequently been held to be a hoax."

"There is a plausible theory on how it got there, though," explained Anne, "that goes something like this. Kircher was a professor of mathematics at the Jesuit Roman College. He built up a huge library and collection of objects, artifacts, devices, and oddities of nature, which became known as *il Museo Kircheriano*, the Kircher Museum. Several catalogs of its contents are published between 1680 and 1773. The Voynich Manuscript doesn't appear in any of them. When the Jesuits are suppressed for the second time in 1870, they've been using the Villa Mondragone for about five years. In order to keep Vittorio Emanuele's troops from seizing a lot of the order's books, they mark them 'private library of P. Beckx,' Peter Beckx being the Superior-General of the order. And, in fact, years later, when Voynich gives the book to the Beinecke, they find exactly this label on it—which Voynich had never mentioned. Kircher's correspondence was also kept at the Villa Mondragone, so it's theorized that the manuscript came into his possession at some point and then travelled with various Jesuit libraries until arriving in the Villa Mondragone, where Voynich found it. It was a boarding school by then, and the Jesuits were secretly selling off some books to restore the building."

"Okay, so what does this all mean for us?" asked Joe.

"Well, it occurs to me that the connection between the breviary and the manuscript seems to definitively be located with the Jesuit community in Prague. We know the breviary came from a Jesuit captured and executed in Britain. Some of the Jesuits of the English Mission—most famously Edmund Campion—spent time at the Jesuit university in Prague. So I think it's not too much of a leap to imagine that our Jesuit comes to Prague and somehow runs across this snippet of Voynich code and its Tibetan equivalent, which have made it with the manuscript from Budapest to Prague by some means. He jots it down, possibly not even knowing what it was. He goes to England, dies, and meanwhile the original key to the manuscript he used is lost somewhere in Prague." She paused a moment and shuddered a little with the thrill of antiquarian discovery. "Or maybe it's still there."

"Neat as that may be, where are we going with this, Anne?" asked John.

"Well, it implies to me that someone somewhere other than the author knew about the book and possibly its contents. So it's entirely possible that our bad guy, perhaps this Monsignor Clairvaux, came by his knowledge of the key through some sort of historical game of telephone, with necromancer passing it down to necromancer. And for the first time in, what, four or five hundred years, someone knows where both the book and the key are."

"What bothers me," said Rafe, "is what he wants it *for.*"

"I just hope to crap it doesn't have to do with Hüsker Dü, or whatever his name is," said Mike grimly.

John looked down at his notes, "You mean Chidag Dü Abaddon-Apollyon, Demon of the Lord of Death, the Angel of the Bottomless Pit? Sounds like a lovely fellow. I mean, just because he's a member of the Apocalyptic-American community, that's no reason to pre-judge him."

"Laugh it up, fuzzball," said Mike. "When's the last time *you* ran into a demon?"

"Let's think this through," said Rafe. "Assuming that this guy wants to summon a demon, even one with a less impressive business card than Mr. Dü, why do you summon a demon in the first place?"

"Power," said Mike. "You make it do stuff for you. Kill your enemies, grant you special favors."

"Knowledge," said Joe. "Like Faust."

"Illusions and sex are big in medieval necromancy too," said Anne.

"Sex?" asked Wilhelmina, speaking up for the first time. "Who wants to get down with a demon?"

"Well," conceded Anne, "you weren't necessarily getting down with the demon—although you might send a succubus or incubus to beset your enemy, who'd then be getting down with a demon. You were usually using their power to let you have sex with some woman you wanted to do—sometimes magically. Sort of a magical rape that made her fall in love with you or whatever. I mean, it's all crackpot, infantile fantasy stuff."

"And yet," said Mike. "Demons exist."

"Even if they didn't," said John, "we'd still be dealing with a guy who's willing to send hit teams to get ahold of mere books."

"*Mere* books?" objected Anne.

Steve cleared his throat and, from the corner in the back of the room where he'd been standing, said, "Does any of this help us actually find the guy? Or do we just now have a faint inkling of what he's up to?"

The various members of the Black Chamber looked at each other.

Anne spoke first. "I don't think it helps us find him at all. We know it's some sort of book of secret knowledge, and we know how to break the code. That's it."

Mike Himmelberg said, "It invokes a very scary demon by two cross-cultural titles. But no."

Joe McManus just shook his head and said, "Nope."

The rest of the crew were silent. John asked, "Any ideas on next steps?"

"I've got a French facsimile edition of the Voynich Manuscript," said Anne. "Maybe we could find a clue by translating more of it?"

"No!" said virtually everyone in the room simultaneously.

Rafe explained, "We're better off not knowing."

Wilhelmina said, "Plus, it's against the rules."

"Yeah, Anne, we really don't need to know what horrible stuff may be in there. We just need to stop the bad guy from doing whatever he wants to do."

"We've got a suspect. We've just got to bird-dog the guy," said Mike. When no one objected, Mike said, "Okay, let's go. Property-search records, cell phone records, whatever we can do."

Everyone rose and left except Claire, who remained in her seat, torqueing her watch around her wrist. Anne noticed, and walked the length of the conference room to sit next to her.

"Are you ok?" Anne asked.

"I'm fine, thanks," said Claire. "It's just … the last time we had something of this magnitude go down, I saw a couple friends die."

"I'm sorry," said Anne. "I mean, I don't even think I get the reality of all of this yet. Necromancers, secret books, all that. It was my harmless little academic sideline. And now, it's real? It's tough to believe."

"It'll always be tough," said Claire. "Even when it's staring you in the face. That's why it's so easy to get killed."

"I have a more serious question, but I wanted to ask you about Rafe—is he okay? I mean, he seemed the worse for wear today."

Claire sighed. "He drinks too much. Occupational hazard, I think. He works out a lot to compensate, I think, but sometimes it shows through."

"Have you told him that you're worried about him? He might take it well from you."

Claire ignored the implication. "I once alluded to it and got the impression that he's just not up to dealing with it at this point. Someday, maybe. But, I mean, we all have our problems. Lily doesn't sleep for days or weeks on end, I'm told. She uses some sort of uppers to keep going, but occasionally she'll crash. Literally. One time she fell down a flight of stairs here."

"My God. Do you guys have any mental-health benefits?"

"Plenty. But it's hard when you can't tell your therapist what's happened." Claire worried her ring violently. "But fuck psychology. This isn't rocket science. We're fucked up because we've seen, and occasionally done, some fucked-up shit. I mean, lately I've been— never mind. You had a question?"

"I didn't want to propose it in front of everyone else because I know it's *verboten*," Anne said, "but that's why I think maybe we should have your friend translate more of the manuscript. If there are spells or rituals in there, there are probably counter-spells, too."

"Let me stop you right there," said Claire. "We don't do any of that stuff. Ever. By law. By rule. For our own good. First of all, it's a form of power, about which Acton was right. Second, it's evil. I don't use that word lightly, and it's not part of my natural vocabulary. But whatever your intentions are, however noble your use, it corrupts and weakens you. Look, I'm a Jew. I don't have the elaborate theology, metaphors, and explanations that our resident Catholics bring to the table on this stuff. But what is dead clear to me is that there are active, weird forces afoot in the world, and almost always, they're malevolent. I mean, they're intentionally, consciously evil. And if you draw on them, they taint you, infect you, seduce you."

"Um, okay," said Anne, drawing back a bit from the darkness in Claire's eyes. "And let me apologize for my ignorance, but what about 'white magic?' Merlin, Gandalf, good-guy wizards? That kind of stuff?"

"Nope. Doesn't exist. At least not that I've seen. The closest thing seems to be things that call on God, rather than other powers. Mike has documented a couple exorcisms that worked. But really, we don't have a hell of a lot on our side, no pun intended."

"So how do you go after someone like this?"

"We make it up as we go along. John will check the Chamber's History and see if there are any precedents and, if so, what worked and didn't, but almost everything we go up against is confusing, strange, and almost *sui generis*."

"Well, say this book tells you how to summon this crazy apocalyptic demon, and this guy does it. What then?"

"A whole lot of people probably die. The end of the world. I don't know."

"Don't you think that's worth having the insurance of knowing what's in the book?"

"No," said Claire. "Sometimes just reading something is enough to make something happen. And as much as he'd readily give his life to save others, I'm not putting my friend Professor Geoffrey or anyone else in danger on the off chance the book can help."

"So what do we do?"

"Find this guy. Stop him. And, in the meantime, pray."

"I'm not religious," said Anne.

Claire smiled for the first time, though there was little joy in it. "We'll see how long that lasts."

10

A couple days later, Anne found herself on the doorstep of Monsignor Clairvaux's Manhattan brownstone with Steve McCormack and Joe McManus. They all had FBI identification in their pockets, pistols under their jackets, and a federal search warrant provided by Claire. Apparently it was a genuine warrant, but the means by which Claire had obtained it remained mysterious to Anne.

Joe and Steve were scanning the doors and windows for some sort of alarm system.

"How the heck does a priest afford this?" asked Anne.

"According to Mike, his foundation owns it, and they're rolling in dough," explained Joe. "Also, he's apparently independently wealthy to begin with."

Anne frowned. "I thought the wages of sin is death, not seven figures."

"Ha," said Steve. "I think it's clear, Joe. You?"

"Yep. Go ahead."

Steve pulled a lock-pick gun out of his pocket and opened the front door's three locks. "Odds that the door is booby-trapped?" he asked.

"Low, I'd guess," said Joe, but he put a hand on Anne's hip and guided her down the stairs. She held her breath, watching

Steve open the door very slowly, peering intently at its sides. He eventually swung it all the way open and waved Joe and Anne in.

Inside, the house was a spacious, high-ceilinged relic of New York's golden age. Its furnishings, however, were much more recent and relatively Spartan. They walked through the downstairs living room, dining room, and kitchen, searching them methodically. Anne was left to go through the converted parlor, which was now a library or study. Joe and Steve went upstairs and searched the bedrooms and the priest's office. Steve came down, reporting that he'd left Joe trying to break into Clairvaux's computer.

"So, library?" he asked laconically.

"That it is, Steve," said Anne. "It's a pretty good one. Mostly theology and history, though that shelf over there has a very nice collection of nineteenth-century literature, including a few first editions. Absolutely nothing about the occult. I've been moving books to see if there's anything hidden behind the rows off books, but so far, I'm just making myself sneeze from the dust."

"Can I give you a hand?" Steve volunteered.

"Sure. Start with that shelf, take each book down and tell me what the title page says. If it's Latin or Greek, just show it to me."

"Yes, ma'am," Steve said with a little salute.

They worked their way through the library methodically. Steve instructed her how to check the bookshelves for secret compartments. After three hours, they were confident that there wasn't anything to be found.

"It's possible we're missing something," said Steve, "but I think we've done everything short of dismantling the place. Want to check the basement with me?"

"Sure, sounds more fun than going cross-eyed over more books," said Anne.

"Oh, just wait," Steve said. "There are more books upstairs."

The two of them headed down into the basement, which seemed very seldom used. Most of the surfaces were covered in a fairly thick layer of undisturbed dust. There were several rooms in the basement, most dedicated to storage of furniture, old paintings and mirrors, and other household goods. There were modern heating, laundry, electrical, and telephone equipment, but nothing unusual or out of order. They checked the walls and doors and tried to find anything anomalous. After an hour or so, they gave up and headed upstairs to the office. They found Joe there, perched behind a computer, his mouth pursed to one side as he worked the keyboard deliberately.

"Anything?" asked Steve.

"Maybe," said Joe. "I cloned the hard drive onto a portable drive, so I can analyze it when we get back, check for hidden files, that sort of thing. I also figured out how this connects to the non-profit's network, so it shouldn't be hard to wander around in there. Right now, I'm just working through a whole bunch of stuff, trying to see if there are any records of properties where the guy could be, mentions of beach houses or retreat centers or whatever. So far, no dice. Oh, I found a cell phone in the drawer here. It seems to be his phone. I cloned the SIM, but just flipping through the address book and call log, there's nothing obvious. And wherever he is, he doesn't have this phone. He could have a prepaid drop phone, though."

"Untraceable. Lovely," said Steve.

"Nobody said bad guys have to be dumb," Joe said.

"It's just so much nicer when they are," Steve countered.

"Amen to that," said Joe. "Anne, what are you looking at?"

"This bookshelf of reference books," Anne said. "This shelf is foreign-language dictionaries and grammars, and there's a big hole right where 'Tibetan' would go alphabetically."

"This is the guy," said Steve.

"Circumstantial," said Joe.

Anne said, "I think I'm with Joe. You know, it's very odd. I haven't seen much religious stuff around the house. Just the one crucifix over the fireplace in the library, and that could just be for show. Just seems weird for a priest, you know?"

"Yeah," said Joe, "although there are all types of priests, and judging from this guy's day job, he's not exactly one of those old-fashioned priests with the giant rosary hanging from his cincture and saying Benediction every Wednesday night."

"What's the deal with the mansion?" asked Anne. "Aren't priests supposed to take a vow of poverty?"

"Only priests in orders," said Joe. "Ordinary, so-called secular priests don't. And even if you're a Jesuit or Benedictine or something and you've taken a vow of personal poverty, it doesn't mean your order can't put you up someplace nice. Okay," he said, rising, "I think I'm done here. We can go."

They let themselves out, and were sitting on the Metroliner heading back to D.C. when Steve's head jerked up from the *Wall Street Journal* he was reading. "Oh, hell," he swore softly.

"What's wrong?" Anne asked.

"We're idiots," said Steve. "Describe the house to me."

"Inside or out?" asked Joe.

"Start with out," said Steve.

"Okay, sort of a sandstone, three-sto—three-story. There was no third story inside. No stairs. What the heck?" Joe slammed his computer magazine against his thighs.

"How did we miss that?" asked Anne.

"There must be some high-quality carpentry in there," said Steve, "to make a whole staircase disappear."

"Or they took it out entirely and hid a dumbwaiter or an elevator in a wall somewhere," said Joe.

"Maybe that was what was giving me that weird feeling the whole time," said Anne.

It was between the walls dividing the bedroom and the office. In the hall, a picture hung between the doors on a wall that opened with a slight pressure, swinging out the whole wall face. There was no obvious light switch, so they proceeded up the stairs single-file by flashlight, guns drawn.

They'd gotten off the Metroliner at the next stop and caught the first train back to New York, but they hadn't gotten back to the brownstone until eleven o'clock. They'd waited outside for some time to check for any lights or sign of movement from inside. On re-entering the house, they'd found it empty. It took them less than half an hour to find and open the secret door.

Steve signalled for Joe and Anne to wait in the middle of the staircase, and cautiously raised his head and gun over the level of the floor. He swept his flashlight and gun back and forth, up and down several times, then said, "Okay, come on up," and holstered his gun.

When they got to the top of the stairs, Anne and Joe saw that the entire third floor had been gutted at some point. It was one large room. Shelves, cabinets, worktables, and a writing desk were arrayed along the walls. Thick curtains blacked out the windows. Steve found a light switch at the top of the stairs and illuminated the room. It was mostly empty, the contents of the shelves and worktable mostly gone. A forlorn Rolodex and a portable phone were all that sat atop the desk. Anne spotted some books across the room and started to walk towards them. Steve reached out and grabbed her arm. She looked over and he pointed to the floor, which was covered in smudged-out chalk marks that must have described various geometries and words, as well as blotches of candle wax and some dark, unidentifiable, troubling stains.

"You don't want to step on any of that," said Steve.

"Oh, right, evidence," said Anne.

"That and hoodoo," said Joe flatly.

Anne's flesh crawled a bit as she navigated her way to the bookshelf. "Junk, junk, junk," she said, flipping through a variety of modern works on demonology, necromancy, and the like.

"Bad taste in reading?" Joe asked.

"No, no, some good stuff. Kieckhefer, Elliot Rose. Just not worth anything. You want to read up on necromancy?" Anne asked.

"Pass," Joe answered.

"Oh my God!" Anne shouted.

Steve and Joe immediately drew their guns and frantically scanned the room. After a second, Steve asked, "What? You okay?"

"Oh, no, sorry. It's this book," Anne said. Steve and Joe looked at each other dubiously as they holstered their guns. "It was just at the bottom of a pile of modern books. He must have forgotten it. This is a fifteenth-century Greek *Key of Solomon.* There's only one known to exist. It's in the British Library. Holy God. This is almost literally priceless. Well, nothing's *priceless.* I mean, if you put this on the block, I'd guess seven figures, easily. Maybe eight."

"Well, congrats. You can take it home, read it in bed, and when you get around to it, add it to the Coolidge Foundation library," said Steve.

"Really?" Anne was a little disturbed and a lot excited.

"Really," explained Joe. "Under the Charter, we get to keep any evidence or goods we deem appropriate. Heck, if we wanted to push it, we could probably confiscate this house. But I think we'll just scrub the attic."

"No wonder you guys don't scrimp on expenses," said Anne.

"Eat, drink, and be merry," muttered Steve.

"So you think he took all his good books, Anne?" Joe asked.

"Looks like it. Don't know how he forgot this one, though. He must have left in a hurry."

"Hey, check this out," Joe said, pulling something large and shiny from the bottom shelf of a worktable. He held it up, revealing a lovely silver serving tray about two feet long and eighteen inches wide. "This has got to be sterling. It's ridiculously heavy."

"Let me see that," said Anne, crossing the room gingerly in a macabre parody of hopscotch. "Look at the lip on it. Do you see any water stains?"

"Sure, a few," said Joe.

Anne sighed with relief. "I think I can look in a mirror again. That's exactly the kind of thing that some medieval scrying spells describe. You put water or oil on it, then say some mumbo-jumbo, wave something over it or drop something into it."

"You think they've given up?" asked Steve.

"I guess so. I mean, maybe he's taken a second salver or something with him, but I think he'd have a lot bigger problem disappearing with that little boy," Anne said.

Joe laughed grimly. "Yeah, that's a quick way to get thirty-seven different police departments coming after you."

"It's possible," Steve hypothesized, "that having obtained the breviary and the Voynich Manuscript, he's far enough along in his plan, whatever it is, that your being able to figure out what he's up to is no longer threatening."

"In other words," said Joe, "we may be in much worse shape than we thought."

"You know, as ominous as all that is, it doesn't overshadow my joy at the prospect of putting on eyeliner," said Anne, as they went back to searching.

A few minutes later, Steve was pulling one worktable away from the wall. "Hey, come look at this," he said. Joe and Anne crossed the room and looked between the heavy table and the wall. There was a strange leathery object that must have fallen down behind the table. Steve reached down for it.

"Don't touch that!" said Anne, alarmed.

"Huh?" said Steve, pulling his hand back quickly.

"Hey, I've been paying attention in orientation. 'Black magic, bad,' right?" she said.

"Right," said Steve and Joe almost in unison.

"Well, that's some bad juju," Anne said, feeling a little like one of the guys, when finally getting to tell *them* something and to indulge in some dark humor. She then explained, "It's a *main de gloire*."

"Amanda who?" asked Steve.

"A *main de gloire*. A Hand of Glory."

"Sick," said Joe, stepping back.

"A what?" asked Steve. "Remember, I'm just the muscle here."

"A Hand of Glory," explained Anne. "You take the severed left hand of a hanged man, desiccate it in some particular salts, and then make a candle out of the fat of his body and set it in the palm. Or just use the fat as fuel to daub on the fingers. See down there, those pointy bits are fingers, and they're scorched on the ends."

"That is sick," said Steve.

"Hey, you're supposed to be the tough guy," joked Anne, punching him lightly in the arm.

"I'm just not big on, you know, mutilated corpses. So, what do you *do* with that?" Steve wondered.

"You rob people," Anne said, to their evident surprise. "It supposedly has two effects. First, anyone in a house where it's lit who's asleep stays asleep until it's extinguished. Second, it casts light that only you can see."

"So, uh, does it work?" Joe asked.

"How do I know? Before I ran into you people, I'd have laughed it off as a particularly gruesome superstition. Now, I don't know. I mean, I doubt it, but do you really want to mess with something like that?"

"Good point," said Steve. He pulled on a pair of gloves, produced a Ziploc bag, picked up and sealed in the Hand, and gave it to Anne. "You're the Librarian. This definitely goes in the Archive."

"Fair enough," said Anne, gingerly taking the bag by a corner, and slipping the grotesque trophy into the black bag she'd brought.

An hour later, and they'd searched the entire room to no further avail. Anne dropped the Rolodex and the portable phone in her bag to take back to the office to go through for information.

"When this is over, we'll have to come back and scrub these floorboards," said Joe.

"My favorite part of the job," said Steve.

"A Hand of Glory. I wonder if he has a *Grimoire of Pope Honorius III*. That's got a *main de gloire* recipe, I think," Anne said, mostly to herself, considering it'd be a considerable addition to the Coolidge Foundation's library, if it were as old as his *Key of Solomon*. Then, suddenly, she said, "Hey, guys, can we stop at an all-night Duane Reade before we check into a hotel? I really want a facial tonight."

11

A few days later they were back in D.C. with no further breaks in the case. There were no addresses in the Rolodex or numbers in the phone's memory that yielded any leads. A general mood of gloom settled back on the Black Chamber, replacing the momentary euphoria of having identified a suspect and brought back such exotica as the Greek grimoire, the scrying tray, and the *main de gloire*, the last of which John was particularly excited to see, as he'd read a fair bit about them but had never actually seen one. Mike was moved to inaugurate a series of awful puns, beginning with attempting to dub the case "The Hand Job," which earned him a welt on the back of the head from a fat paperback C++ manual Joe winged at him.

Anne mostly worked on her Memoranda, which were what the Black Chamber called first-person, written accounts of incidents that were submitted to the Historian, who would draw up a complete, edited third-person account to be entered in the Chamber's History, which also served as a reference. Alas, the History was silent on the topic of medieval necromancy or the lore of Tibet or Mongolia, much less a connection between the two.

That morning, however, Wilhelmina walked into the brainstorming conference with a twinkle in her eye. "I got it," she said, smiling broadly.

"Got what?" asked Claire.

"I've got your next lead," she said triumphantly.

"Really?" asked John. "Please tell."

"The little boy."

"The one I saw in the mirror," Anne said with a sense of realization.

"Right," said Wilhelmina. "I figure he's got to have found the boy somewhere, and he couldn't have taken off with him or murdered him without someone noticing. I know you said he was black, and in even the poorest parts of the community, you'd have a hard time finding a mother, however degraded or desperate, who'd let her child go off with a strange white man, even a priest."

"Maybe especially a priest. The papers make them all sound like degenerates. Most of that stuff was in the '70s and '80s, though," said Mike, warming to a topic.

"Mike," said Joe. "Focus."

"Right," said Mike. "So how do we find him?"

"How do you think the bad guy found him?" asked Wilhelmina.

Joe spoke up. "Was he part of a parish? Because if he was, we should check the parochial school."

"No," said Mike. "I checked all of his institutional affiliations. He's a free agent. He's under the Archdiocese of New York, but they said that he basically does his own thing. He can afford to, as he's got not only his own money, but a big donor roll, with some heavy hitters in the world of liberal philanthropy. The Ford, Gates, and other foundations, that kind of thing."

"Oh, hell," said Claire suddenly. "I know what it is. I was going through his Rolodex, working the contacts. There was one card that said BB&S, and when I called it turned out to be Big Brothers Big Sisters of America. There were a fair number of charitable organizations in there, so I didn't think twice about it. I'm sorry."

"Not at all," said Anne. "None of us thought of it. Including me, who actually saw the kid. Let's see what we can do."

The following day, Anne and Claire, again posing as FBI agents, sat across from Judith Weintraub, the director of the Manhattan office of Big Brothers Big Sisters.

"Let me start by repeating again what I said on the phone, Ms. Weintraub," began Claire. "This is not a criminal matter, nor are we looking to get anyone in trouble. We were asked to look into Monsignor Clairvaux's disappearance by his concerned colleagues when they couldn't get in touch with him. We have no reason to believe there's been any foul play or that his Little Brother would be or has ever been in the least bit of danger. We just want to ask him a few questions to see if he knows anything, and then we're done."

"I understand," said the director. "We'd like to cooperate, which is why we're talking. Our children's privacy is of paramount importance to us."

"We wouldn't have it any other way," said Claire.

Anne spoke up. "Can I ask you one question, Ms. Weintraub? Monsignor Clairvaux was obviously a Catholic priest, and I mean, there have been some problems with Catholic priests and little boys, so how exactly did he get approved?"

"I'm not sure I like your tone," said Ms. Weintraub, "but I understand your concern. First, we don't regard priests as greater risks than your average unmarried male off the street. The statistics bear that out. That said, before pairing him with a boy, we did do a background check. We spoke to a number of Monsignor Clairvaux's former girlfriends, and although most of them weren't particularly well-disposed towards him, to a woman, they all confirmed that he was definitely heterosexual—perhaps voraciously or unpleasantly so—and had no concerns about his taking care of a little boy. And, frankly, he's proved to be one of our best Big Brothers. He took his Little Brother to museums, art galleries, zoos, music recitals, and even an off-Broadway revival of *Little Mary Sunshine* that his Little Brother still talks about as being the funniest thing he's ever seen. He taught the boy the rudiments of playing the piano, and a little French, Spanish, Italian, and Latin. His Little Brother adores him, and since you called, I've been worried about the monsignor too."

Claire and Anne were taken more than a little aback at the director's encomium to Monsignor Clairvaux. They'd both been expecting him to have acted sinisterly or to have put himself under suspicion. Anne couldn't think of what to reply, but Claire, rarely at a loss for words, said, "Well, we certainly hope he's just in a retreat house somewhere outside cell phone range, but it's our job to check. Would it be ok if we were able to talk to his Little Brother?"

"Since we all understand each other, of course. He's waiting in the conference room next door."

Ms. Weintraub picked up a file and led them into the room, where they saw a cherubic, dark-complected black boy of about seven or eight, dressed spiffily in a sweater vest and tie. Anne involuntarily took a half step back in a shock of recognition. His was the face from the mirror. His obviously concerned mother, whose clothes weren't quite up to the mark of those she'd bought her son, sat with her arm around the back of his chair. Anne, Claire, and Ms. Weintraub all sat down.

The director addressed the little boy. "Darrell, these are Special Agents Sotheby and Thatcher from the FBI. They're trying to find Monsignor Clairvaux to make sure he's ok. They just want to ask you a few questions. Is that ok with you?"

"Sure," said Darrell in a soft voice, but with a lilt betraying a little excitement.

Ms. Weintraub turned to his mother. "Mrs. Green?"

"That's fine," Darrell's mother said, with a little trepidation. Ms. Weintraub nodded to Claire and Anne.

Claire took the lead, as usual. "Hi, Darrell. I'm Special Agent Thatcher of the FBI. You can call me Hilda if you like. Here's my ID." He examined it as if it were a precious grown-up thing that he couldn't quite believe he could play with. "We just want to ask you a few questions about Monsignor Clairvaux. Now, no one's in trouble, no one is in danger, do you understand?"

Darrell nodded happily, and showed Claire's FBI badge to his mother, who took it and looked at it intently for a second, then stared closely at Claire. Seemingly satisfied, she handed the ID back to Claire.

"Okay, so Monsignor Clairvaux is your Big Brother, right?"

"Yes. He's *great.*"

"So we hear from Ms. Weintraub. You guys do a lot of fun stuff together, it sounds like."

"Oh yeah! We do *everything*! We go to the Natural History Museum—last time there was this cool movie about this guy Shackleton and his boat that got stuck in the ice at the South Pole. It was very sad because they had to kill all the dogs that they brought because there wouldn't be enough food for the poor dogs and they didn't want to let them starve and the man who took care of the dogs cried. But they got off the South Pole, and not a single person died. I think that Shackleton guy is a hero."

"I think so, too, Darrell," Claire said, smiling. All the adults in the room were smiling, even Mrs. Green, parental pride in her eyes. Claire asked, "Have you ever been to Monsignor Clairvaux's house?" and Mrs. Green's face darkened again.

"A few times. One time he showed me a book he had about some Aztec guys, because we saw this really scary exhibit of Aztec art at the Guggenheim. And I was really scared of Aztecs. But then he showed me this book, and it was only the art they made that was really scary. They looked just like normal people. Sort of like Indians. Not the India kind, but the American kind."

Ms. Weintraub put in, "Monsignor Clairvaux asked for our approval any time before inviting Darrell over, and volunteered to have a supervisor present."

"How many times were you there, Darrell?" asked Claire.

"Um, I don't know. About ten?"

Ms. Weintraub was looking at a paper from the file she'd brought. "We have one dozen approved visits over a two-year period."

"Did you ever do anything interesting there?" Claire asked.

"Sure! We played the piano a few times, a couple times Monsignor showed me some magic tricks, and one time he showed me this awesome book about trains he had. It was real big, like one of those table-coffee books, and it had pictures of every kind of train in the world! His one grandfather was an engineer back when all they had were steam engines, but this book has all the diesels and electrics and even had some stuff on the maglev train they have in China and the TGVs in France, those aren't maglev trains, but regular ones that go about as fast. TGV means *train à grande vitesse*, which means 'train of high speed.'"

Claire smiled. "That's very good! *Tu parles français bien.*"

"*Monsignor Clairvaux est un bon professeur. J'espére que je suis un bon étudiant.*"

"I'm sure you are a great student, Darrell," praised Claire. "Your accent is great and your grammar is perfect."

Anne leaned in. "*Et linguam latinam discis?*"

"*Disco,*" Darrell smiled, very pleased with himself.

"That's fantastic. I hope you keep up with those languages. They can be really helpful in life," said Anne.

"The monsignor got Darrell a scholarship through high school in the Catholic school system," said Mrs. Green. "He's taking those languages in school now, too."

"They're pretty fun," said Darrell. "But I like math best."

"Yikes," said Anne. "Not me. Can I call you when I'm doing my taxes?"

Darrell looked shy. "Sure."

Claire said, "Darrell, did Monsignor Clairvaux say anything to you before he left town?"

Darrell nodded vigorously.

"And what was that?"

"He said that he was going away for a long time, and he wasn't sure when he'd be back, but when he came back we'd go to another Yankees game."

"Did he tell you where he was going?" asked Claire.

"No, not really. Some place up north in Canada."

Claire and Anne looked at each other in surprise. "Canada?" Claire asked.

"Uh-huh. One of his grandparents or great-grandparents or something used to live up there."

"Did he mention the name of a town or a province or anything?" Anne asked.

"Nope. Just Canada," said Darrell. "Do you think he'll be back soon?"

Anne felt her heart sink. "I don't know, Darrell. I really don't. If he does, I'm sure you'll be one of the first people he calls. But if not, you just keep doing what you're doing in school, and being good for your mom, and being so polite and gracious to strangers like us. He will be very, very proud."

"Thanks," said Darrell.

"It was a pleasure to meet you, Darrell," said Claire, reaching across the table to shake his hand.

"Thank you, the pleasure was mine," Darrell said carefully, as if trying to remember the pleasantry exactly.

"Mrs. Green, you've got an amazing son," Anne said, shaking her hand as they all stood.

"I know. I wish his father were alive to see him," she said, choking up a little.

"I'm so sorry," said Claire, shaking her hand.

"My dad died in Afghanistan," said Darrell. "He was a Green Beret and he was really brave and he saved six other soldiers and killed nineteen Talibans. They came to our house to thank Mom and me. And then we got a medal for him from the President."

"Medal of Honor," said Mrs. Green in a low, tight voice, her eyes bright with tears.

"My dad was a hero. Like Shackleton. Only he died. We were really sad. I still miss him. I wish I remembered him a little better, but I have a great picture the other soldiers gave us."

Anne swallowed a huge lump in her throat and said, "It sounds like your dad was a great, great hero. I'm really proud to meet his son," offering her hand for him to shake.

Darrell took it solemnly, then smiled. "Can I tell you a secret?"

"Sure," Anne said, bending down, as he stood on tiptoe and cupped his hand to her ear.

He whispered, "I remember you from the mirror trick."

Anne whispered back, "I remember you, too," and then, before she knew what she was doing, she hugged him.

ཀ ཌ ལ

Claire shut off her cell phone and slipped it into her pocket as the Delta shuttle's stewardesses passed by checking her and Anne's seat belts.

"What did he say?" asked Anne.

Claire lifted an eyebrow. "Verbatim? He said, 'Canada? Oh, shit.'"

"John doesn't like Canada?"

"No, it's just that we don't have the slightest jurisdiction in Canada. We're a branch of the U.S. government. Our legal authority stops at the border."

"Oh, right. So, does Canada have a, you know, *chambre noire*?" She spoke softly and circumspectly, though the flight was only half full.

"No. At least we don't think so."

"That leads me to a question. Who does have similar agencies?"

"That's a very good question. Again, we can't be sure that there aren't ones out there below the radar, but we know of a handful. The British do, and they have been known to operate in places like Canada and India, so there may be some Imperial or Commonwealth connection. The Russians do, but we're really not sure what they're up to these days. In the Soviet days, they were after power and dedicated to stamping out evidence of the supernatural, lest it discredit the state cult of atheism. Nowadays with the whole weird Caesaropapist alignment of the Kremlin and the Orthodox Church, we're not sure if that's affected their mission. In fact, it's possible that they've dropped below the Kremlin's radar. They were part of the GRU, not the KGB, so the Kremlin probably isn't as wired into them as they might otherwise be. Or they could have been abolished. Though that's never a safe bet with shady, spooky organizations.

"France does, but they're much more about the science of the supernatural, near as we can tell. Mostly gathering information, rather than running around with guns like we do. If you look in the library there's a volume on the biochemistry of lycanthropy produced by them that we obtained. It's very interesting. That said, if they've got a former French special-ops guy or two, that makes them as dangerous as we are with Steve. Steve always says that despite the French reputation for cowardice, his experience with their special forces is that they are very, very good and very, very ruthless.

"Um, let me think, who else? We're a little sketchy on East Asia. The Japanese might, but if they do, they play it very close to the vest. The Chinese do, we believe, and in fact, if you read some ancient texts the right way, it's arguable that they've had one for a thousand years. The Communist government is so closed, though, that we have no idea what's happened to them since 1949. Remember Herbert Yardley, our founder? He documented that an organization existed called the *Pai Tse Ko*, the Cabinet (or Chamber) of the White Marsh, and even saw their library, which he said had an amazing number of very old documents that he was told were written by members of the organization. But, of course, Mao might well have burned the place to the ground and killed everyone. Or they all packed up and moved to Tibet until the Commies got there in 1959. Or they're still there, hiding. Or, perhaps, they're actually out in the service of the People's Republic, keeping down all the hungry ghosts left over from the Great Leap Forward. It's one of those big 'who knows?' questions."

"Why 'White Marsh?'"

"Ah, that's actually very interesting. *Pai Tse* not only means 'white marsh' but it's the name of a legendary creature who dictated a book to Huang Ti, the Yellow Emperor, in which it described the appearance and behavior of the eleven thousand five hundred twenty supernatural creatures in the world and how to defeat and dispel them. The book, the *Pai Tse T'u*, was lost in antiquity, but fragments of it crop up in other works."

"Aha. So it's a not-so-subtle clue that they're attempting to do the same thing."

"So Yardley thought."

"Wow."

"Let me think, who am I missing? Ah, the Germans. That's an interesting case. You've heard of the *Ahnenerbe*, I assume?"

Anne smiled. "You assume incorrectly."

"Ah, ok. All the big Nazis were freaks for the occult. Himmler was one of the biggest kooks on that score. He believed in these oddball historical theories whereby the Aryan race had been the most glorious civilization in world history until it was beaten down by those evil Romans, Christians, and Jews, more or less in turn."

Anne nodded. "I've heard that. You run across a lot of b.s. occultism when you're going through estates or auction catalogs trying to find the good stuff. And it seems like you could slap a swastika on a washing-machine repair manual and get a bestseller, given the number of books about the Nazis out there."

"Probably true," Claire said. "So, in 1935, once the Nazis were firmly ensconced in power, Himmler, some of his race-theory buddies, and a historian of prehistoric antiquity set up the *Forschungsgemeinschaft Deutsches Ahnenerbe*, the 'Research Society for German Ancestral Heritage,' a body for obtaining and scientifically documenting evidence of these prehistoric-Aryan-glory theories. They sent out expeditions to Sweden, France, Tibet, Finland, and the Middle East. They're what the *Raiders of the Lost Ark* villains were based on. Now, although many of them were crackpot Nazis, they had some very well-trained scholars with them who came up with all sorts of fascinating archaeological, anthropological, and paleontological stuff, though most of it was within their framework of race-war drivel. During the war, especially in Poland, a lot of their activities were flat-out looting. But they always clung tenaciously to a veneer of science. As did their medical-research branch, which did a lot of hideous experiments on Jews in concentration camps."

"Oh dear God," said Anne, her hand flying to her mouth.

"I know, right? Anyway, most of their bigwigs were found guilty of war crimes at Nuremberg—they hanged the boss—and the *Ahnenerbe* disappeared."

"So what does this have to do with B.C. kind of stuff?"

"Well, here's the interesting thing. In 1942, in the middle of the war, the *Ahnenerbe*, a private organization—partially funded, get this, by royalties from a patent on a bike reflector that Himmler made mandatory on all bikes made in Germany—sets up a sort of branch office in Cologne, right across the square from the cathedral. To run it, they choose Joseph-Maria Wilhelm de Hódmezővásárhely-Csongrád."

"Say that three times fast."

"Not on your life. This is the first sign that something odd is up. JMW is no Nazi. In fact, he was a devout man who'd opposed both the Horthy regime and the Nazis on religious grounds, as well as an aristocrat of a very old Austro-Hungarian family. He'd been a colonel in the First World War and is widely credited with some brilliant maneuver warfare and guerrilla-like tactics in their Romanian Campaign. I'll take the peanuts, oh, and a glass of red wine," Claire said to the stewardess, briefly confusing Anne.

"I'll take the peanuts too," Anne said. "Coffee for me, please."

"So, JMW returns to the ancestral estate after the war and finds himself a citizen of the new country of Hungary. When Admiral Horthy allies Hungary with the Axis in exchange for some lost territory in Romania, JMW resigns all his remaining ranks and so forth, and disappears into his manor house. Then, suddenly, in 1942, he's in Cologne, going to Mass at the cathedral every day, hanging around with Archbishop Frings— one of the loudest voices against Nazism—and working for this *Forschungsgemeinschaft Sankt-Dionysius-von-Paris.*"

"Wait, how's that possible? He's doing all these über-Catholic things on the Nazis' dime?"

"Apparently. Moreover, although the *Ahnenerbe* was an SS organization, this *Forschungsgemeinschaft* had no SS or Nazi Party members. And whatever he was doing, it never got him in trouble with the law after the war. Why the Nazis, to their doubtless chagrin, picked JMW to do whatever he was doing is the sixty-four-thousand *Reichsmark* question. The sole clue we have is that there was a novel privately published in Bratislava in 1919 by an infantryman who'd served under JMW. It told the story of an Austro-Hungarian unit in Romania in the First World War that took a position in an ancient castle and then was slowly decimated by a vampire whose castle it turned out to be until the colonel in charge managed to trap it with holy water and a crucifix, then impaled it with a saber, cut off its head, stuffed garlic in its mouth and burnt the remains. It's a pretty good read, though a little crude, stylistically. It was very popular in Slovakia and even made it into German in Vienna in the late '20s. We have an English translation in the Archive. It's generally considered an interesting, if minor, derivative of Bram Stoker's *Dracula.*"

"Let me guess, it wasn't a novel; it was a memoir."

"Maybe. Also suggestive is the fact that there was a hideous series of murders in Cologne that stopped not long after he got there."

"So this guy was *Freiherr* Buffy von Vampire Slayer?"

"Your guess is as good as mine. But he also manages to flip off the Nazis by naming his organization after the patron saint of France, St. Denis of Paris, whose name was a battle cry of the French, whose royal standard, the *oriflamme*, came from Denis's abbey and was supposedly consecrated in his blood."

"Ick."

"Ah, but it's a great story. The Romans decapitated Denis on Montmartre. He got up, picked up his head, and walked two miles to his grave, preaching all the way. They built a church on the spot, and that's where they buried the kings of France."

"Heh. Good one, JMW," said Anne, toasting him with her Styrofoam cup.

Claire tapped her plastic wineglass on it and said, "And there's another suggestive fact about St. Denis. He's a patron saint of the possessed, invoked against demons."

"Ah, another coincidence."

"So after the war's over and they set up the Federal Republic, the FGSDP, as it's known, kind of disappears. No one's sure what happened to it, exactly. However, there exist a couple photographs from the mid-1950s of the incredibly old JMW having lunch with Konrad Adenauer at the latter's house. Adenauer was a Rhineland Catholic and former mayor of Cologne who doubtless learned of JMW through Cardinal Frings, whom he'd known before the war."

"So you think it's still around."

"It's got to be. They're Germans, the best managers in world history. The initials FGSDP have appeared a couple times in German budget documents, and there is a JMW GmbH that's ostensibly a boutique management-consulting firm in Cologne, but we have our doubts."

"That's pretty crazy," said Anne.

"Yeah, but it's of a piece with what we do," shrugged Claire.

"Can I ask you a sort of personal question?" said Anne.

"Well, I'm sort of a person. Fire away."

"You're Jewish, right?"

"Yep. An *ekhte yiddische maydele*, as my grandfather used to say."

"Do you believe in God?"

"Yes."

"Okay. I've just been noticing that in all this stuff, there seem to be a lot of Catholics. What's the story with that?"

"Don't you watch horror movies? No one says, 'My God, it's a vampire! Call that nice lesbian Episcopalian minister down the street to whip up some holy water!'"

"I'm serious. I mean, I'm not Catholic—well, not really religious at all—and it's always seemed a little weird. And now I'm surrounded by it. I mean, what's the deal?"

"Well, a couple of things. First, it's kind of their franchise. I mean, they've got a couple thousand years of teaching that supernatural evil exists and that it preys on people. Whatever the theology, that's sort of close to what we're doing: protecting people from weirdness. So I think they have less cognitive dissonance than a lot of people. You hear since you were a kid that you have to 'reject the devil and all his pomps and works' and when some spooky stuff that looks like a devil pops up, you've got a frame of reference. Plus, on the demonic front, Jesus charged his apostles with going and driving out demons. So it makes sense that the organization they started would have some sort of institutional demon-fighting procedures. The fact that they seem to work does give me the occasional bit of pause that, you know, oh crap, the *goyim* may be right.

"But my theory is that they're just picking up where the great rabbis left off. They're worshipping our God, even if they're a little confused on His nature. But, although it doesn't come up a lot, there's a ton of rabbinical literature on all sorts of demons. Ashmodai and Samaël, Lilith, Agrat bat Maḥlat "the dancing roof-demon," Keṭeb Meriri, Azazel, Shamḥazai, Belial, Alukah the vampire, and on and on, down to garden-variety evil spirits.

We had our own demon-fighters like Abba José of Zaintor. And Jews held, back to Egypt, that all magic was demonic. Miracles were from God, but magic was messing with malevolent forces. In fact, interestingly enough, the Pharisees accused Jesus and the Christians of casting out demons by means of demonic power, so that there always seemed to be more and more demons around. Still, it was never a central part of the Jewish worldview, unlike the battle between God and Satan for Christians, so my theory is that over the last couple centuries, it's slipped out of sight and out of mind, leaving the field to the Catholics, who seem to be a little more hard-headed about resisting the ontological claims of modernity." Claire laughed.

"So who in the Chamber is Catholic?"

"John, Mike, and Joe. They usually go to Mass every morning at St. Matthew's, and breakfast afterwards. Wilhelmina is high-church Episcopalian. With a name like McCormack, Steve might be nominally Catholic, but good luck prying out personal information from that guy. Rafe's Jewish like me, and Lily's Presbyterian, I think, but I'm not entirely sure what her stance on the metaphysical is."

"Okay, but there aren't any problems with not being Catholic, are there?"

"No. It's not a big deal. Although I have to say, having ins to a large, international organization that believes in the existence of the supernatural is awfully convenient for our purposes."

"And you don't have any religious or philosophical problems with it?"

"I might if I thought too deeply about stuff, but this job isn't about deep thought. It's about staying sane and alive, and doing some bits of good in a very murky, very strange world."

12

By the middle of the next day, Mike Himmelberg had found the deed for Clairvaux's Canadian property. His mother's family had made quite a lot of money in the lumber industry and owned an estate outside of a small town in north-central Ontario called Nicton. Joe McManus had a large satellite image of the house and ranging, wooded grounds up on a large flat-screen monitor in the conference room. Steve McCormack was alternately staring at it intently and scribbling notes on a yellow pad.

"You guys don't have a satellite, do you?" asked Anne, slightly incredulous.

"No, this is Google Earth. I've enhanced the image somewhat with some neat software they use over at the Navy Yard," said Joe, "but the military and CIA don't do surveillance of rural Canada."

"So what are we doing about the fact we can't legally go in there?" asked Mike.

"I think we've got to go anyway. We'll try and get in and out and not do anything to upset the Canadians," said John. "Steve, you have a plan?"

"Yes. Shouldn't be hard, tactically, as the grounds of the house are so heavily wooded. Unless they've got heavy security or lots of armed guards, we should be able to get inside without much trouble. After that, we're probably through the looking glass, so who knows? Who's coming? Mike? You're our demon guy. You want to try and line up an exorcist, just in case someone starts spouting Aramaic and pea soup?"

"Yeah, fine, I'm in. Fuck, what am I going to tell my wife?" Mike muttered.

"Same as always, dude," said Joe.

"You should tell her you're not going," said Wilhelmina with a ferocious stare.

Mike put his head in his hands. "Wilhelmina, I know you don't think married men"

"Fathers. I don't care if your wife weeps on your grave. She chose you, so much the worse for her. But you got *kids*."

Joe said peaceably, "We've had this conversation before. I don't think anyone's changed their mind."

"Look, you can make me out to be the crazy old black lady, but dammit, you two should *not* be going out in the field. Hell, I don't go out there because I'd get myself or one of y'all killed. You should have at least that much regard for your kids."

A hostile silence descended upon the room, Wilhelmina and Mike glaring at each other, Joe staring pointedly at the floor.

"This is why we need a clear chain of command, John," said Claire.

"Good God, Claire, why don't we hash out *all* the stalemated arguments that the Chamber's had over the years? Anyone want to discuss again whether what we did to that meth head in trying to find little Madison what's-her-name in that haunted-house case was justifiable? Crap. Let's focus, people. Wilhelmina, objection noted, as always. Mike, you're in?"

"Yes. And my family life is pri—"

"Got it, Mike," John said testily. "Joe?"

"Steve, you want me there in case there's any complicated alarms that you can't take out?"

"Couldn't hurt. And we know these guys play for keeps, so having another gun is always good. John?"

"Sure," the Historian nodded.

"Rafe?"

"Sure. Who wants to live forever? Oh, incidentally, I was flipping through the Torah the other night and I found two more instances of something called 'the destroyer' or 'the destroying angel.' The first was about the thing that killed the firstborn of the Egyptians, and the second about something that killed seventy thousand Israelites when David had displeased God. So we got that goin' for us."

"Claire?"

Claire took a deep breath. "Yeah, what the hell. Back on the horse."

"Lily?"

"Pass."

"Wilhelmina?"

"I'm a homebody, Steve."

"Okay. Anne, you want to skip this one until you're a little better oriented?"

"No. I want to go. This guy tried to kill me and blew up my office."

"Okay, fine," Steve said. "I want you all down on the range for at least an hour after work. I'm going to give you all a refresher course—and a crash course for you, Anne—on some guns a little heavier than your pistols. These guys were packing serious weapons, so everyone's got to get up to speed and fast so we're not outgunned. I can probably have transport ready by late tonight or early tomorrow."

"Let's go tomorrow," said Mike. "If he's doing something tonight, we're going to miss it anyway. And we can all sleep in our beds."

"I second that," said Claire. "I'm going to have to draw up all sorts of fake papers for us. I'll probably be here most of the night anyway."

Steve turned to John. "I think you should stay with Lily and Wilhelmina under Rule 14."

"Okay," shrugged John.

"What's that?" asked Anne.

"We have to keep enough people out of harm's way to ensure that we can rebuild the unit, if the worst comes to pass."

"Oh," said Anne.

"Anything else?" asked John.

"You sure we shouldn't get a rush translation of more of the Voynich Manuscript?" asked Anne.

"Killing's not the worst thing curiosity can do to the cat," said John with a distinct note of sadness in his voice.

༄ཉྫ

That afternoon and evening, Anne got a short course in commando etiquette. Steve ran her through the equipment, hand signals, and some of the tactics they used. She took to it naturally and even had fun, thinking it was exactly the sort of game she would have liked to have played with her all-boy mob of cousins in the high mountains of New Mexico. Then, inevitably, the realization that this was potentially a life-and-death matter would leach all enjoyment from it. Oddly, she found the lessons harder to learn when she was deadly earnest; having fun, they seemed to stick a little better in her muscle memory.

Firing a submachine gun might have been the easiest to learn, as she was a good shot to begin with. Getting used to the fully automatic weapon's rate of fire was a little tricky but came quickly to her. The gun, a .45-caliber Heckler & Koch UMP, Steve explained, fired very smoothly and had fairly little recoil. After not very long, Steve declared her adequate in all departments and strongly suggested she go back to the safe house and sleep as much as she could. Not being able to think of a single helpful thing to do, she agreed.

On her way out through the main office, John called out to her from his office, where he was hand-transcribing a printed report into one of the large bound volumes of the Chamber's History.

"Hey, Anne. You done with Steve?"

"Yes, I was just going to take a cab back to Kensington."

"Stop off and have a nice dinner on the way. Can you sit down for a second?"

"Sure."

"I appreciate your wanting to go along, but you know you don't have to, right?"

"I understand. I would like to see this through, though."

"Okay. Well, I want to tell you a couple things that I really should have gotten out of the way right when you were hired on, but I haven't had a chance to."

"Okay."

"Um, let me ask you a question. Do you have a will?"

"No. I probably should, though, right?"

"Yeah, what I'm saying is, I may not have informed you of just how dangerous this can be."

"Don't worry. Claire has been more than emphatic."

"Oh, yeah. That was an awful thing."

"What happened?"

"Well, about five years ago we had an incident with, well— people thought there was a werewolf loose in northern Nevada. They were more or less right. Claire was the lead investigator and took Steve, Mike's predecessor and Rafe's predecessor to check it out. She and Steve came back. It was bad."

"So why is she going out now?"

"Well, I think she knows that, in general, the more people go, the lower the odds of any one individual getting killed. So she's doing it out of a sense of duty to the rest of us, being willing to take the bullet, so to speak. Although this is the first time in a while bullets are definitely in play. It's why Steve's running the show. Okay, well, if you're aware that, to be honest, you may not come back from this trip, I don't really have anything else to add. Go have a nice dinner, call your parents and tell them that you love them, take a nice bath, and get some sleep."

"I will," said Anne, and did.

༄ ༅ ༄

The next day, the team assembled at the Black Chamber. Claire handed each member two manila envelopes. "The first set of identification is for the flight. The second is for once we cross the border."

Anne opened hers. The first set was a set of Central Intelligence Agency identifications in her own name. The second envelope held some Canadian Security Intelligence Service identifications under a false name. Anne held her CSIS ID up to Claire and said, "Again? Christie Sotheby?"

"Come on, you worked in auctions. I'm supposed to resist that? Otherwise, I was thinking of Annabel Lee Bookbinder."

"Christie it is. So why Canadian intelligence whatever?"

"If we get stopped by Canadian authorities, it should give us enough time to get out and get back here."

"Okay. Why the CIA?"

"Because we have to get there," came Steve's deep voice over her shoulder. "And none of us can fly a plane. Fortunately, the CIA has a fair number of well-equipped private jets that they use. And that we can use."

"How's that possible?" said Anne.

"Easy," said Claire. "Remember how Joe was telling you that he's got access to all the different computer networks? It's the same sort of thing. We're older than all of the other agencies, and when they were getting set up, we made sure that we were in on it. So I hit a button on my phone, and I'm effectively calling from Langley or FBI headquarters or the White House or wherever. The call routes through their switchboards from a perfectly legitimate extension."

Steve explained, "I call a non-official-cover front company with a plane from a Langley number, tell them where we need to go, and they take care of the rest without asking any questions."

"What about billing the costs and so forth?" Anne wondered.

Claire laughed and Steve smiled. "Cost accounting isn't really an issue in the black-ops world."

Several hours later, the team of six was flying north in comfort on a Gulfstream V jet. Steve had arrived first thing in the morning with their equipment, weapons, and clothing. They took turns changing in the surprisingly spacious head, made sandwiches, and microwaved miniature pizzas. All in all, the mood aboard the plane was very much like kids on a field trip to a hospital—excited, but with an undercurrent of worry about what they might see.

The sun was setting as they crossed the Canadian border. "Okay, folks," Claire announced, consulting a GPS map of their progress and holding out a black pouch, "switch to CSIS IDs. CIA ones go in here and stay on the plane. The pilot has instructions to destroy them if we don't come back."

Steve then handed out some thin file folders. "Okay, everyone. Take a good look at these, because I'm collecting them once we hit the ground. First page is a large-scale map. You can see the marked location of the little airstrip we're using. To the southwest is Nicton, and to the southeast through the forest is Wystan House. It's going to be about a two-hour walk through the woods, so I hope you all brought comfortable shoes. It's a full moon tonight and the weather's supposed to be clear, so I don't think we'll need night-vision or infrared equipment, though I'll carry a set in case. Second page is a close-up of the house and grounds, labeled with all the obstacles that Joe could identify. You'll want to remember the various outbuildings' and gates' locations, in case we need to hide or flee.

"We go in through the woods, over the wall, and across the grounds to the house. At that point, we'll pick a likely entry point and go in. What happens next, who knows? If we're lucky, we grab the guy in his sleep and drug him. But if he's doing that late-night black-magic thing, it could be a circus. There are two ways to extract yourself. First, walk back the way you came. It's a ways, but it gives you the least chance of being seen. The airstrip is eight point three miles or thirteen and a third kilometers north by northwest from the front gate of the compound. If you're separated, use the compass you've got. If that's gone, guess with the North Star.

"Worst case, get your street clothes out of your pack, get rid of all your equipment—bury it with the little trowel in the pack if you can—and walk into town. Get a cab out to the airstrip— everyone's got a thousand bucks Canadian in their pack—or flash your CSIS badge at a cop or a cabbie and tell 'em it's critical you reach your flight. Not ideal, especially if there's a mess back at the house, but it'll get you out of the country. We leave an hour before sunrise, no later, so if you're not back by then, you're on your own. Call us at the Chamber and we'll do what we can, but in the meantime, keep a low profile and have a good cover story."

"I've got one thing to add," said Mike. "My buddy the D.C. exorcist put me in touch with an exorcist up here, and he's willing to accompany us. He's apparently reasonably fit and not a hundred and fifty years old, so I think we might as well bring him along, unless anyone thinks he'll be more of a burden."

Steve thought for a second. "Well, we'll take a look at him, and decide then."

"Fair enough," Mike said. "Though I want as much divine assistance as I can get."

"Noted," said Steve. "Okay, folks. Get yourselves ready, hit the head, whatever you need to do."

As Anne involuntarily took a deep breath, she noticed everyone else doing so as well.

13

The plane touched down without lights on a cracked and pitted concrete airstrip with tufts of grass scattered through it. It looked like God had dropped an errant slab of pavement into the middle of the Canadian wilderness. The team climbed off the plane clad in tactical 'ninja' suits, black knapsacks in hand. No one spoke as they milled around for a moment, shouldering the packs and stretching their legs—Claire in impressive, yogic fashion.

A slim man, also clad in black save a mahogany-and-silver pectoral cross, walked purposefully out of the wall of trees around the airstrip towards the plane. Mike went out to meet him, shook his hand, and escorted him back to the group.

"People, this is," he pulled a piece of paper out of his pocket and read, "Father Thomas-Joseph Jean-Baptiste Amédée-François Lamy of the Dominicans and the Archdiocese of Montreal."

The priest, a young man with the fine features of Burgundy, said with only the slightest Québécois accent, "Call me Tom."

Mike said, "Father Lamy is an exorcist and a former professor of epigraphy, Assyriology, and Egyptology at the *École biblique et archéologique française de Jérusalem*."

"No offense, Father, but how old *are* you?" asked Claire, in mock surprise.

"Older every day," the priest smiled.

"Wait a second," said Rafe, "Assyriology and exorcism? How often do you get Pazuzu and Max von Sydow jokes?"

"All the time," said Father Lamy. "Well, from those who know I'm an exorcist, at any rate. My mother's particularly bad about it, but she had a crush on von Sydow since *The Seventh Seal*. Me, I could take or leave Bergman and I tend to think of von Sydow as Ming the Merciless in *Flash Gordon*. I'm more of a Luc Besson guy. So how can I help you all?"

"We're going into a situation where there's a risk of encountering something demonic," Mike said.

"Ah. Well, shall I come along?"

"How are you at hiking in those shoes, Father?" asked Steve.

"Fine."

"Okay, then, if you want to come along, you're more than welcome."

"What should I do with my car?"

"Good question." Steve pulled out a map. "Okay, park it about here, then walk this way, and wait here by this creek. We'll meet you there." He held up the map. "Everyone, Father Lamy's car is going to be about here. If you find yourself needing out quickly, that's another option. Leave the keys under the mat, will you, Father?"

"Of course."

Joe spoke up. "Father, would you mind offering a little prayer for us before we go?"

"Not at all." He raised his hands in the *orans* posture and, as the Catholics bowed their heads and the rest looked at each other out of the corners of their eyes, said, "*Sancte Michael Archangele, defende nos in prælio; contra nequitiam et insidias Diaboli esto præsidium. Imperat illi Deus; supplices deprecamur: tuque, Princeps militiæ cælestis, Satanam aliosque spiritus malignos, qui ad perditionem animarum pervagantur in mundo, divina virtute in infernum detrude. Amen.*"

Anne surprised herself by joining in when everyone murmured, "Amen."

"Okay, folks, let's go," said Steve. "Come over here and get your weapons."

Father Lamy walked back off through the trees, as the Black Chamber team holstered pistols on their hips and slung submachine guns over their shoulders. When everyone was armed, Steve said, "This way," and headed off into the woods.

Under the sheltering evergreens, the moonlight was much reduced and they waited five minutes for their eyes to adjust. Once they were accustomed to the dimness, they followed Steve, single-file, through the trees. Anne occasionally caught herself wondering, *What am I doing here?* but tried to let it go immediately, lest she get distracted and do something to endanger herself or the others. Ordinarily, the hike through the forest would have been a charming nature walk, even at night, as badgers, raccoons, bats, nocturnal birds, and lizards regarded them impassively, wild enough to show no fear of humans deep in the middle of the dark, dark woods; but the walk quickly became a test of concentration and focus, as Anne noticed her focus slipping every so often. *How do soldiers do this?* Anne asked herself. *Well, the bad ones probably get killed quickly, leaving only the stealthy ones. God, I'm in trouble.*

About an hour and a half into the walk, they came across Father Lamy, sitting quietly on a log next to a shallow creek. He put away the rosary he'd been fingering and tucked his pectoral cross under his shirt. Steve pulled a Glock out of his knapsack and offered it to the priest. The priest paused, then took the gun and put it in his jacket pocket. He fell in between Anne and Rafe, who guarded the rear of the line. Unlike the rest of the team, Rafe carried a gun that looked very strange to Anne. When she'd asked him about it at the airport, he'd explained it was a Tavor rifle. He collected Israeli weaponry and was more comfortable with his own guns than the ones Steve issued. He'd wanted to bring an Uzi, which was smaller and lighter, but Steve had said that, if he was bringing something non-standard, he might as well bring something with greater range and a larger caliber. The Tavor wasn't much longer than the UMP, but because its magazine sat behind the handgrip, it had a full-length rifle barrel and fired the same bullet as an M16. Rafe seemed to handle the weapon very confidently, so Anne felt much safer with him at her back.

After what seemed like forever, Steve signaled for the group to stop and get down. They'd reached the edge of the forest and he was cautiously scanning the open space in front of them. He took out a pair of goggles and looked through them, then stashed them. He moved silently across the grass to the base of a high stone wall about a hundred yards away, staying stock-still, then walking its length and peering around both corners. Then he signaled the group forward.

Crouching, they all hurried deliberately to the base of the wall. Steve threw a line with a grapple to the top, then scaled the wall to peek over. He pulled out the goggles again and scanned one more time, then signaled the others to follow. They all went over with aplomb. Anne watched with amazement as Claire went over like a cat. *Oh hell, there's no lower bar for girls*, she thought. When it was her turn, she climbed awkwardly, her long legs occasionally splaying in different directions. She was grateful, not offended, when she felt Rafe's hands on her backside, pushing her up to the top. She swung her legs over the wall and let herself down as gently as she could. It still hurt. When Father Lamy came over, he whispered in her ear, "I was even worse," and smiled conspiratorially. Anne smiled at him and then looked across a wide lawn dotted with trees and shrubs to an 1890s Norman Revival mansion built of stone and heavy timbers but shaped with a grace that made Anne silently admire the architect. Once Rafe dropped to the ground, they moved out, one at a time, using individual trees and bushes as cover.

Suddenly the night's stillness was rent by a hideous, deafening blast and roar. Anne braced herself, thinking something had exploded, but instead of a burst radiating outward from the house, she had the sensation of the air around her being drawn powerfully towards it. She felt Rafe's hand grab her pack and pull her to the ground. She turned her head and saw him between her and Father Lamy, his left hand on the priest's windbreaker. The strange winds ceased and the air was unnaturally, perfectly calm.

After a long, long moment, Steve signaled the group to rise. Anne was just on her knees when it hit. It felt like a shock wave, but it was black. The world went dark, and she could only glimpse the dim silhouettes of her colleagues being tossed onto their backs as she crashed onto her backpack, her gun flipping on the sling and hitting her in the face. She was vaguely aware of the pain and the blood, but her mind was overwhelmed by a horrific series of impressions, none of which made sense, but all of which felt as if jagged talons were tearing across the fabric of her consciousness. Skull. Hunger. Rot. Flame. Ice. Hate. Acid. Sulfur. Slave. Prey. Blood. Rape.

Death.

Then it swept away. Anne rolled over, pushed herself up on all fours and vomited, shaking. When she managed to get her body under control, she looked around and saw the rest of the Black Chamber team rising, staggered. They all made their way together to the base of a large oak.

Father Lamy pulled his shirt up, exposing the pectoral cross burnt into his chest. He pulled it out, tearing bits of flesh with it. "*Sacre ciboire de tabarnac de Calvaire,*" he swore, then looked around. "Sorry."

Mike pulled some Neosporin and a bandage out of his backpack and began dressing the priest's wounds. He whispered, "Don't worry, Father. Let me capture our common sentiment. *What the fuck was that?!*"

Claire tugged at a pocket on her vest. "Shit," she hissed. "It's fucking melted."

"What is?" asked Joe.

"My amulet. I have a Syro-Egyptian amulet from 200 B.C. with a protective petition to the Lord of Hosts. The pocket melted around it. I'm going to have to scrape all this fucking plastic off it."

"Let me reiterate," said Mike. "What the fuck was that?"

Father Lamy said, "It was evil."

"No kidding, Father," said Joe.

"No. I mean, it was evil-with-a-capital-e. Active, searching Evil. Some sort of major, major demon or something. I've never felt anything *close* to that."

Steve looked from face to face. "So, is everyone still up for going in there?"

No one said anything. Finally, Mike spoke up. "Well, if we don't, there was no point in coming up here."

"He's right," said Rafe. "That was some crazy shit, but who's to say there isn't worse to come."

"Worse than *that*?" said Claire. "All in all, I'd rather be ... anyplace else."

"Okay, well, if no one wants out, everyone please make sure your weapon is loaded, cocked, and ready to fire," said Steve.

Anne looked around and then sheepishly pulled back the cocking lever above the barrel of her gun. She clicked the safety/selector lever from the safe symbol to the four bullets that meant "fully automatic" and carefully set her index finger on the side of gun just above the trigger.

They spread out and slowly made their way across the lawn. They were less than twenty feet from the back door when it burst open, and six men with guns in their hands and long robes over their clothes ran out, screaming. Things started moving in very choppy impressions for Anne. The screaming men started firing wildly, and the Black Chamber returned fire in short bursts, the heavy .45 bullets tearing into the crazed men's flesh. Anne was paralyzed at the sudden, chaotic violence and the horrific gore spurting from holes in the men's bodies, or pieces that simply blew off. Before she knew it, one of the men was right in front of her, screaming, and raising his gun. She fumbled vainly with her gun, but suddenly there was a hole in his chest, and his throat, and the left side of his face was gone.

Something flared in his remaining eye before his body crumpled, and Anne felt something forcing its way into her head, shoving her mind aside. She felt cold intelligence and hot malevolence. *Dear God, help me!* she thought but could not enunciate. She heard her voice say something she didn't understand. Then she was pulled to the ground. Suddenly she felt a cloth wrapped around her shoulders and Father Lamy knelt next to her, his hands on the sides of her face, a purple cloth around his neck. She felt herself fighting him, though she had no volition in it. She felt like a small, powerless spectator trapped in a cage with a pack of lions. In the distance, she heard gunfire. *I wonder what that is*, she thought. Then, suddenly she felt a wave of sensation—and pain—and she was herself again.

Anne rolled over and tried to vomit, but only had the dry heaves. Then the thought of the carnage she'd just witnessed, the sight of that be-robed sack of bloody meat on the ground in front of her, and the memory of that *thing* in her head ... caused her to pass out cold.

She woke up to find Claire holding a cold, wet towel on her forehead and staring intently at her, her brow furrowed with concern. "Hey," Claire said softly, "you're back. You okay?"

"I feel like shit," Anne said weakly, "but I'm okay. What happened?"

"Short version, bunch of crazy guys come out of the house, start shooting. You freeze up, Rafe blows away a guy who's about to kill you, all of a sudden you're screaming crazy stuff, so Rafe tackles you. Then more crazy guys come around the house, we kill them. Joe and Steve get shot—nothing serious, thank God. Turns out crazy guys have shitty aim. Meanwhile, Father Tom is performing a battlefield exorcism on you. You calm down, retch, and pass out. Which brings us to now."

"Exorcism? My God. I can't believe it, but that makes sense. There was something … in me. It took over. It hated me. Hated everything."

"Yeah, we think the reason the guys were crazy and crappy with guns is that they were just recently possessed. Sort of demon puppets."

Father Lamy hove into Anne's view. "Are you all right, Anne?"

"Not great, Father, but Claire tells me I'd be a lot worse without you. Thank you."

"You're welcome. Do you remember anything about what happened?"

"Only vague impressions. I sort of remember watching things as if they were very far away, and all the sounds were muted. I remember the feeling of having something inside my head. It was a little like that blackness, though not anywhere near as strong. It just sort of pushed me aside and I couldn't do anything."

"Do you remember what you told me?"

"No. Did I tell you something?"

"Yes. Just as I was beginning the exorcism, you said, '*O prædicator, Bel-Namtar kašid.*'"

"Well, I know Latin. 'O preacher.' But you lost me after that."

"Right. I'm a Dominican, we're the *Ordo Prædicatorum.*"

"Spooky."

"Not as spooky as saying, '*Bel-Namtar kašid.*' That means 'Lord Namtar is arrived.' In Akkadian. You don't know Akkadian, do you?"

"Hardly."

"I think the demon was taunting me, because it knew I speak Akkadian."

Claire asked very deliberately, "Father, who's Lord Namtar?"

"Namtar is the messenger of the Goddess of the Underworld. He's Death."

Claire's eyes opened wide, "Chidag Dü, demon of the Lord of Death. Lord Namtar, messenger of the Underworld. Abaddon the Destroyer. Apollyon the Destroyer. It's got to be the same thing."

"I don't follow," said Father Lamy.

"I get it," said Anne. "Those are all names for the Blackness."

"*Sacre câlice*," Father Lamy swore. "Sorry."

"Father," Claire asked, "why do you keep swearing with religious terms?"

"I'm Québécois. Old habits die hard. And, really, I don't do it except under circumstances *extreme*. This qualifies."

Mike, Steve, Joe, and Rafe came over. Joe had a fresh bandage on the left side of his neck, and Steve's left pant leg was bloody and torn. A white dressing showed through the gash. "These guys are ready to go now," said Rafe. "You guys set?"

Claire and Father Lamy looked down at Anne. "Sure," she said, reaching up for Claire's hand. She got to her feet, tottered a bit, checked her gun, her clothes, and wiped the blood off her chin. "What's next?"

Steve pointed his UMP at the open back door of the house, past a half-dozen dead men. Anne recognized one of the gunmen from the Times Square Marriott, his abdomen shot to hamburger. The iron stench of blood filled her nose and mouth, and she felt queasy. It didn't abate when Steve spoke.

"We go in."

ༀ༷ༀ

The back door opened on a kitchen. Rafe, Anne, and Father Lamy stayed put while the others cautiously went from room to room on the first floor, exploring the large, spacious house furnished in a somewhat haphazard combination of Arts & Crafts and nineteenth-century Gothic-revival furniture. They were surprised to find it neat and looking lived-in. When the first floor proved empty, they headed up to the second, then third floors, with not a soul to be found. The servants' quarters on the top floor had been occupied, presumably by the men they'd killed outside.

Returning to the kitchen, they reported it was all clear.

"But where's the monsignor?" asked Claire.

"Monsignor?" asked Father Lamy, surprised.

"Necromancer," said Mike.

"*Baptême de la vierge*," swore the priest. "Sorry. I really have to stop that," he muttered, mostly to himself.

"Unless he got out, he's got to be here somewhere," said Steve.

"Basement," said Joe. "We haven't found a basement."

The door was at the end of a small hallway off the walk-in pantry. The Black Chamber investigators shouldered their weapons, Father Lamy drew his, and they followed Steve single-file down the old, wooden stairs along the exposed stone foundation.

The main room of the basement was an open space, with several doors in the brick walls. The room smelled of blood, incense, and smoke. Anne fought the urge to retch. No lights shone except several guttering candles placed around the floor and along the walls. Two bodies could be discerned in the middle of the floor.

Steve signaled for the others to stay back and cover Mike, Joe, and him while they checked the bodies and the side rooms, the tactical flashlights under the barrels of their UMPs cutting through the gloom. Steve approached the bodies, which appeared to be covered in blood, then knelt beside one, his gun still readied. When Joe and Mike gave the all-clear, Steve said, "Someone turn on the lights, please, we've got a survivor."

Claire found a light switch at the bottom of the stairs, and rows of tubes in the ceiling flickered and fluoresced. They all blinked in the harsh brightness, then were wide-eyed at what it revealed.

The basement floor was entirely covered by four concentric circles crossed by several lines at angles to each other, not a pentagram but something similar. The candles sat at the intersections of the lines and circles. Latin, Greek, and Hebrew words appeared between the circles, as well as various symbols that looked like, but were not, zodiacal sigils.

At the nexus of the lines in the innermost circle lay the prone body of a man, drenched in blood. His throat had been cut to the spinal cord, almost decapitating him. Anne almost wished he had been decapitated, so obscene was the sight of his head lolling off his body at that atrocious angle. Behind him lay another man, supine. Rafe and Claire were rushing to his side, pulling first-aid equipment out of their backpacks, Father Lamy in tow. Steve kept his gun warily trained on the man, who hardly seemed in a position to resist.

Anne put the safety on her gun and walked across the nightmare room. When she got to the man's side, Rafe and Claire were a blur of medical activity. Claire looked down at the man's face, which was half-covered in gore, the skin torn from the muscle and bone beneath. It was Monsignor Clairvaux. The remaining handsome features were unmistakably his. His limbs were wrecked, lying at unnatural angles. He wore odd vestments, a Roman collar underneath robes covered in odd symbols made obscure by the copious amounts of blood congealing on them. Two books lay beside him, their covers spattered with crimson. Anne picked them up and carefully slipped the familiar Jesuit breviary and the Voynich Manuscript into her backpack.

Suddenly, Clairvaux stirred, his eyes fixing on something, and one claw-like hand trying to push away those treating him. His voice, almost inaudible and hoarse as if his larynx had been damaged, began repeating a word, as he pointed upwards. Claire leaned over his mouth. "'Priest,'" she said, "he's saying 'priest.'" Everyone looked at Father Lamy, who was, in fact, directly in Monsignor Clairvaux's sight line, his collar peeking out from under his black jacket.

Father Lamy knelt down, and asked the man, "Do you wish to confess, Father?" Clairvaux closed his one good eye in confirmation. "I'm going to have to ask the rest of you to step back, please," said Father Lamy, almost apologetically.

The Black Chamber team huddled in a corner.

"Any chance he's telling Lamy how to destroy the demon?" asked Steve.

"Or how to control it," said Rafe mordantly.

"It's a pain, but you gotta respect the confessional," Mike said, and Joe nodded. The rest looked slightly askance.

"What's he doing now?" asked Steve. The priest had pulled a bottle out of his pocket and was daubing something onto the monsignor's forehead.

"Extreme Unction," said Joe. "Last rites."

Father Lamy waved them back. "Monsignor Clairvaux will talk to you now." His face black with anger, he stalked off to the stairs and sat with his head in his hands.

"What did you do?" demanded Mike.

"Demon," whispered the priest.

"Chidag Dü? Abaddon? Apollyon? Lord Namtar?" Claire said. The priest nodded.

"And your men?"

"Little demons followed."

"Who's this man here?" said Rafe, indicating the corpse on the floor.

"Sacrifice."

"You murdering son of a bitch," said Steve.

The priest seemed to nod sadly, but said, "Volunteer. Had cancer. Greater good."

"Greater good?!" said Mike. "What are you talking about?!"

"Needed power to remake Church. Remake country. Remake world. Better. Just. Perfect. Abaddon is power." The priest started coughing blood. When he stopped, his eye fixed upon Anne. "Sorry," he croaked.

Anne ignored his apology and said, "Look, that thing is out there somewhere. What did you tell it to do?"

"Nothing ... it wouldn't be bound."

They all stood in silence for a moment, thinking of the malevolent force they'd felt and what it might do unconstrained. Choking a last time, the bloodied priest spouted a further gout of scarlet from his mouth, then shuddered and went limp.

"God, if we'd been here sooner, we could have stopped him," said Claire.

"Just bad luck," said Steve.

"Maybe we were too deliberate," said Mike.

"Save it for your Memoranda, guys," said Rafe. "We've got to clean this place up."

An hour later, they'd rendered the basement spotless and stacked all the bodies, save Monsignor Clairvaux's, inside a tool shed, stripped of their occult vestments. Apparently a CIA asset could be called to come dispose of them, as well as all the cartridge cases they raked off the lawns. Steve and Rafe took off Monsignor Clairvaux's robes as well, put hiking boots and a jacket on him, and carried his body off into the woods to drop into a ravine they found on a map. All the occult paraphernalia were packed in trash bags, and Anne added a few necromantic texts she'd found in Clairvaux's study to her now-burdensome backpack.

On the hike back to the airstrip, Anne found herself next to Steve.

"Is this job always so bloody?" she asked.

"No, not always," he said, less than reassuringly.

After a pause, she voiced a question that had been nagging at her. "So this guy wasn't a supervillain after all? He was just a misguided idealist?"

"From here, they don't look much different."

"I keep finding myself thinking of that little boy, Darrell. He loves him. It'll break his heart when he finds out he's dead. And he confessed to Father Lamy, right? So that meant he was sorry?"

"I don't know."

"I'm almost sorry he died," she surprised herself by saying.

"Saved me a bullet," said Steve.

She turned to him, shocked. "You would have shot him?"

"Look, Anne, there's no hoodoo jail. And even if there were, maybe he finds a way to get his buddy the Destroyer to bust him out. It's an impossibility. When someone's messing with stuff like that, they've got to go."

"That can't possibly be legal—much less moral."

"It's not only legal, it's mandatory under our charter. Ask Claire or John or Mike about morality. Me, it's just my job."

"You can't possibly kill people all the time," Anne said, agitated. "You'd be a sociopath."

Steve fixed her with a stare. "I don't kill anyone that I'm not compelled to kill by law or who isn't a threat to myself or others. I don't like killing people, but nor do I keep myself up nights worrying about the poor demon-summoning necromancer who may have unleashed God knows what horror on the world because he really wanted to have his stupid church ordain women or something. We aren't assassins, Anne. But it's a hard truth that some people have to be killed. So I do it, I don't regret it, and I don't lose sleep over it."

"Jesus Christ," said Anne, and fell back a bit in the line of people. Eventually she came abreast of Father Lamy. "Father," she said, "I know you can't talk about what people confess and all, but, I mean, was he sorry about what he did?"

The priest, who'd looked stricken since the basement, stared at his shoes. "He seemed sorry. The thing is, I wonder if that's enough. Even if he's genuinely repentant and God is infinitely merciful, how can God treat a man who not only committed a human sacrifice but brought a powerful diabolical being into the world, then confesses to those enormities—and more—when dying? How many more deaths will be at his feet before this ends? How could his confession be sincere? I granted him absolution, but the magnitude of his sin is crushing. I would not want to be in his place in judgment before God. Nor can I quite bring myself to pray for mercy on his soul. Whatever his intentions—and I suspect I'd not find them worthy in any case—he was consumed by pride and the Devil from whose hands he may never escape." Seeming to snap from a reverie, he looked up at her. "*Ciboire et câlice de tabernac*, I can't be telling you this. There is the seal of confession. Now I'm going to have to go confess to this. *Maudit.*" He shook his head and fell into silence again.

Anne tried to give him a reassuring hug when he left them at the stream that led to the road where his car was parked, but he just said to the group, "God bless you, my children," and wandered off in morbid taciturnity.

When their plane took off into the night, Rafe, Steve, and Joe were asleep before wheels-up. Everyone else sat in silence with their thoughts. When Anne saw the sky pinkening with dawn, she felt her despair lift a little, as the beauty of the sunrise seemed to testify against the world's depravity.

14

Around noon, having been home long enough to catch a couple hours of sleep and shower, Anne went to work, although it was the last thing she wanted to do. She grabbed a coffee, pastry, and sandwich to go at the crowded little Tea Room in Kensington and lunched *en voiture*. Heading underground from the office front, she found herself sharing the elevator with Joe McManus, who'd been signing in when she arrived.

"How are you doing?" she asked.

"Terrible," he smiled. "All I want to do is stay home, pull my kids out of school and take them down to the Smithsonian and out for ridiculous amounts of ice cream. And to convince my wife that this cut here was really nothing serious." He pointed to the bandage on his neck. "She was, um, excited to have me back safe, but she's not dumb. She knows I'm doing something dangerous, and she's not really happy about that. This really is no job for a family man. I keep thinking, that bullet's an inch or two off, and my kids are burying me."

"You going to quit?"

"Ha. We don't quit, Anne. I may take a powder from the front lines for a while, you know?"

"I do. I was thinking about taking a powder altogether."

"Don't do that. You've been the key to this whole thing. Without you, we wouldn't even know that thing is out there …"

He finally saw the sadness and fear in Anne's eyes. "Hey, on a lighter note, did you see the highlights of that Capitals game last night? God, Ovechkin is unbelievable."

They chatted on innocuous topics for a while, until they got to the main office. When they walked through the double doors, only Mike Himmelberg was at his desk.

"Hey, slackers, you must have some awesome Posturepedics to sleep in so late. Or is it the Sleep Number bed?" Mike asked.

Anne just shook her head, while behind her, Joe silently mouthed, "Eat me."

"Sorry, sorry. But you guys have missed some stuff. I mean, unless you were at home monitoring Canadian radio frequencies, news reports, and cell phones."

"They think something happened at the house?" said Joe, concerned.

"No, no, we covered that up just fine. They haven't even found Monsignor Clairvaux's body yet."

"What's happened?" asked Anne.

"Well, it's circumstantial, but I have no trouble figuring out what's going on. First, a village in northern Ontario north by northwest of Nicton is hit by what's described as freak wind shear. Six people dead, seventy injured. Then there's a huge fish kill northwest of there on a three-hundred-plus-mile stretch of the Hudson Bay between East Pen, Manitoba, and Walrus Islands, Nunavut. And just now the NSA picked up that some WWF types in the Central Barrens came across an entire herd of caribou dead, with their flesh ripped off and bones crushed."

"Holy crap," said Joe. "That's our … thing."

"That's my guess. It seems to be getting stronger."

"Any idea how fast it's going?" said Joe.

"Well, it's probably covered over a thousand miles in under a day."

"Where's it going?" asked Anne.

"No idea," said Mike. "Rafe's been working on a plot of all the incidents, starting at Nicton, and has a pretty clear idea of the path. But where it's actually headed, provided it's heading somewhere specific, isn't clear at all. Especially since it's heading towards the Arctic."

"Hyperborea?" joked Anne. "Ultima Thule?"

Joe's eyes looked at a spot on the ceiling to his right. "Somewhere in ... Asia," he said. "Airliners fly trans-polar routes all the time. It's faster. Look, has Rafe gotten into the government's geospatial databases, yet? Satellite imagery?"

"No, I think he's working on Google Earth."

"Okay," said Joe, grabbing a flash drive out of his desk drawer. "I gotta go find him and hook us up. Sorry to run, Anne."

"No problem," she said. She asked Mike, "What am I supposed to do?"

"Go see John. Figure out how to stop this thing."

Damn, Anne thought. *I was hoping you'd say, "Go into the ladies' room and cry for an hour or two." Because that's about all I feel up to doing.*

ᠣᠢ ᠵᠢ

John Ashton sat in his office, his desk covered with piles of books, with only space for his computer and a yellow pad. He looked up and saw Anne in his doorway, miserable.

"Time for homework," he said in an exaggeratedly perky voice, hoping to get a rise out of her.

Anne nodded. "Mike Himmelberg said that we're supposed to figure out how to stop that thing. It's apparently destroying its way across Canada."

"Abaddon the Destroyer. That's what he does. It's on his business cards."

"How can you joke? People are dead!"

"I can't do this job unless I joke. I'm going through the History trying to see if past cases have any clues. Honestly, I don't think we've ever been faced with an entity like this before, so I'm looking for smaller, maybe analogous cases. But I'm not finding much."

"So can I help?"

"No, I've got this. What you've got to do is really get to work on the Library ... by which I mean the Archive as well."

"I haven't been a very good Librarian, have I?"

"You haven't had time. But what you need to do is start scanning the summaries of all the books and artifacts and so forth and see if you can figure out something that can banish a very, very powerful demon, for lack of a better word. Then, if you find something, you get to go down to the Library and open up the brown-paper wrappings and dig through the book or check out the thingamabob or whatever seems useful. You get to peek into some weird stuff. Enjoy it, if you can."

"It actually sounds really fun, if only I weren't panicked about what could happen if I don't find anything."

"Have some soothing tea, or head down to the firing range and put a couple hundred rounds through a machine gun, whatever works for you. Just get your head in the game as fast as you can."

Anne scowled. "What about the Voynich Manuscript? Is it possible that it contains the answer on how to dismiss this thing?"

John laughed. "That would be a great I-told-you-so!"

"I didn't mean it that way."

"No, I know." John kept laughing. "Still, it'd show that the best-intended rules can have some bad effects. I actually thought of that just after I heard what happened. I had Lily take one of the transliterations of the V.M. into arbitrary Roman letters that's on the Internet, swap in the rest of our letters, and see what turns up. When I checked last night, she had filled in the remaining consonants and was working on translating anything that looked like 'dismiss,' 'send away,' 'banish,' 'defeat,' or the like in proximity to that 'Chidag Dü-Abaddon-Apollyon' sequence. So far, she was stumped, but was still working on it."

"Can I e-mail it to Professor Geoffrey? He could read the whole thing inside a day, I expect."

John looked hesitant, then said. "Why not? Who knows how long we have with this thing? Give me his e-mail address and I'll get it to Lily and we'll send him an encrypted copy. Also, tell Claire that when this is all over, I'm going to need her help in setting up a file on him as an official Collaborator."

Anne nodded. "I'll have her send you his e-mail address."

"And then get down to the Library and see what you can do."

�ོ51

Anne walked down the spiral staircase that led to the Librarian's office. She flicked on the lights and saw a tidy, well-organized office lined with books, and a large flat-screen iMac on the desk. Still on the desk were an enameled fountain pen and a pair of cat-eye glasses in a slipcase. *Mrs. Garrett*, she thought, tears welling in her eyes. *I miss you. If you're around, please help me figure something out.* Wiping at her cheeks, she walked over to the shelf where the large, handwritten volumes of the Index to the Library sat. There were a good number of them, she thought, for an institution less than a century old. When she opened the first volume, she saw a complex list of topics with an unusual set of numbers and symbols below them. She scowled, not knowing what to make of them. Then she noticed a little notebook-sized book on the same shelf. Opening it, she saw it contained the key to all the symbols and showed how a given topic could be explored and a list of relevant books and objects could be drawn up with relative ease, though a lot of flipping through the large registers' pages was involved, and it provided no analysis of what the categories actually connoted or might imply. For a system apparently designed to conceal the totality of its holdings, even from its maintainer, it was surprisingly useful. She felt rather unsure of how well she'd be able to update the Indices in the future, but the bold strokes of at least six hands told her that competence lay out there somewhere to be found. She hefted two volumes over to her desk, then pulled the Voynich Manuscript and the Jesuit breviary out of her ninja-suit carry bag, which someone, presumably Steve, had left next to the desk for her. She looked at them, a tad amazed that a couple small books could unleash such a powerful evil. Books had always been her Eden, and she stared at these two like serpents.

Then she got to work.

She had no idea how much time had passed when the phone on the desk—she couldn't quite think of them as *her* phone and *her* desk yet—rang. The display said HISTORIAN.

"Hello?"

"Anne, it's John. Come on up to the conference room. Rafe and Joe have something."

"Okay, I'll be right there."

She checked the clock. Five o'clock. And she still hadn't found anything. *Dammit.*

Up in the conference room, Rafe Stoll and Joe McManus were standing next to the large screen. Anne and Steve McCormack were the last to arrive.

"Okay, everyone," said Rafe. "Here's what we know. We've got a more or less straight-line path between all these awful incidents in Canada. Assuming it started in Nicton, this is what we've got." A number of spots lit up on a map of Canada. Then a line shot from Nicton, slightly to the left of the village dot, over Hudson Bay, then slightly to the right of the caribou-kill dot. "We're assuming it's traveling this path, with the odd slight deviation to kill stuff. Based on the times of these incidents, we're guessing that it's traveling about sixty miles an hour."

"Hey, wait a second, Rafe," Mike Himmelberg interrupted. "Just got something out of the NSA." He was sitting with a set of wireless headphones held up to one ear. "Two things. Okay, first, we got a call from an electrical engineer doing routine maintenance on some of the early-warning radars on Jenny Lind Island. Hey, Jenny Lind, the "Swedish Nightingale"—she got an island. Good for her. Anyway, he reports seeing a dark cloud or fog or shape sweeping rapidly through the air and a whole flock of birds exploding and dropping out of the sky when this cloud hit them."

Rafe scrolled the map north. "The eastern part of Jenny Lind Island is on our line. What else do you have?"

"This one's a little worse. I have a sat-phone call from a guy who seems to be part of an Eskimo hunting party on Victoria Island. He's describing this weird weather front or something coming in, then he just starts screaming, saying, 'We're all dying,' then the phone goes dead."

"Dear God," said Claire.

"Do you have coordinates for the call?"

"They'll be on my computer. Let me go get them." He came back a moment later and read off a string of numbers, which Rafe typed into the computer. "Christ, they're exactly on the line."

"Let me ask a question," said Claire. "So, we know which direction and how fast this thing is going. But do we have any idea *where* it's going?"

"Let me turn that over to Joe," said Rafe.

Manipulating the map to illustrate his words, Joe said, "Okay, the path takes us over the pole, then down into Russia. Fortunately, it's way out in Yakutia, which is one of the most sparsely populated places in the world, then across the Chinese border into Inner Mongolia, and then across the very eastern tip of the country of Mongolia, then back across the Chinese border. Then it crosses these mountains and so forth—that's the Great Wall—until we get to Beijing."

"Peking," Mike Himmelberg interjected.

"Peiping," said Claire.

"Whatever," said Joe. "So I'm guessing that's not an accident."

"No, makes sense," said John. "I mean if you're going to kill a lot of people, why not head for a big city? Although wouldn't New York or Mexico City have been closer? And with lots of delicious cities along the way?"

"Well, I have a theory about that," said Joe.

"It's a doozy," said Rafe.

"Okay, let's see. Here's the refined plot of the line." He zoomed the screen into a view of Beijing with individual buildings visible. "See how it tracks into the city between the Olympic stadium over here to the east, and the Summer Palace to the west?"

"Wait a second, Joe," said Mike. "How confident are you in this super-exact track? I mean, this thing could go right, left, or hang a U-turn at any point, right?"

"More than moderately, based on what data we have and the assumption that this thing is making as much of a beeline as possible for its destination."

"Okay," said Mike.

"So, you'll notice that the line leads right across this big office complex here. This is a northern suburb of Bei—the capital. I'm told it's pronounced Ch'ing-ho or something, but it's spelled Q-i-n-g-h-e on all the maps, so no 'ch'ing ho' jokes, Mike."

"Damn," Mike said.

"Anyway, this office complex is the headquarters of the Second Artillery Corps, and if I were a betting man, I'd say that's where it's headed."

"Why?" asked Steve. "It wants some howitzers? What does artillery have to do with anything?"

"The Second Artillery Corps," Joe said, his voice sinking, "controls China's nuclear arsenal."

The room erupted in oaths, questions, and the sound of Anne crashing into the wall behind her and sliding to the floor when she unconsciously took a quick step back. Anne got back to her feet and everyone else began to calm down.

"Wait," said Mike, his voice loudest. Everyone turned to him. "Why would this thing fly all the way to China when it could have just gone to SAC in Omaha or the Pentagon or the White House? Isn't that going out of its way? And doesn't China have a lot fewer nukes?"

"They do," said Joe evenly, "but they're a lot less loosely controlled. They still have a top-down command structure, in which no one does anything without the order of the guy above him. So they don't have a lot of redundant checks on a launch. My theory is this thing will go in there and take over the people or whatever, and launch everything they've got. It's the Destroyer, right? What's better to destroy with than nukes?"

No one said anything.

"Plus," Joe continued, "as far as anyone knows, China's nukes are targeted three ways. At us, at the Russians, and at the Indians. Maybe Taiwan gets one, and maybe Japan is also on the list. But, if they launch everything in all directions, they get retaliatory strikes from Russia, us, and India—and maybe Japan if they've got secret nukes. If Russia is panicked, who's to say they don't fire a few at us and Europe for good measure? And we, the French, and the British would fire back on them. I'm just guessing, but with India and China being so densely populated, a general free-for-all like this could kill more than a billion people, and wreck civilization as we know it. Leaving the field clear for whatever else Chidag Dü has up his sleeve. Or some of the stuff in Revelation. Or ... worse."

"Okay, thanks, Joe," said Mike. "I'll be changing my pants shortly. But putting aside what could happen, what do we do next?"

"Stop it," said Joe.

"How?" said half the room.

"I don't know," Joe said. "I'm just an engineer."

"Anne?" said John.

"I've got nothing. And nothing from Professor Geoffrey yet."

"Lily?" John asked.

"Nothing. Though my Tibetan's getting better."

"Well, that'll be nice when we're all hiding from the Four Horsemen in the Himalayas," John chuckled.

Steve McCormack spoke up. "Ignoring the hoodoo aspect of this, we're likely going to have to intercept this thing, right? I mean, we can't just sit here and say, 'Mumbo-jumbo,' and it'll disappear half a world away, right?"

"Probably," shrugged John.

"So, let's work on that for a minute. Now, we're dealing with some big, empty spaces, right? So could we risk a landing in Russia or China?"

Mike Himmelberg said, "I don't know about that. We'd have to get some crazy high-level CIA authorizations. Claire?"

"Eesh, I don't think so."

"So that leaves us exactly one option," Steve said. Looking around the room at his colleagues' confusion, he said, "Mongolia. The eastern tip. Was I the only one listening?"

"I think we were all distracted by the fiery nuclear holocaust, Steve," said Claire.

"So when does this thing get to Mongolia?"

Joe stared at the ceiling. "Okay, it's up in the Canadian Arctic now. It left Nicton around midnight, say. At sixty miles an hour. It's about twelve hundred miles out of Canada, and about twenty-three hundred miles to Russia. I'm gonna say it's going to hit Russia in about a day and a half. From Russia to Mongolia is …" He typed a few keys and the relevant arc on the path lit up. "About nineteen hundred miles. That's another, say, thirty-two hours. And it'll be in Mongolia for … a hair under sixty miles. So we have a one-hour window before we're chasing it into China and maybe causing an international incident. Which beats the end of the world, but, still…. If we do miss it in Mongolia, it's four hundred ninety miles to Qinghe. So we'd have about eight hours to get to our cave in the Himalayas," he joked grimly.

"How do you say 'abominable snowman' in Tibetan?" Mike Himmelberg joked.

"*Mekö*," Lily said, dead serious.

"So we've basically got three days to figure out how to stop it, get to a remote location in eastern Mongolia, then take it on," said Steve. "Plus, it's probably twenty or thirty hours in the air to Mongolia. So we've really got less than two days here, then we have to be on a plane." Everyone blanched. Steve smiled a little and said, "How about I go out for some coffee?"

15

A nne read her American Express number into the phone again, thanked the other party, then hung up, thinking, *Well, so much for my savings. Though at this point, saving seems a little dumb.*

She dialed her parents' number in Albuquerque and made some small talk with her mother. Then she got to the point. "Mom, I have a surprise for you and Dad. I've got this great new job and they gave me a big bonus, so I'm sending you on a vacation!... No, seriously. It's this great place called Apache Lodge up in the mountains above Taos. It's in this secluded little valley, totally surrounded by mountains. They've got their own wells, electricity, the whole deal. They have satellite TV, phones, radio, and Internet. And it's five-star all the way. Food, suites, and all sorts of awesome activities.... No, no, I got a special rate..." *Ten grand a day for last-minute reservations.* "No, it's not too much at all. No, it's just because—" her throat closed and tears squeezed from her eyes, as she forced cheerfulness back into her voice, "because you've been such great parents. I couldn't ever have done any of this without you.... No, no. Really, it's not too much. There is one thing, though. My rate applied to an immediate vacancy. You have to get there by tomorrow. But it's two full weeks. I know Dad must have a ton of vacation saved up. Is that going to be a problem?... Oh, good, good. Now, here's the thing, Mom, they have a ton of excursions and the like, but you still probably want to pack the trunk with food and water and stuff, in case you want to picnic or stuff separately. I'm sure the hotel could provide you with stuff, and I think it's all-inclusive, but you never want to end up paying fourteen bucks for an eight-ounce bottle of Evian out of the minibar. Go by Costco and stock up. Oh, and tell Dad that they not only have guided hunting parties up in the mountains, but they've got shooting tournaments as well, so he should pack a lot of his guns and tons of ammo.... No, no, you're totally welcome. Really, it's my absolute pleasure. I just—love you guys so much, I want to do a little thing for you like all the huge things you've done for me over the years.... Don't cry, Mom! You're going to make me cry!... I love you too. Kiss Dad for me and call me when you get there. I'll e-mail you directions."

Anne hung up the phone, wiped her eyes, then dialed again before she broke down. "Hey, Lindsay, it's Anne. You still at H&E? No? Awesome. Have I got a present for you. I won this cruise in a raffle, and I'm so tied up here at the Foundation, I can't get away. But I figured that since you're done at H&E and haven't started down here, you could use it.... You can? Awesome. You'll love it, though you've got to pack fast. There's a flight down to Montevideo, Uruguay, tomorrow, and the ship leaves the next morning for Patagonia and the Antarctic....Penguins! Yeah! This is all through National Geographic and the Smithsonian, so it's a whole bunch of serious adventure-science types and so forth who can hike and hunt and build campfires and birdwatch and all sorts of stuff. Which means to me lots of hot young guys in great shape.... I know! So cool, right? I think you even get to stop in at the Falkland Islands.... Right, maybe some cute British soldiers down there? Oh, I'm so glad you can do it. I'm FedExing you the tickets. Have an awesome, awesome time.... You're so welcome. Just send me some postcards, ok? Love you too, babe."

Anne hung up and cried.

ᴅ᷈᷉

A couple hours later, she was poring over some books she'd pulled from the Library to run down some ambiguous references in the Index when John came down the spiral staircase into her office.

"Hi," she said.

"How you doing?" he asked.

"Been better. Crying a lot. Tried to get my parents and a friend out of harm's way, if that's even possible."

"That's what I wanted to ask you. Do you want to go to Mongolia, or is there someone who needs you here?"

Anne was tempted to take to the mountains with her parents. Even if she died there, at least her last day or so would have been luxurious and in the company of those she loved most. But she took a deep breath and said, "No, I'll go. If I go, someone else can stay."

"Yeah, looks like it'll be you, me, Steve, Rafe, and Claire. Mike and Joe are married with kids, and Wilhelmina and Lily have elderly parents they want to take care of."

"Can they get somewhere safe?"

"Sort of. There are some FBI safe houses in the Blue Ridge Mountains and up in West Virginia and western Maryland that aren't being used at the moment. That's the best we can do by car. They're pretty nice. Furnished, modern appliances, et cetera."

"How about you?" Anne asked.

"I'm single, my parents are dead, my brother lives in Finland, and my sister is on a UN mission to Burma, God help her. There's not much I can do, except give 'em a call and say 'hi,' pretending it might not be 'bye.'"

"It really sucks not being able to tell anyone that you're scared."

John nodded. "This is a scary, lonely job sometimes. Although to be fair, you've walked into a particularly scary situation."

"You guys don't face the end of the world every day?"

"Oh, two or three times a year, tops," John laughed. "No, this is easily the biggest—and almost the craziest—thing I've ever been a part of. And the History doesn't show anything of this magnitude."

"Well, lucky me!" Anne joked.

"No," John said seriously. "Lucky us and lucky world. Without your getting involved, this would be happening, and we'd have no idea. The end of the world just would have popped up, unannounced."

"Be serious with me, is this a suicide mission?"

"No, not in the least. I mean, unless it needs to be. And if that turns out to be the case, you can un-volunteer whenever you like. The problem right now is that we don't know what the mission is going to be."

"Well, I might have something for you on that front. There's a story in this grimoire about a Russian sorcerer who called up something he couldn't put down. He knew it would be heading for the next village after it had wiped out his, so he took a bunch of posts, had them consecrated and engraved with various symbols and planted them in a V pattern." She grabbed a pencil. "Like this:"

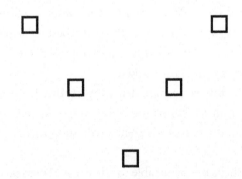

"The monster came down, got funnelled down the V, then his assistants moved the posts at the end of the arms of the V into post holes they'd dug so the posts made a circle. Like this:"

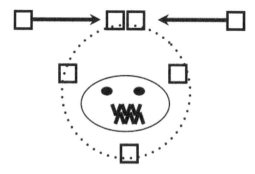

"It trapped the monster within it. Then he basically made a magic circle of some sort all around the perimeter and cast this exorcism-type spell that 'banished it whence it came.' Do you think that'd work?"

"Do you have the banishment spell?"

"No. It's not in the text. I'm thinking I might be able to improvise something along the lines of a magic circle that would be inhospitable to a creature like that. There's a *ton* on magic circles. The trick is figuring out what's real and what's just made up."

"Wow, that'd be great, if you could pull it off. And I really like the trap idea," said John, picking up her phone. "Hey, Joe, take Mike and head to Home Depot. We're going to need some posts. How many?" He looked at Anne.

"Five would do."

"We need five, but get ten just in case.... At least four-by-four. Bigger if they have 'em. And bring some of your wood-shop tools in with you. Anne's got some decorative carving for you to do. And tell Mike we're going to need a priest with some discretion to bless the finished product and not ask questions." John hung up. "Excellent work, Anne. Can I help you look through some books? I've kind of run out of parts of the History to look through, and even the Library of Congress is a little short on practical demonology."

"On one condition," Anne said.

"Sure, what?"

She held up her empty cup. "Bring us down some strong, black coffee."

དར༷ར

By the next morning, they had five eight-by-eight-inch posts, each carved with a different combination of Hebrew, Greek, Slavonic, and occult sigils sitting amidst a pile of wood shavings in the middle of Rafe and Lily's lab. Anne ran her fingers across the smoothly cut letters and signs as she checked them against the old Russian book. "Very nice work, Joe," she told McManus, who was standing nearby looking on proudly.

He said, "Hey, bring 'em back with you and I'll make you a nice pergola for your backyard."

"Thanks. I would, of course, need to buy a house first."

"Good point. How do you like Kensington?"

"Very nice. Quiet. Homey."

"Yeah, we love it too. We're on the other side of Connecticut Avenue."

"What are you going to do when we go?"

"Take my wife and kids up to West Virginia. Mike and I are both set up with safe houses up there. Lily and Wilhelmina are headed down into the Blue Ridge. I'm hoping to make it a fun surprise vacation for the kids, so that no matter what happens, we'll all be together and happy. My wife's going to suspect something bad is up, and I'm going to be a nervous wreck, but we're masters at hiding stuff from our kids. It's a basic parental skill. Do me a favor, though. If it all goes wrong and you're still alive, call me and let me know that it's going down. I want to hug my kids."

"Will do. You'll hear from us either way. God willing."

"I'll be praying for you all. I know Mike and Wilhelmina will, too. And Lily, too, I suspect."

"Thanks. Do you know when our plane is leaving? I've got a bunch of books I've got to pack with various rituals and spells and stuff that might or might not work. I keep feeling like I've got to pick a card out of a deck, and if it's not the eight of diamonds, the world ends."

Joe put his hand on her shoulder reassuringly. "It's ok. Just do your best. I have faith in you."

"Thanks. I do wonder if my best is good enough."

"I think it will be. I think the plane's leaving around noon. You packed?"

"Yeah, Steve said we'd probably camp there briefly before pickup, so I really only need one change of clothes, if all goes well. I'm bringing extra underwear, though, in case we're trapped in the Mongolian wilderness with no way out."

"Always prepared. The Boy Scouts and Coast Guard would be proud."

"Thanks. But I am so not an outdoorsman," Anne said. "I camped a bit as a kid, but you know, at campgrounds. So when does the thing hit Russia?"

Joe looked at his watch. "About two this afternoon, our time. Two in the morning there, I think."

"How much time will we have once we land?" Anne asked.

"If everything goes right, about three hours."

Anne worried her fingers through her hair. "Jesus, that's cutting it close, isn't it?"

"Oh yeah. Unfortunately the Destroyer is setting the schedule, not us."

"Are you guys going to stay here for a while, or just leave when we do?"

"We'll be here for a while, but I think we all want to get going first thing tomorrow, so we're sure to be out of Ground Zero."

"Well, if I don't get the chance to tell you before we go, good luck. I can't imagine having children to worry about at this point."

Joe smiled, pain in his eyes. "Kids are the best, but," his voice caught and he looked fiercely at his shoes, "the thought of them … you know." He cleared his throat and picked up a pen to fidget with. "We'll be ok, Anne. You just go and kick Aba-dabba-doo in the ass for us."

"I'll wear my biggest boots."

Later that morning, Steve called to ask Anne what sort of gun she'd like to carry.

"Does it matter? We can't shoot this thing."

"No, more in case we have to shoot it out with Russian or Chinese border guards."

"Oh. I dunno, that submachine gun was fine."

"Okay. See you soon." Steve hung up.

John tidied his office. Anne packed up a case with books, then sat in a chair, absently drinking coffee. Claire paced like a panther on Benzedrine, ostensibly looking for something but not knowing what. Steve cleaned and packed weapons with intense concentration. Rafe continued his work on an experiment, just walking away as if for a cup of coffee when the call came.

Late that morning, they said their goodbyes. Steve handed Mike and Joe ominous black cases. Anne thought of them sliding them into the backs of minivans next to their children's toys, and tears stung at her eyes. The strain of holding back emotion showed on Wilhelmina's, Joe's, and Mike's faces, and Lily, outwardly calm, picked at her cuticles unconsciously. One bled.

Their goodbyes were mostly restrained. Wilhelmina took Anne's face in her hands and whispered, "You're so *young*. Pray to Our Lord and come back to us safe, little girl." Lily told her, "Good luck. Stay safe." Joe just smiled and hugged her. Mike said, "Get back soon. I need someone to show me the dirty books in the Library. Mildred never would."

16

On the CIA plane—a jet appointed with desks, Internet-connected computers, a large galley, a head with a shower, and a room with six large, curtained bunks, three on each side—Anne stowed her clothes and spread her books out on a desk in the main compartment, settling into a comfortable chair.

"Not bad," she joked, breaking the silence.

"Yeah, the intelligence community has some nice toys," John joked, logging on to a computer.

Steve and Rafe sat down with a deck of cards. "Claire, you in?" Steve asked.

"Can you wait a couple? I'm sorting these shotgun shells. Salt. Silver-alloy slugs. Magnum double-ought buck. Should stop anything short of Chidag Dü."

"You do like your shotguns," joked Rafe.

"You boys can play sharpshooter all you like. I'm blowing anything that gets near me to hamburger."

"She's got a point," said Rafe.

"She does, indeed," said Steve, shuffling the deck.

Anne immersed herself in the grimoires and magical texts she'd brought, comparing and contrasting various rituals for summoning and dismissing demons, for creating protective wards and traps.

"Hey, jackpot!" shouted Claire, waving a fax. "Well, sort of."

"*Qu'est-ce que c'est?*" asked John archly.

"Professor Geoffrey found something in the Voynich Manuscript!" she said. "Listen to this," she added unnecessarily.

�᠊五

My dearest Claire,

You know what they say about being careful about the things for which one wishes. Alas, I fear my wish to read your mystery manuscript is one of those whose fulfillment brings sorrow. It is a very dark, disturbing work, Claire. I cannot recommend your reading it. I will send a complete and unique transliteration and translation as soon as it's complete, and rid myself of the thing with no little relief.

However, you mentioned in your facsimile (burned, of course) that there was some urgency in obtaining information inimical to the entity named in the short excerpt you provided as **Chidag Dü Abaddon-Apollyon**. Immediately upon completing the automatic substitution of the letters I'd already established, I searched for those names. In a section which was written in Mongolian consonant with the fifteenth-century date given in the document, I found the following reference.

Jehoël, erkim ["supreme, chief"] **of the seraphim, restrains Matar** ["monster, sea monster, crocodile," which I take as a calque for the Biblical Leviathan] **who consumes the souls of the damned after the Last Judgment. He** [*Matar*] **is called Abaddon-Apollyon Chidag Dü. Against him only sakighulsunnar** ["the group of angels," perhaps "the heavenly host"?] can stand.

To stop him, Jehoël orders his noyad ["noblemen, princes"] to stretch out their hands to permit his entry.

Raphaël and his *nököd* ["comrades, friends, companions"] Miël and Seraphiël stretch out their hands to Sachiël and his nököd Castiël and Asasiël or to Torquaret and his nököd Tarquam and Guabarel.

Cassiël and his *nököd* Machatan and Uriël reach to Gabriël and his *nököd* Michaël and Samaël or to Anaël and his *nököd* Rachiël and Sachiël.

Sachiël and his *nököd* Castiël and Asasiël reach to Michaël and his *nököd* Dardiël and Hurapatel or to Torquaret and his *nököd* Tarquam and Guabarel.

Samaël and his *nököd* Sataël and Amabiël reach to Anaël and his *nököd* Rachiël and Sachiël or to Cassiël and his *nököd* Machatan and Uriël.

Anaël and his *nököd* Rachiël and Sachiël reach to Sachiël and his *nököd* Castiël and Asasiël or Samaël and his *nököd* Sataël and Amabiël.

Michaël and his *nököd* Dardiël and Hurapatel reach to Gabriël and his *nököd* Michaël and Samaël or Sachiël and his *nököd* Castiël and Asasiël.

Torquaret and his *nököd* Tarquam and Guabarel reach to Cassiël and his *nököd* Machatan and Uriël or Sachiël and his *nököd* Castiël and Asasiël.

Thus joined, they deny Chidag Dü Abaddon-Apollyon repose and life. They will protect the pious chanting "*Boghda boghda boghda.*"

This last chant, I believe, refers to the seraphim's chanting, not that of the pious. *Boghda* means "holy, sacred, divine," and three *boghda*s is very likely Father Boiohæmus's gloss on the *Sanctus* (*Sanctus sanctus sanctus | Dominus Deus Sabbaoth | Pleni sunt cæli et terra gloria Tua | Hosanna in excelsis*), or its predecessor, the Hebrew *Kedusha* (*Kadosh kadosh kadosh Adonai Tz'vaot melo kol ha-aretz kevodo*), the traditional hymn of the seraphim, as described in their single mention in the Bible:

In the year that King Uzziah died I saw also the LORD sitting upon a throne, high and lifted up, and his train filled the temple. Above it stood the seraphim: each one had six wings; with twain he covered his face, and with twain he covered his feet, and with twain he did fly. And one cried unto another, and said, "Holy, holy, holy, is the LORD of hosts: the whole earth is full of his glory." (Isaiah 6:1–3)

Please accept my apologies for the length of time it took me to compose this. My pre-modern Mongolian isn't what it once was, and my Judaic and Christian angelology was nigh non-existent.

I apologize more abjectly for my inability to shed the slightest insight as to what this means. Take care, darling Claire, and I hope and pray— yes, this dire tome moved me to prayer for you, something I have not been able to do since the occasion of Alma's death—that I shall see you again soon, whole, hale, and undefiled.

With profoundest solicitude,

Lewis

"Well, that bothers me to no end," said Claire, biting the corner of her lip. "Not least because the good professor doesn't scare easily. He spent World War II in Burma, killing God knows how many Japanese and being shot six times, though never seriously."

"So what the heck *does* that mean?" asked Rafe.

John said, "Well, I recognize some of the names of angels as standard Christian angels, but some of them seem kind of off the wall. Tarquam? Are they from Jewish lore?"

Rafe and Claire looked at each other and shrugged. Claire said, "If they are, it's awfully obscure."

Anne said, "Can I see that?" Claire handed her the fax. "These sound really familiar. I mean, like I've run across something like this very recently. Of course, these books are just packed full of gobbledygook names of angels and devils. It's the groups of three that jump out at me. Wait!" She grabbed one of the tomes off her desk and flipped quickly through it, scanning the pages through a squint of concentration. "Aha!" she shouted, stabbing at a page with a finger. "Okay, this is from *De magia mathematica*, or *On Mathematical Magic*, by Giordano Bruno, a serious heavy hitter in the field. *Nomina angelorium dierum et primo die Solis.* 'Names of the angels of the days and the first day, Sunday.' More or less. Okay, I'll spare you the Latin. 'The foremost three angels of Sunday are Michael, Dardiel, Huratapel (says Peter de Abano in his *Elementa magica—Elements of Magic*, page blah blah blah). The names of the angels of Monday. The three are foremost Gabriel, Michael, Samael. The names of the angels of Tuesday. The three foremost are Samael, et cetera.' That's his *et cetera*, not mine."

"Those match up," said Claire, having picked up the fax.

"Now, he only names the main angel of every other day, but they match up. Hold on." Anne dug in her satchel of books. "Ha! I thought I packed this. *Heptameron, seu Elementa magica!*" She flipped through the pages. "Yep. Look here. They all match up. Except that Torquaret joker and his homies Tarquam and Guabarel. Not on the list."

"So they match up to *days?*" asked Steve.

"Yeah, how do days reach out to each other?" asked Rafe. "I mean, space-time is curved, but ..."

"Hey, here they are!" said Anne. *"Angeli autumni*: Tarquam. Gualbarel. *Caput signi autumni*: Torquaret. So Tarquam and Guabarel—he misspells it—are the angels of autumn, and the head of the sign of autumn is Torquaret."

Rafe drawled, "So that means ..."

"Beats the hell out of me," said Anne.

"Yeah, days of the week and a season don't really help us out, do they?" frowned Claire.

"Wait a second," said John. "Anne, you've read a ton of these books. Don't they attribute multiple associations with various angels?"

"Oh sure." She opened another book. "This is the *Key of Solomon.* You've got hours of the day, days of the week, archangels associated with angels, planets, metals, and colors, and that's just one book."

"Metals?" said Rafe. "Maybe it's a metallurgical code of some sort."

"Could be," said Anne. "Alchemists were notorious for using all sorts of metaphors like that."

"Okay, let's take one," said Rafe. "Okay, we've got my namesake Raphael—woo—reaching out to Sachiel. What 'days' are those?"

Anne looked down at the *Heptameron.* "Wednesday and Thursday."

"And what metals are those?" Rafe followed up.

"Hmm. If he's using the *Key of Solomon*, it's tin and mercury," said Anne. "What does that make?"

"Uh, you can make a mirror out of that. Or dental amalgam. Or an amalgam for a fluorescent lightbulb," said Rafe.

"So, maybe we need to shine a fluorescent light on it? Or a mirror or something?"

"I'd think a mirror is more fifteenth-century technology," said Claire.

"What's the next one?" asked Rafe. "Cassiel and Gabriel."

"Um ... Saturday and Monday ... lead and silver," said Anne.

"Well, you could make solder," said Rafe.

"Next?" said John.

"Sachiel and Michael ... Thursday and Sunday ... tin and gold."

"Geez, either a hard solder, or a covering for electronic components. Electroplate?" said Rafe.

"Okay, folks, I'm out of my depth," said Steve, standing up. "I'm going to go start dinner." He walked back towards the galley.

"Samael and Anael," continued Anne. "Tuesday and ... Friday. Iron and copper."

"Steel or cast iron," said Rafe. "But I'm seriously baffled as to where this is all going."

"Hold on," said Claire. "You don't have any correspondence for Torquaret, do you?"

"No," said Anne.

"So if this is a chemical formula, we've got some mystery ingredient here that we don't have the key to."

"Shit, good point," said Rafe. "Autumn. Hmm. Dried leaves? Pumpkin spice?"

"Let's try something else," said John. "We can come back to metals."

"I'm pretty sure, though, that if it comes down to it, I can scavenge all those metals from somewhere or other on this plane," said Rafe.

"Good to know," said Claire. "Okay, what else do we have?"

"Um, colors, planets, and archangels, at least in this book."

"Well, they could be intermediate points of a color wheel or spectrum," said Rafe. "One color 'reaches' to the other."

"Let me look at the colors," said Claire, bending over the books.

"I'll put the planets on the monitor there," said Rafe. "I have a cool program."

Anne and Claire discussed the various colors and their combinations, asking John and Rafe if they had any associations with them, but nothing coherent came of it. Anne looked up at the monitor, where Rafe had put up a picture that showed a circle with planets and stars surrounded by land.

"What's that?" said Anne.

"Oh, this is what you'd see standing in my backyard and looking straight up. I mean, if there were no atmosphere. I turned that off. I can move the view around all different ways." Rafe pressed some keys and it resolved into a more traditional perspective.

"No, no, go back to the first one," said Anne. "The circle."

"Okay. Here you go."

"Can you draw some lines on there?" Connect planets?"

"Sure," he said. "Like this?"

"No, extend them all the way to the edges of the circle."

"Like this?"

"Exactly." She pulled out an ancient-looking volume and opened it to a page full of inscribed circles crisscrossed by lines at odd angles. "Does that look like a magic circle?"

"It looks *exactly* like a magic circle," said John. "And that's what you use to protect yourself from a demon you summon, right?"

"So they're planets," said Claire. "But how do we figure out which ones, and when?"

Anne had anticipated the question. "I think we figure out where the planets are at the time and place we need the circle."

Rafe said, "Oh, ok, so …" he pulled a GPS out of his pocket, "47° 9′ 47.05″ north latitude, 118° 57′ 15.76″ east longitude," he typed the coordinates into the program. "At, say, nine a.m. local time on the day in question," he typed more. "Bam."

"Neat," said John.

"Dude, that would have taken like three days with pencil and paper."

"*Very* neat," replied John.

"Okay, what do we have here?" said Claire. "We've got Mars over here near the horizon in the—what is this, north … east? This is disorienting."

"East northeast," said Rafe.

"Okay, the sun and Venus are high in the southeast quadrant right on top of each other," continued Claire.

"Venus is actually beyond the sun and a little south and west," said Rafe.

"And Mercury's there just to the north and west of them," pointed John.

"Okay, the moon's really high in the southeast quadrant, closer to the south line," noted Anne.

"Uranus and Neptune are here in the southwest," said Claire.

"Yeah, but they won't be in Anne's book," said John.

"Yep, weren't discovered until the 1700s and 1800s respectively," said Rafe. "And Saturn and Jupiter are below the horizon, so I'm guessing we get to ignore them. I'll bet that's why there are two different options for each one, in case the primary one isn't visible."

"Okay, so Michael, et al., Mercury, is connected to … Sachiel or Torquaret. Jupiter or … autumn," said Anne.

"Not helpful," said John. "Let's get back to that."

"Okay, Cassiel and Sachiel … Saturn and Jupiter," read Anne.

"Skip," said Claire.

"Okay, Samael reaches out to Anael, Mars to Venus," said Anne.

"Hey, we have a winner!" said Rafe, then plotted a purple line through the two points across the circle.

"Michael to Gabriel, Sun to Moon," said Anne.

"Done and done," said Rafe, connecting them with a green line.

"Okay, and we can rule out that last one," said John. "Torky is reaching out to Saturn or Jupiter."

"Wow, you did that in your head?" said Anne.

"What? I'm paying attention," said John.

"So...Torky," said Claire ruminatively. "Autumn."

"I got it," said Rafe. "Fomalhaut."

"You sure you're not remembering that thing out in L.A.?" asked John.

"What thing?" said Anne.

"My first big gig," said Rafe. "There's a big star out in Hollywood who famously belongs to a cult."

"I think I know who you mean," said Anne.

"Almost certainly. Over two years, sixteen people who'd crossed him in some way or another were burned to death, either their houses burning down around them, or almost spontaneously combusting, with nothing around them touched. Of course, he was the obvious suspect, but he had airtight alibis in every case, being miles away, on TV, at a party with dozens of witnesses, et cetera. So the thought was maybe the cult was doing it for him. But there was never a single scrap of evidence, no forced entry, no fingerprints, no footprints, no trace evidence, and—this is what made the arson guys crazy—no accelerants, ignitors, or any evidence of arson. The one pattern I found out was that the burnings started the night Fomalhaut entered the night sky and stopped when it left. But that was it. It still haunts me. Whoever or whatever was doing that could start again anytime."

John said, "So you see why I tend to think Rafe has Fomalhaut on the brain."

"Ha," said Rafe. "Not in this case. I just happen to know *much* more about Fomalhaut than most people. Like that its name comes from *fam al-janûbî*, 'mouth of the southern whale.' And another thing I know is that it's the only first-magnitude star in the fall sky of mid-northern latitudes. Hence its nickname: the 'Lonely Star of Autumn.'"

Claire applauded, and John and Anne joined in.

"So where's Fomalhaut?" said John. "I don't see it."

"It's … um … uh … aha!" said Rafe. "See this star just south of the southwest line right above the horizon?" Everyone nodded. Rafe pressed a button and the green-grass graphic disappeared around the edges. The label FOMALHAUT revealed itself next to the star.

"Ho-o!" John shouted. "Woo! Yeah!" said Anne and Claire.

Rafe plotted a red line through Mercury and Fomalhaut.

"Can you flip that around so the compass points are normal?" said Anne. "It'd be much easier to use as a guide if so."

"Your wish, madame …" said Rafe, and seconds later a color copy came out of a printer.

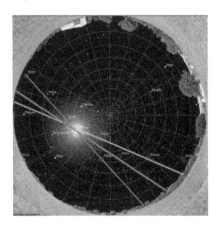

"All right," said Anne. "I think we got it. Let me just hit the books a little bit to figure out what to draw around the lines." She had covered two pages of a legal pad with notes and sketches when she was overwhelmed by the smell of food. She looked up.

"Oh my God, that smells good. What is it?"

Claire looked up from a surveyor's map of eastern Mongolia. "Steve stocked the galley from a bunch of awesome restaurants. I think it's steak for dinner tonight."

Well, if we're going out, we're going out in style, Anne thought, smiling. "Sounds wonderful. I'm famished."

The food was outstanding, and their conversation was animated, inconsequential, and funny, as they all were happy to shrug off the oppressive foreboding with the aid of several bottles of a rich Zinfandel.

Around eleven Eastern Time that night (they hadn't reset any clocks), as they were still sitting at the table chatting, a phone rang. Silence fell; it was a death knell.

John stood up and answered the plane's phone.

"Hello?… Oh, man. Let me put you on speaker." He hit a button.

"Mike, you there?"

"Yep," came Mike's voice.

"Why don't you repeat what you just said."

"Okay, we think the Destroyer made landfall about eight hours ago. Joe says it's right on track, geographically. It's in the Sakha Republic—also called Yakutia. About an hour ago there was a burst of panicked radio and phone activity from Ese-Khayya, a town of about three hundred people about four hundred miles inland from the Arctic Ocean. Then nothing at all.

"Two more towns got hit, but not wiped out. Let me try and pronounce these things. Boronuk and Verkhoyansk. The latter, incidentally, is the coldest inhabited locale on the planet. In case that comes up on *Jeopardy!*. The only phone calls we've had intercepted and translated through NSA basically claim some sort of horrible weather system swept into town and destroyed most of it, killing almost everyone."

"Don't play the audio, Mike," said Claire, yanking on her ring.

"No, no. I heard it, and even in Russian or Yakut or whatever the heck it was … not good. Fortunately, there isn't a lot else out there in terms of people. At least until the thing gets near Yakutsk in about seven hours, which is a bit east of the tracking path but has a population of about two hundred forty thousand."

"After that, just towns called Aldan and Amazar, still in Russia. Then Beijicun in China, Makho in China, Ignashino in Russia again, then Derbur in Inner Mongolia—that's China. Then some villages called Gen He, Erui Zuoqi, Yetulihe, and Tulihe. Then towns called Shangkuli and Hailar and Monggon Qulu and Yimin. Then it crosses into Mongolia, where you get to say hi."

"Jesus," said Steve, shaking his head.

"Joe's sending the more precise estimate of its path on the computer. He's got a zippy little graphic that shows about where it is along the line."

"What's the timeline look like?" asked Rafe.

"You'll be landing around 18:00 Eastern tomorrow, which is six a.m. the next day local time. It should cross the Mongolian border around nine a.m."

"So we'll have about three and a half hours on the ground before showtime," said John.

"Yes," said Mike. "And if, God forbid, it gets by you, it'll be in Qinghe eight hours later."

"Okay, thanks, Mike," said John. "Take care of your family, ok?"

"Will do. Go get it."

The click from the phone's disconnecting was the only sound in the plane for some time.

John turned to Anne. "So, Anne, do we have a plan?"

"Getting there, yes. Your guess is as good as mine if it'll work." She downed the rest of her glass of wine.

"We've got faith in you. Hey, Steve, you have any dessert back there?"

"Oh yeah. Hazelnut-infused crème brûlée."

"Awesome," said John, standing. "Come on. You get that, I'm going to break out some port and brew some coffee."

"I don't know ..." said Claire.

"Hey," smiled Rafe, "eat, drink, and be merry."

"For tomorrow ..." Claire left the thought hanging.

John said, "C'mon, Claire. It's horrible. But if we can stop it, it'll have killed fewer people than your average African civil war."

"African civil wars bum me out, too, John."

"Yeah, but Latin American border wars make you want to salsa!" said Rafe, cracking Claire up.

"Fine, fine," Claire said. "Bring on the port, coffee, and crème brûlée. I'll choke it down."

"Back to our last topic," said Rafe. "Worse movie sidekick: Short Round or Incredibly Gay Robin in *Batman & Robin*?"

17

Anne slept poorly. She couldn't decide whether it was the rich food, the wine, or the impending apocalypse. She showered, dressed for the outdoors, and got back to work on her books. Steve brought her a tray with coffee, a sweet roll, quiche, a cinnamon scone, and some deliciously salty Smithfield ham.

"Steve, if we do keep the world from ending, I'm going to have to go on a serious diet. Thank you," she smiled.

"Hey, nothing but the best. Gotta keep the protein and caffeine coming. The carbs are just a bonus."

"A delicious one. Cheers." She raised her coffee cup to him.

The day passed quickly, Anne thought. Mike Himmelberg called in from his safe house with another damage report. Yakutsk had been hit. There were hundreds, maybe thousands dead. The Destroyer continued relentlessly along its path.

Anne studied while everyone else alternately played cards or morosely watched the blip estimating the Destroyer's position. They ate another good lunch and an early dinner, and stared out the window as the landing gear touched down on a Mongolian grassland, and the plane rumbled to a bumpy stop. Everyone checked his or her watch. Six twenty-two—p.m. on the east coast of North America, a.m. there in the land of Mongols, Manchus, and Khans.

"Ready?" asked Steve, rhetorically. They all thanked the pilots and climbed off the plane quickly, taking all their gear with them. When they were done, the pilots took off for Ulan Bator, where their flight plan had them landing in a few hours. They'd refuel and return at noon local time. No one was quite clear what the contingency plan for failure was, if anyone survived. Chase the monster in the plane to China, risking being shot down by the J-11s of the 7th Fighter Division out of Zhangjiakou Air Force Base? Or high-tail it for the Southern Hemisphere, hoping to survive the potential nuclear exchanges? Or figure that's too far to go in the amount of time left, and risk being shot down on an unauthorized flight to Tibet or somewhere else in the Himalayas unlikely to be devastated? Steve reported there were two mountain-infantry brigades in Tibet, but nothing of likely strategic importance to the Russians, Indians, or U.S., with Chengdu being the most likely nearby military target. The Black Chamber agents had talked vaguely and indecisively among themselves about the options, but they'd never brought them up to the pilots, who still believed this was a simple, discreet CIA/NSA operation.

Anne set her satchel of books on the ground next to the pile of Home Depot lumber with which they hoped to stave off the eschaton. Steve handed over her UMP and a Velcro belt with extra magazines. She slung the gun over her shoulders and secured the belt, then picked up the yellow legal pad she'd covered during the flight. Anne turned around to see what the others were doing and was a little unnerved to find they were all looking at her. Steve and John had slung futuristic-looking Belgian assault rifles on their backs, Rafe cradled his equally science-fictiony Tavor rifle, and Claire held an evil-looking SPAS-12 combat shotgun, yet for all their lethal implements, they looked vulnerable and small under the enormous Mongolian sky.

John smiled. "What's the plan, Anne?"

Anne took a deep breath. "Okay, first step is to take GPS readings and find out where we think the thing is coming through, as exactly as possible."

"I'm on it," said Rafe, pulling out a pocket GPS system that looked very classified to Anne's untutored eyes. He began walking off to the east.

"Second thing is to schlep these posts, tools, bags of flour, and jugs of distilled water over to wherever he calculates."

"Got it," said John and Steve, grabbing the heavy fifty-pound bags of flour.

Claire and Anne grabbed the ends of some eight-foot posts and carried them along. Eventually all the gear made it to the point where Rafe had stuck a long stick in the ground.

"Okay, part the third. We dig a post hole here for—let me check." Anne flipped through her notes then examined the sigils on the posts until she found the one she wanted. "*This* post. It has to be mounted so that the Aleph is facing north directly in the thing's path. Then, let's see, *these* two need to be mounted say, fifty yards away to the northeast and northwest so that they form a right angle. Then these two, here, have to continue the V arms northeast and northwest out to a hundred yards. So they'll be …" she flipped through her notes, "a hundred and forty-one point five-five yards apart." Seeing their gapes, she smiled a little. "Approximately. It doesn't have to be bang-on exact. I mean, if you can do sixty *sazhen*, two *arshin*, that'd be great, but I think our Russian wizard will forgive us if we're a couple inches off here or there.

"Okay, on the middle posts, the Greek letters need to be facing each other across the V. There's a theta and a chi. And on the last ones, the Slavonic letters face south. That's these squiggly things," she said, pointing to a Ⱑ on one post and a Ȝ on another. "Okay, I think we want the theta post facing east, and the chi facing west. And the backwards three with a tail goes on the northeast point of the V and the octopus with a walking stick goes on the northwest point."

"So everybody grab a shovel," said Steve.

"You got it. Except me. Consistent with our lifestyle of international intrigue, I'm going to be spreading damp flour on the ground."

An hour later, they had the stakes in the ground at the right points, and two hours later Anne had finished drawing a giant circle of moist flour which intersected the V at its vertex and the two posts fifty yards out, then added concentric circles a foot inside and a foot outside them. Carefully comparing her work to the printout of the star chart, as exactly as she could, she laid three lines across the circles corresponding to the lines on the chart connecting the planets invisible behind the sky above them. Last, she crafted letters and words in several alphabets in the odd wedges formed between the circles by the angled lines.

"Okay, now we need a double post hole *here,* said Anne, at the northernmost point of the middle circle, the one intersecting the other posts. Steve obligingly got out his spade, dug the hole, and tested it with the two posts from the ends of the V, then replaced them in their original position, while Anne walked around the circle to the vertex of the V and kicked a foot of flour off of the outermost circle directly behind the post.

Everyone dragged their shovels back to the vertex and sat on the ground.

Anne looked at them and said, half joking, half despairing, "Look, folks, let me apologize in advance if this gets us all killed and ends the world. It's the best I could do." Everyone nodded in silent sympathy. "Here's the plan. We need to bait Abaddon, and the only bait around here is us. So what we do is stand inside these posts. Doesn't matter who stands where, though we probably need the two strongest guys at the farthest points of the V." Steve and Rafe volunteered. "Okay, that'll put Claire and John at the middle posts, and me at the vertex," Anne continued. "Stay there as long as you can, then at the very last minute, duck behind the pole. John and Claire, watch your feet. Do *not* kick any of the flour around. I can't stress that enough."

"Noted," said John.

"I am tattooing 'do not kick flour' on my wrist as we speak," deadpanned Claire.

"Excellent. Now once Abaddon hits the Aleph, it's supposed to stop him. I'll shout when he's there. At that point, and not before, Steve and Rafe, pull up your posts and run as fast as you can to the double post hole at the top of the circle, and plant the posts. I have no idea what you'll have to face in trying to do this, but it's absolutely critical that you do so. Otherwise, it can get back out the way it came. As long as you're closing the gap and then sealing it with the posts, it's not supposed to be able to get out. In theory. And again, let me emphasize that when you get near the top-of-the-circle post hole, do *not* kick the flour."

"Hey, I have an idea," said Claire. "How about we each take some flour with us to our posts—ha, literal as well as figurative—and then if we do mess up the circle, we can fix it? I mean, we'll have to try and memorize our area in advance, of course, but it's a fallback, right?"

Oh thank God they're buying this, Anne thought, starting to get a little excited about the prospect of actually trying this lunatic science project from Hell. "Excellent idea. Anyone have buckets?" asked Anne.

"Shovels will do just fine," said Steve.

"Okay, everyone take a shovelful of flour," said Anne. "Thanks, Claire. Okay, and then the grand finale is my connecting the circle at the bottom. The posts should trap him in the circle, and once the circle's complete, Abaddon shouldn't be able to exist within it. I have no idea what will happen, but the guy who did this near Nizhny Novgorod in 1408 said that 'the wood shall be a bower,' by which I'm guessing he means 'hide behind the posts.' And that's all I've got."

"Okay, thanks Anne," said John. "Let's just go over it a couple times to make sure everyone's got it cold." They reviewed the plan pro forma, but with their adrenaline-fueled focus, no one needed the repetition.

"How much time do we have?" John asked, merely curious, but sounding like a terminal patient.

Rafe said, "Twenty minutes, more or less."

"Well, let's go to battle stations," said Steve, "in case the son of a bitch is early. Turn on your throat mikes and earpieces so we can all hear each other."

They looked around at each other, and nodded in silent valediction. They embraced each other solemnly in turn, knowing it might be the last human touch they'd feel. When it was his turn, Rafe looked longingly into Claire's eyes, pain and regret comingled. Claire put her hand on his cheek and met his gaze with understanding. He embraced her fiercely. When John approached Claire a few moments later, she began, "John—" with brow furrowed, as if to explain or apologize for something. He just shook his head and waved his hand in open-handed acceptance. She nodded in tacit agreement and relief, and they embraced.

Goodbyes technically unsaid, they walked silently out to the posts, tiny vertical sprigs on the vast, empty horizontal of the grassland. They gingerly stepped over the lines of flour and positioned themselves inside the posts, minnows baiting a shark.

Five minutes later, Steve, at the northwesterly end of the V, said, "Does anybody hear that thumping noise?" Everyone checked in 'no,' agitation in their voices.

"I hear it," said John a minute later. Then Anne heard it. "Me too," she radioed.

"It's not coming from the north," Steve said. "I think it's from the west."

They all turned away from the horizon they'd been glued to and saw a strange, inhuman figure coming across the plain towards them. They had to squint behind their sunglasses, as the figure seemed to radiate light. Its outline was approximately man-sized, but much more hulking, and long, brachiating horns sprung from its head.

"What the fuck is *that?*" John asked, and Anne heard him cock his rifle.

"Easy," said Steve authoritatively. "Fingers off triggers, everybody. Let's not overreact. Anne, looks like he's heading towards you."

"Um, ok." Anne shouldered her gun as the figure and the rhythmic thumping got closer and louder.

The figure seemed to glide across the plain towards her.

"Does anyone else think that looks like Obi-Wan coming to scare the Sand People away from Luke's landspeeder?" asked Rafe.

"*Quiet!*" said Claire. "But, yes."

"Hello?" Anne shouted.

Anne saw an arm raised in salutation. *Well, that's good.* She heard the jingling and clanking of metal. *Huh?*

When the figure got close enough that Anne could make out details around the light it was emitting, she realized it was a man in a strange costume.

"It's a guy," she radioed. "I'm not sure what he's wearing, but I don't see any weapons. He's got a big walking stick."

She watched as the man got closer, fascinated by his outlandish garb. He was wearing a kaftan covered with little metal plates and jingle bells, a tiger-stripe apron of alternating orange-and-black cotton strips, a wide leather belt with nine mirrors attached to it, and one large circular mirror over his chest like a pectoral cross. The mirrors had been reflecting the morning sun back towards them. His hulking shape came from a large, heavy deerskin cape. His horns were a magnificent set of antlers on a helmet. Under the helmet, his head was wrapped in a cloth of red silk. In his right hand was a long staff, with horse and wolf tails atop it. In his left was an unusual curved drumstick, one end a horse's head, the other a hoof. He was beating a constant rhythm on a round drum on his belt; iron rings jangled from the drum.

"Anne?" came John's concerned voice.

"Ah, stand down? I think?" said Anne. "It's a guy in a weird costume."

She lowered her gun as the man got closer. When he was about ten feet away, he looked at her with kind, intelligent eyes out of an ageless, weathered Mongol countenance and nodded. He looked over the arrangement of posts and flour and smiled. He said something in Mongolian, pointed to Anne, pointed to himself, and then pointed to the northern horizon.

"You're here because of the monster?" Anne asked, knowing the question was futile as soon as it was out of her mouth. The Mongol just smiled.

"Ah, guys," Anne said, incredulously into her mike, "he seems to be some sort of Mongol shaman or something. I think he's here to help."

"Awesome!" said Rafe.

"Oh, that's great!" said Claire.

"Hey, we'll take all the reinforcements we can get," said Steve.

John finally stopped laughing and said, "Tell him the *koumiss* is on us afterwards."

Anne went back to her position. The Mongol's drumming continued. After a while he began chanting softly to the sky, then making what sounded to Anne like birdcalls.

After what seemed like a long, long time, Steve's voice came over the radio. "He's late."

Rafe said, "Fucking apocalypse demons can't keep to a schedule. Buy a damn watch, Golgoroth. I got a bus to catch."

Another age passed underneath the Eternal Blue Heaven, which the shaman doubtlessly invoked. Then Claire's voice came over the radio. "There. See it?"

Anne couldn't at first, but then, "Yes," she said, "dark cloud, due north?"

"You girls have better eyesight," said John.

"Better everything," said Claire.

"Ah shit, I see it," said Rafe.

"Roger that," said Steve.

"Hey, now even I can see it," said John.

The Mongol raised his voice in a series of cries.

"Come on, you son of a bitch," muttered Steve. "Get over here."

"HEY!" screamed Rafe off the radio, but loud enough Anne could hear him just fine a hundred yards behind him. "ABADDON! APOLLYON! HÜSKER DÜ! OVER HERE, YOU BASTARD!"

Suddenly, like a football team before a big game, all the Black Chamber agents were all yelling and screaming at the top of their lungs, taunting the specter of death, jumping up and down. Anne realized she was close to jumping on some flour, and dialed back her catharsis.

It took the cloud a half an hour to close, which seemed as long as the rest of their lives. It was huge and black and coming right for them. It howled deafeningly. It swept into the V, and Anne saw Rafe and Steve spin outside the posts, and John and Claire slip behind theirs, watching their feet. She saw John drop to his knees to grab some flour out of his shovel and frantically pack it on the ground.

Anne waited a fraction of a second and spun around her pole. The front of the cloud hit her post like a freight train. The post didn't move, but a shock wave knocked Anne off her feet. As she fell, she peered through the blackness to see if Rafe and Steve were moving the posts closed. She couldn't see a thing.

"Rafe! Steve!" she screamed into her microphone. "Run! Run! Run!"

As she feared, the blackness began to recede like a tide, the evil attempting to find a clear path.

Suddenly she heard the howling of a wolf next to her, and turned to see the Mongol shaman letting out the spine-tingling cry of a lone wolf, then of a pack of wolves. His drumming was so loud and fast Anne could barely hear the rhythm. He planted his staff in the ground in front of him, then drew from a pocket what looked like the scapula of some large animal carved and painted with symbols. He screamed a horrible cry and threw it into the blackness. Flames erupted where it hit. The blackness surged again towards Anne and the shaman, coming through the gaps in the posts, like a prisoner lunging out between jail bars. Anne shrank down behind her post, where the air was oddly still. She saw blackness to either side of her, but nothing but blue sky above and behind her, a wedge-shaped anti-shadow of sun and light stretching out from the post.

"THEY'RE IN! ANNE! NOW!" shouted Rafe and Steve semi-coherently over the radio.

Anne grabbed her flour and, hands shaking, carefully connected the last arc of the magic circle she'd derived from examples in the *Key of Solomon*, Bruno's *Triginta Sigilli*, Kircher's *Œdipus Ægypticus*, the *Testament of Carnamagos*, and the *Grimoire of Pope Honorius*. She screamed as much in surprise as pain when the wet flour of the completed circle burst into searing blue flames inches under her fingers, burning her wrists and scorching her face. She fell back, and through her tearing eyes watched in amazement as the blue flame spread across the whole of the circle.

A sound like a million cows being slaughtered and a train being shredded and a bomb going off and Hell's purest, thundering rage blasted out of the circle. Anne saw the blackness twitching and thrashing, huge strange distorted shapes appearing in the cloud, wings, an eye, a huge, fanged mouth, more eyes, and shapes geometers couldn't describe. Pure hate flowed from the circle. Anne could almost taste it in her little lee. She looked over at the shaman, who chanted and drummed on, seemingly entirely unaffected, as if in a bubble of his own.

Then the blackness became flame. A pillar of blue fire shot up into the sky from the circle, poisonous-smelling black smoke billowing in the wind.

Then silence.

Anne slowly got up off her backside and looked around. The air was vile with black smoke. The entire circle was a solid black, charred waste, the posts eerily unscathed. The shaman stopped drumming.

Then she heard the screaming. The happy, cheering screams of the other Black Chamber operatives running across the steppe towards her, ecstasy on their faces. They gang-tackled her like she was two yards from their end zone and bawled crazed congratulations. Anne closed her eyes with relief, felt any number of people kiss her cheeks, eyes, and lips, and let herself collapse.

When they'd regained their senses, they got up off the ground and dusted themselves off, as the thick, oily, foul black smoke dissipated in the gorgeous azure of the Mongol sky.

John pulled out a satellite phone, and he, Steve, Rafe, and Claire took turns shouting the good news down the line to Mike, Joe, Lily, and Wilhelmina.

Anne, feeling a little like an outsider, just looked around at the landscape, thinking it was the most beautiful sight she'd ever seen. She noticed the Mongol shaman putting away his drum and taking off his helmet, stashing them in a large sack that he slung over his shoulder like an Altaic Santa Claus. He smiled broadly, a beautiful, joyous, gap-toothed smile that warmed Anne's soul, then raised his hand in valediction, calling, "*Sain suuj baigaaray!*" in a high, tight voice. Anne waved back. He turned and began walking off into the west.

"Everyone in one piece?" asked Claire.

"I burned my wrists and singed my eyebrows and lashes," said Anne, raising up her raw, red wrists for inspection.

"When one of those shock waves hit, I fell hard on my shoulder," said John. "I think it popped out and back in the joint. I need about a pound of Advil."

"Yeah, I got knocked on my ass," said Claire. "My leg got twisted under me, but yoga saves the day once again. I'm just sore."

"Guess we took the worst of it," said Steve to Rafe.

"Oh no, are you guys okay?" asked Anne.

"Well, your Russian wizard failed to mention that you don't want to have your fingertips on the *inside* of the poles when the thing is trying to get out," said Steve. He lifted his hands and showed that his gloves were completely destroyed above the second knuckle of his finger. His fingers were bloody and little bits of metal embedded in his flesh sparkled in the bright sun.

"Oh shit," said Claire. "Are you okay?"

"Yeah, I was wearing gloves with steel mesh in 'em. I think I've just got to pick the bits out and dunk my hands in iodine or something. Rafe's worse off."

Rafe held out two small white pebbles with traces of blood in his right palm.

"What are those?" asked Anne.

Rafe raised his left hand, his middle and ring fingers one joint short. "I think they're called distal phalanges."

"Oh my God!" said Anne.

"Jesus, what happened?" said John.

"I don't know exactly," Rafe said. "One second I'm carrying the pole, the next—wham—it feels like someone drove a semi into my hand. The pole didn't move at all though, which was really weird. Once we finally got the poles in place, I looked down and the tips of my fingers were just pulped. There were just shreds left holding the dangling bones." Anne felt faint. "So I pulled the bones out and tried to bandage the tips so I didn't lose much blood. Hurts like a son of a bitch, and I think my career as a harpsichordist is over."

"Can I ask why you're still carrying your finger bones around?" said Claire, squinting one eye in repulsion.

"Are you kidding?" said Rafe. "Lucky charm. Conversation piece. Heck, I might put some pips on them and make them into dice like the Romans used to. Of course, these are pointier than real 'knucklebones.'"

"Gee, too bad you didn't lose one from each finger. You could play Yahtzee," snarked Claire.

"Very funny. Of course, Roman dice weren't really made from knucklebones. That's just a slang term. They were made from the anklebones of oxen, cattle, and whatnot," Rafe said.

John incredulously said, "Dude, you just lost your fingertips and you're talking about *dice*?"

"Dice are awesome. And you know, with a little sanding, these might make some cool barrel dice ..."

"Oh dear God!" said Anne.

"I'm just kidding, Anne," said Rafe, putting his phalanges in his pocket. "Mostly. But seriously, you want to talk dice sometime, I can show you some amazing polyhedrals I have. Plus, talking about anything distracts me from the fact that my hand is throbbing like you wouldn't believe."

"Come see my polyhedrals?" said Claire. "Is that nerd for, 'Come up and see my etchings'?" They all laughed like they were drunk.

"Holy crap, I thought we were all dead when that thing showed up," John said. "I mean was it me or was it bigger and nastier than in Canada?"

They all burned off the rest of their adrenaline excitedly recounting, sometimes repeatedly, what they'd each seen, heard, felt, smelled, tasted, and thought at virtually every second. Anne, Claire, and John reassembled all their gear for loading on the plane when it came, Steve and Rafe being excused from manual tasks. Steve wouldn't let them pack up the guns, still worried about a potential cross-border incident in case the Chinese somehow detected something on their radar and came to investigate, knowing that there were no effective border controls.

The entire PLA might have shown up and taken them back to a State Security dungeon, and they'd never have known. When the pilots arrived back at noon, they found the agents of the Black Chamber sound asleep, dead to the world, on the green steppe grass under the gaze of *Möngke Kök Tengri*, Eternal Blue Heaven.

18

When the plane landed to refuel in Honolulu, they took Rafe and Steve to Tripler Army Medical Center to have their hands repaired. As they were sitting in the waiting room of the pink coral building on Moanalua Ridge on Oahu, Claire came in and announced, "I just got off the phone with the Four Seasons resort on the Big Island. I've booked us all in for three weeks. I'm going to go call Joe, Mike, Lily, and Wilhelmina, and tell them to get out here with their families. I think we all deserve some vacation."

"Fantastic idea," said John.

"I don't know if I can afford that," said Anne.

"Oh, it's all on the Chamber," said Claire. "We do things right."

"Then I've got to go buy a couple bathing suits," smiled Anne.

ཨ༦༼༦

The Hawaiian sojourn was a marvelous restorative. Rest, relaxation, and simple fun, especially once Mike and Joe's children had arrived. Anne went out of her way to be friendly with their wives, as she suspected that a youngish, not unattractive single woman who's working with your husband on matters clandestine was pretty high up on a wife's list of anxieties. They seemed a tad wary at first, but by the time they flew home, Anne felt she'd removed any suspicion that she might be angling for their men, and they all got along terrifically.

Tanned, rested, and still marveling at the details of everyday life that she'd taken for granted, Anne returned to work at the Black Chamber. Everyone was in a marvelous, lighthearted mood. Joe, Mike, Claire, Steve, and Wilhelmina sat at their desks in the central office composing their Memoranda on the events of the past few weeks, laughing and joking with each other. Rafe and Lily did the same in the lab, in between tossing various designs of paper airplanes at a target at the far end of the long room.

Anne worked on her Memorandum, and began work on Library entries for the *Brevarium dæmonologicum* and Professor Geoffrey's transliteration and translation of the Voynich Manuscript. She had decided to file a separate entry under her own name for the magic circle she'd derived, with citations back to the works she'd used. Last, she had decided that the five wooden poles deserved to be filed away in the event, however unlikely, that another demon cropped up and needed trapping. She had told Joe that she'd love a duplicate set for her (still-hypothetical) backyard as a memento. And she'd called a Professor of Altaic and Inner Asian History at Georgetown and found out that the Mongol shaman's valediction, *sain suuj baigaaray*, meant "live well." *I will*, she thought, *and* sain suuj *to you, friend, wherever you are.*

The phone rang, its screen announcing HISTORIAN. Anne picked up with a cheerful, "Hi, John!"

"Hey, Anne. You sound chipper."

"You know what, I am. Something about billions not dead in a fiery nuclear holocaust gives me a spring in my step," she laughed.

"Me too," he said. "Can I come down and have a word with you?"

"Sure, just bring coffee! I'm thinking I'm going to have to buy a little machine for down here."

A few minutes later, John came down the spiral staircase and sat in the leather guest chair. "Okay, Anne, here's the thing. We saved the world. No, actually, *you* saved the world. We helped."

"Everyone did what he was good at. I just happened to get stuck with the how-do-you-kill-it problem and lucked into that Russian story that turned out not to be a folk tale," Anne demurred.

"Well, I won't argue. But, bottom line, I talked to everyone else in the Chamber, and we've decided to make an exception to the Charter for you. We're all willing to look the other way and break the law. You got dragooned into this job like no one else here. We usually cultivate potential replacements, and all of us were happy to sign up when we got the offer. You never really had a choice. So we all decided to give you a mulligan. You can step back out and into your old life. We'll write you an official letter from an unspecified government agency saying that you've been doing great service, we'll cut you a check to cover your expenses and your partnership buy-in fee, and we'll pay Hathaway & Edgecombe for the damage to your office. With that, you should be able to step right back into your old life, no questions asked. Just don't mention us, ever, and you'll be free and clear for the rest of your life. What do you say?"

"I say no."

John's brows knit together. "Give yourself a minute to think about it."

"I don't need it. Look, John, everything you say is right, and I'm touched profoundly that all of you would give me the option, given that it's technically illegal under the one law you guys seem to have to follow. But you can't un-ring my bell, to use a really lame metaphor. I'm in. And *we saved the world*! What's more exciting than that? If I left, I'd have no one to talk to about it! And worse, I'd constantly be worrying about other spooky phenomena. I'd probably end up as one of those crazy people who tries to read between the lines of the *Weekly World News*."

"It's out of business," John said.

"Really? Aw, too bad."

"Don't worry, we have Bat Boy in a secure facility in North Carolina," John said seriously.

"You what?" Anne said.

"Kidding."

Anne took a playful swat at him with some papers from her desk. "That's exactly the thing. If I left, I'd be thinking, 'Maybe there was something to Bat Boy ...' and they'd eventually lock me up, if I wasn't already devoured by the thirty-nine cats I'd amassed to defend me from hobgoblins."

"Are you sure? This is a one-time deal. We can't ever offer this again."

"I understand. And, no, I like it here. I like the people, the job is ludicrously interesting when it's not making you wet yourself in terror, and frankly, saving the world from a discarnate entity of overwhelming evil has spoiled me for anything else."

"What about your old job?"

"It was fun. I liked it a lot. But what I really liked was the books. And I can stay in that world, just from the other side of the transaction."

"Last chance."

"No, I'm in."

John broke into a smile. "Then we're elated to have you. You've been amazing, and once you actually know what you're doing, you're going to be scary good." He stood and offered his hand.

"Thank you, John," Anne said.

John leaned down and kissed her cheek chastely. "No, thank you."

He went upstairs and Anne sat lost in thought for a few moments. *What have I done?* she thought, then knew, *Something good. What will it be like here? And what was that he was saying about cultivating your own replacement?*

པ༵ ༵

Anne unlocked the doors of the Coolidge Foundation and ushered Lindsay in.

"Check it out, Linds."

"Oh my freaking God. And it's got lots of rare volumes, esoterica, and general weirdness? This is *amazing*."

"I know, right? Well, it's all yours now. I'll show you our offices upstairs, oh, and John's office. He's the vice president. One thing I'll have to warn you about is that the terms of the Foundation are extremely strange, and John and I will be out of the office a lot, maybe for longish stretches, and we're not allowed to disclose to anyone, even you, where we are."

"Ooh, very cloak-and-dagger."

"Well, no. But those are the rules. Will it bug you to be here alone a lot?"

"Not in the least. At least until I've read everything here," she laughed, cracking Anne up.

"Wonderful! I'll be here working and hanging out for at least a couple hours every day, but what I'd really like is for you to really be running the place, in terms of managing the library, loan requests, and eventually, of course, scouting and acquisitions."

"Anne, this is so totally cool, I don't know what to say."

"Say you'll do it."

"This is a dream job, but I don't have an MLS or anything."

"Well, if you think you need one, or an advanced degree in anything else, let me know. The Foundation will pay for it. We're all about employee development."

"That's so cool!"

"You'll do it?"

"Of course I'll do it!"

"I'm so glad. Let's poke around here a bit, and then I'm buying lunch. There's an amazing French-Vietnamese place not far from here."

"Thank you so much for this opportunity, Anne."

"Thanks for taking me up on it," said Anne. Then with just a hint of rue, she said, "Who knows, maybe you'll take my job when I'm not around anymore."

19

One Monday morning, John, Mike, and Joe were sitting in their usual pew at St. Matthew's Cathedral waiting for the seven o'clock Mass to begin. They were surprised to see Anne slip in next to them. Anne was herself surprised to be there. She sat (and periodically stood) through the Mass, and then walked out onto Rhode Island Avenue with her colleagues in the diffuse morning light, as the previous evening's fog burned off.

"Hey, Anne, good morning," said Mike. "What are you doing here? Want to cross the Tiber?"

Anne laughed. "No, not hardly. I don't know. I just thought, you know, that since I can't argue that demons don't exist, there's a pretty damn good chance that God exists too, and, if that's the case, I ought to say thanks. I've had a very good life, and I've never been more conscious of how little I did to earn it—or how lucky I was in Mongolia. If God has something to do with that, He deserves a thank-you."

They walked down Connecticut Avenue towards Farragut Square.

"We're here every morning, so you're always welcome to join us," said Joe.

"Breakfast is always on the Papists," Mike announced as they turned into a chain bakery for coffee and a small pastry.

"Are you trying to convert me?" Anne grinned. "If so, I'll put you in the queue. At the moment, Mongolian shamanism has the pole position." They all laughed.

The three men sarcastically kicked around the stories in the morning's *Post* and *Times*. Anne chimed in from time to time, but mostly just enjoyed watching their silly masculine camaraderie.

Anne got a refill of her coffee and returned to the table as the guys were getting up.

"Ready, Anne?" John asked. She nodded. He smiled and said, "Let's go to work."

Acknowledgements

Tales from the Black Chamber was written some years back to amuse myself while waiting to start a Ph.D. program. No one is more surprised than I that it has emerged, vampire-like, from the grave (ok, drawer), where it sat, mostly forgotten, and will beat my dissertation into print.

Given the passing of time, I may well have forgotten some of the people who read and commented on the story. If so, sorry, folks. I certainly apologize to those named below, for not having taken it as seriously as they did and improved it as much as their comments would have allowed me to. In this regard, I am particularly indebted (alphabetically) to Claire Berlinski, Tucker Cawley, Aaron Elkins, Eric Haanstad, Nick Pelling, and Kate Schulz.

Jonah Goldberg indirectly pointed me to the folks at Liberty Island, for which I must thank him.

The merry band at Liberty Island has been an undiluted pleasure to work with. Adam Bellow, David Bernstein, Abbey Brill, Jay Merwin, David Swindle, and Elena Vega have all contributed materially to this book's seeing the light of day—in better shape than it's ever been. I am very grateful. (And you should be too.)

I thank you, dear reader, for your time and treasure. Let's hope this is the beginning of a beautiful friendship.

Finally, as this was originally an amusement and *passe-temps*, some characters were loosely based on real friends of mine whom I wished to entertain, parts of whose personalities remain in forms distorted through the lens of my whimsy. I both apologize to and thank them for their forbearance in allowing me to pay homage to them even in such silly form. Thanks, Claire, Joe, John, and Rob.

About the author

Born in Washington, D.C., Bill Walsh has spent the intervening decades collecting history degrees, foreign languages, and other cognitive miscellany. He lives in a 1920s house in Wisconsin with his very understanding wife, their kids, and a cat named after St. Methodius

Made in the USA
Coppell, TX
10 April 2020

19739419R00144